Stephen Oram writes science fiction and is lead curator for near-future fiction at Virtual Futures. He's been a hippie-punk, religious-squatter and an anarchist-bureaucrat; he thrives on contradictions. He is published in several anthologies and has two published novels, *Quantum Confessions* and *Fluence*. His collection of sci-fi shorts, *Eating Robots and Other Stories*, was described by the *Morning Star* as one of the top radical works of fiction in 2017.

ALSO BY STEPHEN ORAM
Fluence
Eating Robots and Other Stories
Biohacked & Begging and Other Stories

IN ANTHOLOGIES
Best of British Science Fiction 2020 (NewCon Press)
Vast (Orchid's Lantern)
Once Upon A Parsec (NewCon Press)
Near-Future Fictions Vol. 1 (Virtual Futures)
Fairy Tales and Folklore Re-imagined (Between the Lines Publishing)
Dream City Blues (theEXAGGERATEDpress)
Mountebanks (theEXAGGERATEDpress)
Versions of the Future (sBooks)

Visit stephenoram.net
Twitter @OramStephen
Facebook Stephen Oram Author

STEPHEN ORAM

QUANTUM CONFESSIONS

SilverWood

Published in 2014 by SilverWood Books
Reprinted 2019 and 2021

SilverWood Books Ltd
14 Small Street, Bristol, BS1 1DE, United Kingdom
www.silverwoodbooks.co.uk

ISBN 978-1-78132-263-5 (paperback)
ISBN 978-1-78132-264-2 (ebook)

British Library Cataloguing in Publication Data
A CIP catalogue record for this book is available from
the British Library

Page design and typesetting by SilverWood Books

To Penn, a wise and wonderful woman

Part 1

1

Aled

2019 – 2024

Perfect trust is like a pure glass sphere. It's beautiful, precious and fragile. The perfect trust I had in my parents had just suffered its first hairline crack. I was six years old, I was moving country and I was dreading the future.

There had been lots of arguments between them and, although I was too young to understand, I knew something wasn't right. Ma had made it quite clear that never again would she take me into the hills on her shoulders, never again would I feel the cool Welsh wind on my face.

I looked out of my bedroom window. The spring sunshine was sparkling off the cars lining the street, each one plugged into a blue neon socket in the kerb, charging up, upgrading itself and uploading the day's news and weather. Wherever there was a car, the kerb had turned itself brown, signalling to the authorities that all was okay, that this car was registered at this address. Only our kerb was yellow, the colour of illegal parking. An old bright red, battered van decorated with hand-painted rainbows and the words 'Carmarthen Community Church' was parked outside. Someone had dropped it off the night before and we'd spent the evening trudging back and forth, moving a pile of possessions from the front room to the van.

Our house was slightly different from all the rest, lacking their paraphernalia of solar panels and wind turbines. Ma was so proud that it was still the same as when Grandma had lived there – still painted white with a little slate roof that jutted out over the front-room bay window and a lounge with french doors that opened on to a carefully manicured lawn bordered by a high hedge.

I'd only been awake for a few moments when Ma, carrying my baby brother Sean, came into my room, gave me a hug and ruffled my jet-black hair as only mothers can. Even though we'd both inherited Ma's blue eyes and the splash of freckles across the bridge of our noses, Sean was her favourite.

'Aled, be brave for me,' she said through her tears.

'Okay, Ma,' I replied, not really knowing what she meant.

Downstairs there was the same strong smell of bleach as there was upstairs, but the atmosphere was different. My dad beckoned me over as I walked into the living-room, throwing me an ancient pair of 3D goggles.

'Son, look what I found. Come and watch it with me. It's my favourite, you'll love it. When I was a little bit older than you, my daddy, your granddad, took me to see it in Cardiff. We spent all day together, taking the bus into the city, having lunch in the castle and then finally going to the cinema. Granddad was so embarrassing. He kept commenting on the way the big city people were dressed and how silly they looked. Ever since then it's been my favourite film. Come on, you'll love it.'

I flopped down next to him and he gave me a big manly squeeze, pulling me close. I was very pleased but a bit wary of this change of attitude towards me. My dad could be very volatile – his tongue could be as soothing as honey one minute and suddenly switch to being as sour as vinegar the next.

Mousehunt, the film he was so enthralled by, was a classic and Lee Evans's face made me giggle all the way through. My favourite bit is when he is being outwitted by a mouse which, having carefully tiptoed its way through hundreds of mousetraps, triggers them all to snap shut, attaching themselves to the mouse-hating Lee Evans like a shoal of flying piranha fish. This was the first day of my love affair with slapstick and in particular with Lee Evans, who has the same parentage as me – an Irish mother and a Welsh father.

The film was almost over and my dad was playfully punching me on the arm as we rolled about laughing, when Ma came storming into the room.

'Dylan, will you please stop,' she said through clenched teeth.

He just looked at her and quietly said, 'Sure, of course. Sorry.'

When my dad's friend turned up to drive us, we all squashed into the van and set off on our journey.

Ma was looking out of the window. 'Turned their back on us. Sorry, Mum, I can't believe we had to leave so much of your stuff behind,' she said in a quiet voice.

'Tell me about it. I still don't see why I couldn't bring the theology books from my course,' said my dad.

'Really? Dylan, you're unbelievable,' said Ma.

We wound our way along the country lanes and it wasn't long before we reached the big motorway that would take us to London. We trundled along with the wheels clanking, the engine screaming and my dad singing along to old Country and Western songs on the radio. Occasionally Ma would make a sarcastic comment about some particularly sincere lyric, but mainly she just kept quiet, only once getting really agitated as we passed a motorway exit.

'Care to take a detour, Dylan?'

'I made my choice,' he replied and then carried on singing, albeit a little quieter than before.

As we crossed the Severn Bridge, my dad and his friend were complaining.

'The English collect all the money, you know?' said my dad.

'It's only collected on one side of the bridge.'

'Only because they know better than to try and charge anyone to get into England.'

They shook hands in one big exaggerated shake and their

belly laughs reverberated around the van.

'I'll get charged on the way back, you know? If only you had a decent car, I'd be able to speed through like the rest. You know the bridge and the car talk to each other and take the money from your account?'

'No chance of that with me, I can assure you. Let me give you the toll money for the way back,' said my dad. He fumbled around in his pocket. 'Don't seem to have the right change,' he said.

'I bet you don't. No worries, I'll pay. It's worth it just to get rid of you from our beautiful country.'

They both laughed again. Ma sat there, stony-faced, hugging Sean close to her.

When we were about halfway, my dad's friend suggested we stopped to, 'top up the tank' and 'let loose a leak.' We pulled into the service station, but as we got out of the van to go and buy some sweets, there was an almighty commotion. A baby-minding blanket – originally designed to detect passive smoke, but now able to identify a whole range of pollution – was pulsating between scarlet and black. A loud shrill alerted everyone that it had detected our van's emissions.

A young, well-dressed woman carrying the baby with the blanket shouted, 'Get away from my baby with your evil dirt. Typical god-botherers – think you're too good for us, don't you? Want to see the world destroyed.'

My dad was laughing.

Ma was angry and shouted back. 'Hypocrites! The amount of Earth's resources that go into keeping you up-to-date with the latest shiny car is far more than the diesel we need to keep this old thing on the road. And what if God did bring it all to an end – would that be such a shame?'

'C'mon. We must be over the legal limit. It'll have alerted the police,' said my dad's friend as he quickly ushered us back into the van. We 'topped up the tank', but that was all. I desperately needed a pee all the way to London.

*

London was very big and as we negotiated the web of city streets everyone in the van was quiet, except for a touristy gasp of recognition as we passed St Paul's Cathedral.

Finally, we pulled into our new road and my dad's friend began pointing out all sorts of useful things.

'Look, lad, there's a sweet shop on the corner and there's a fancy dress shop, too.'

'What's that?' I asked, pointing at two towers with crescent moons on top.

'Fertile ground,' said Ma.

We turned into a car park surrounded by a block of new buildings and pulled up in a space with 111a painted on the ground.

'That's it then, our new home,' said my dad, pointing in the general direction of the flats. Ma leant over and whispered in my ear.

'Be brave, Aled. We still have an upstairs and a garden.'

Once we'd finished moving our stuff into the flat and waved goodbye to his friend, my dad grabbed hold of my hand and with a bounce in his step said, 'Come on, son. Fancy a kick-about?'

He took me to Victory Park and we spent the final few hours of daylight kicking a ball between us. I think he only pretended to fall over as the ball whizzed passed him into the goal, time and time again. He was so carefree and so different to the dad who'd always seemed to be looking over his shoulder, as if he expected something to grab him from behind.

When I was worn out, we walked to the shops and he sat me down. In a serious voice he said, 'This is a new start for all of us. Things are going to be much better now. I've found a church for us to go to that's the right sort of church. Not one of those backwater ones that don't understand what makes men tick and are far too quick to judge.'

I didn't understand the implications of what he was saying, but I knew it was important because of his slow voice, his solemn face and the fact that he'd bought me an ice cream – which was a rare extravagance that signalled something important was happening.

He didn't spend much time at home, but it seemed to me that my dad was really happy that we'd moved. He disappeared for days on end and then came back full of stories about miracles he'd performed and people he'd met. Ma scoffed and tutted at how stupid and naive the Church was to make him an elder.

Ma wasn't at all settled and one of her recurring themes was how Sean wouldn't have to share a bedroom with me if we still lived in Lammas Street. She kept referring to the fact that purely on account of my dad's selfishness we'd had to move to this cage in a suburban concrete jungle. She was a woman of routine who believed that cleanliness was still next to godliness and sadly, unlike most people, didn't trust cleaning-bots to do a good enough job. Every Saturday evening she would clean the kitchen with copious amounts of bleach, making sure every corner was scrubbed. Regular as clockwork, my dad would come in with a bunch of flowers or herbs or sometimes even a plant. His gifts would often be a little the worse for wear but he'd present them to her as if it was a surprise. She'd smile, but it was a smile that didn't reach her eyes.

'Oh, Dylan, thank you!' she'd exclaim, letting out a big sigh.

Just before my eleventh birthday, Ma came in from the shops and, without unpacking the shopping, wept uncontrollably on the kitchen floor. She'd been harassed by the local lads who hung around the parade of shops and, despite the fact that she was a tough woman who would normally give as good as she got, this time she'd kept quiet and scurried home.

My dad buzzed around her, asking, 'What's wrong? What can I do?'

After crying for some time, she snapped at him, 'It's too late, Dylan, you did more than enough ten years ago and now we're here. What's to do or say, eh?'

I had no idea what had happened; every time it was mentioned, I felt a little more distance creep in between me and them, making me desperately unhappy. To emotionally survive,

I had to create an inner shell to protect myself from the fact that this was the way of my world – my dad out and about with his Church, Sean and Ma often together in their own private world and me without any friends, because I was known as the religious Welsh nut.

On the day of my eleventh birthday, my life changed dramatically – the Church considered me old enough to have my own confidante and I moved to the big secondary school. I realised I couldn't rely on my family and that I had to be self-sufficient or wither away and die.

2

Kate

My dad was an almost mythical character to me. Mum never spoke to me about him. Occasionally I heard her telling someone that he was a lovely man who just couldn't break free.

'Kate,' my Aunt G would say, 'he's a good-for-nothing who can charm the coal out of the ground.'

My mum was forty years old when she had me and her career, as an academic and theologian, was well under way. She was clear that she didn't need a man to make her whole and although she loved me to bits, she wouldn't let the raising of a child get in the way of her work. Unlike my mum, Aunt G was fond of saying about herself that she was, 'sadly, without child or man.' They were so different from one another but, as sisters, they were close and had decided to bring me up together. It was brilliant. I had two mums and I loved them both.

Aunt G was a senior biologist for a biotech company in Cardiff and she was great. Most people thought she was all prim and proper, but actually she was just meticulous and precise. Everything in her house was orderly and in exactly the correct position.

Once, when it was her turn to look after me, she had some friends come to visit her. They were sitting around chatting and drinking tea when one of her visitors commented, 'You always wear the same clothes.'

Aunt G replied with her usual answer. 'If I like something, why wouldn't I take every opportunity to wear it?'

It was the first time that these particular friends had been to Aunt G's house so she showed them around. I loved watching the way that she followed them, making the necessary, and often slightest, re-adjustments to ornaments they had unwittingly moved.

Mum always defended Aunt G's eccentricities, pointing out to people that underneath the veneer of austerity, she was actually one of the most thoughtful and generous people around – generous with her affection, her tolerance and her money.

Mum was at the other end of the organised spectrum. Suddenly doing things on the spur of the moment. One rainy day – I must have been about five years old at the time – I was sitting at the window watching the rain-drops trickle down the glass, forming patterns as they slid the last few inches of their long journey from the heavens.

Mum came bursting through the door like a rainbow pushing the clouds to one side. 'Kate, let's go and have a picnic by the sea,' she said, holding a picnic hamper packed full of crisps and sandwiches. 'After all, skin's waterproof,' she added.

Off we went, in the pouring rain, to the seaside. All alone on the beach and in swimming costumes, we sat and ate our picnic. That was what she was like.

These two powerful women were shaping me, helping me form my own wonderful uniqueness of two strong and sometimes opposing sides to my personality. A side that thrives on detail and gets totally engrossed and a side that is wildly imaginative, that can picture a world of humans with enhancing technology, such as replacement eyes that can see in the dark.

My mum, who was absolutely ace, had been teaching me a bit at weekends and she was always one step ahead of the teachers. Mr Gold, the mathematics teacher, was standing at the front of the class asking us simple questions and I was bored.

'I need fifty apples but they come in packs of eight. How many packs do I need?' he asked.

Because I was the only one answering, supposedly not giving anyone else a chance, he made me work on my own while he carried on teaching the others. So, when Miss Wicks came in saying the Head wanted to see me, I was up like a shot, following her out of the door and along the corridor. As we approached the Head's office I could hear raised voices and as we went through the door, the Head was telling Mum how I was too clever for my own good. Disrupting the other children's education. Apparently, I refused to take part, took over or made smart comments that made the teachers look foolish. The Head was taking umbrage at the fact that I'd refused to recite my three times table out loud. She called me "passive aggressive" and wanted to know what my mum was going to do about it.

Mum stood tall and proud. I loved the way she looked, with her short bleached hair and her tattoo of a thousand tiny little stars that burst from a crown of thorns on her wedding-ring finger, wound their way up and around her left arm, across her shoulder and back down her chest. What nobody else could see, but I knew was there under her tee-shirt, was the rest of the tattoo – a final flourish of multi-coloured fireworks exploding around her nipple. It was one of those tattoos that made people stare and, more often than not, ask where it ended.

Mum was furious. In her best calm, slightly raised lecturer's voice she said, 'I agree with Kate. It's a stupid thing to ask a seven-year-old to do and just goes to show how poor the standard of teaching is in this school.'

'Really? Well, I am so sorry we do not come up to your standard, Mrs Davies. But as I said – I want to know what you are going to do about Katherine.'

'It's Ms not Mrs but you can call me Ruth. I was hoping to talk through an idea with you, but I can see there is no point. I'll tell you exactly what I'm going to do – I'm going to take her out of school and teach her at home. Satisfied?'

Without waiting to hear the answer, Mum grabbed my hand and walked me out of the school – forever. I knew at that moment that my life would be special.

I was so excited and so was she, gabbling on at a rate of knots.

'We're going to move. I've found us a great little place just outside Narberth, on a caravan park. It's a wooden lodge with a veranda all the way round. It has loads of open space around it and it's built on a slope so you can see right across the valley. You'll have your own room, which you can decorate however you want, and the best bit is that there's a home-schooling community already there. You'll have lots of friends. I can work from home and look after my theology students almost entirely online. It's got loads of craft shops and lots of quirky people. It's so perfectly us. It'll be fab!'

'But what about Aunt G?'

'Full of "wannabe alternative types, with brightly coloured hair", according to her. Anyway, you're old enough now to look after yourself and she needs a life of her own.'

It was soon after that I met him for the first time. The brass knocker banged exceptionally loudly and the house intercom announced, 'Katherine's father.'

As Aunt G opened the front door, a booming voice bounced off the bookshelves, rolling down the hallway.

'Hello, Gerry. It's me. Nice to see ya! Thanks for the call. Is she here?'

'No need to announce yourself. You're in my contacts list – the door recognised you,' said Aunt G.

'Damn. How did it do that?'

'Oh. Just some stuff we're playing around with at work. Tapping into face recognition databases, finger-prints, bit of DNA if possible.'

'Where will it all end? It's not right, if you ask me.'

'I didn't. She's through there. Don't think I'm happy with this, but it's what Ruth wants,' replied Aunt G.

She introduced him to me as 'your father,' and then sat in the corner of the room, watching. He kissed me on the cheek. His breath was beery and his chin was rough with stubble. He talked a lot but didn't say much and seemed awkward, which made me shy.

I was fascinated by him. He brought with him the most wonderful old Barbie doll that he said had been my grandmother's, his mum's. She was absolutely gorgeous, with a titian-red ponytail and bright blue eyes – exactly the same colour of hair and eyes as me. However, unlike my broad face and high cheek-bones, she had a pointy face with a little pointy nose and a long slender neck. She had bright red lips, red toenails and a stunning long red dress with a white feather boa. I treasured his gift, even though I wasn't into dolls, being more of a tomboy than a girly girl. In fact, a few days before that, I'd hurt myself playing in the old derelict shopping centre. It was a really hot summer and as usual I'd been mucking about with some of the lads from our street. We'd been playing at demolition men, knocking down walls and crawling into the boarded-up buildings to pretend we were laying explosives. As I'd squeezed my way out of a tight hole, I'd caught myself on some barbed wire and gouged a couple of two-inch cuts into my left arm. I was really proud of them, especially as the hospital told me they would form nasty scars. And so, once he'd left, I carved two cuts into Barbie's left arm and painted a little red mark on her right cheekbone to match mine.

I had mixed feelings about moving from Pontypridd to Narberth and leaving Aunt G behind.

It was fantastic, though, and so much better than Mum had described. It was the most beautiful wooden house you could imagine. As you approached it, the sloping lawn of luscious green grass rolled away from the front of the house down to a gravel path. On the other side of the path was a square, marshy area with the prettiest celandine flowers, poking their fragile little yellow heads out from the tall marsh grass. The earthy smell of the grass mixed in with the scent of the flowers seemed to cover me from head to foot as I spent day after day in the summer rolling down the lawn, tumbling head over heels and landing with a crunch on the gravel path at the bottom.

As a final treat before I moved, Aunt G had taken me to a Hadron Collider exhibition in Cardiff where I'd bought a poster of a computer-simulated proton-proton collision – producing a Higgs Boson – which Mum faithfully copied on to my new ceiling for me. She also wanted me to have some inspiring art, so she framed a copy of a mosaic by Mat Collishaw, a famous artist she'd been at college with. This Madonna had one of the saddest but most serene faces I'd ever seen. With an intense and haunting beauty, my Madonna looked across my room in bewilderment. I sat on my bed for hours just staring at her face, imagining her thoughts. The solitude of my bedroom was a perfect sanctuary where I could withdraw to contemplate, safe in my cocoon.

I got completely hooked on William Blake's *The Fly*; his painting and his words were so evocative of the loneliness and hopelessness of life. While I was out playing one day, Mum scanned and uploaded it into the prototype living-wallpaper that Aunt G had given me as a moving-in present. The words are written in the sky and framed by leafless trees under which a little girl, with her back to the others, is playing badminton on her own while a young boy is being helped to walk by their mother. Their clothes, the yellowy clouds, the green hills and the branches of the tree all flow with the same curves as the printed words:

Little Fly
Thy summers play,
My thoughtless hand
Has brush'd away.

Am not I
A fly like thee?
Or art not thou
A man like me?

For I dance
And drink & sing;
Till some blind hand
Shall brush my wing.

If thought is life
And strength & breath;
And the want
Of thought is death;

Then am I
A happy fly,
If I live,
Or if I die.

Although my room had two beds, the only person that I ever allowed to stay, apart from Aunt G who hardly ever came, was my best friend, Cleo. As usual, Mum cooked us pikelets when we'd finished our schooling for the day and the others had left. Cleo and I read to each other while the batter was whisked and dropped, a spoon at a time, into the hot pan. After quite a difficult day, learning about social norms, we sat down with our favourite book – *The Silver Chair.* Together, as we often did, the three of us – me, Cleo and Mum – recited one of our much-loved passages.

I started, then Cleo, then Mum and then, all together, we shouted the last line about staying in the play-world. It was a celebration of the private world of our home-schooling.

After tea, Cleo and I went to my room. I loved it when we did this, especially when we talked about what we'd been learning, helping each other fathom out some particularly knotty problem.

'Do you reckon that if we're cool, and, like, learn a lot, we'll be able to change the world?' said Cleo.

'Don't see why not,' I said.

'That'd be awesome. Eh?'

'Yeah. I reckon it would.'

We rambled on about how we were going to learn as much as we could, so that when we grew up we could change the world.

'And we could, like, get some robot code off your aunt. Couldn't we?'

'And we could have it scrolling across the wall. That way we'd be able to learn it,' I said.

'And, like, recode the robots to do what we wanted.'

'Yeah. Cool.'

'Trouble is,' said Cleo, 'the other kids would pick on us. Better to, like, fit in.'

'No way. I'm my own girl. I'll be my own woman. And, in some ways I'll fit in and in others I won't. I'll decide which is which, though.'

'My dad gets really angry if I don't do what all the other girls do.'

'What other girls? That's what made today so difficult. We hardly know anyone else. How are we meant to know what social norms are?' I said.

'Dunno. He seems to have a good idea, though.'

It was hard to concentrate because all I could think about was how much I ached to have my dad around. I sat there listening to her, longing to be able to talk about my dad and desperate to share my life with him.

3

Aled

2026 – 2027

'Aled. Look at you. You're only thirteen and already the girls won't leave you alone. You're cursed for life, just like your father. You're both very attractive men, but you should learn to control yourself. Avoid sexual immorality.'

I was sitting opposite my confidante on low red chairs that would have been more suited to a waiting-room in an up-market office block than this small room which, in contrast to the soft chairs, was cold and bare. On the small rickety table between me and my confidante were some leaflets.

'Don't ever forget, God loves you. He won't let you be tempted beyond what you can bear,' she said as she shook her head. 'I feel sorry for you pitiful men. Read this,' she added, thrusting one of the leaflets at me.

This was typical of her guidance through the previous two years of my puberty. Once a week, or more frequently if I'd had an emergency, we'd meet in this plain room. I loved and hated these sessions because on the one hand they were excruciatingly embarrassing and made me realise how bad I was, but on the other, I truly felt the firm and loving presence of my creator.

Today we were talking about Simmone, who was the only posh kid from that part of our street to mix with the rest of us. Although us kids didn't all hang out together, we still lived happily alongside each other – a mix of black, brown, white, rich and poor.

These streets, the little parks and the industrial estates were ours, it was where we belonged. Occasionally some of us would venture as far as the Westfield shopping centre. The 'concentrated opiate of consumerism,' as Simmone called it.

There was nothing unusual about our particular street in comparison with those around us. We had a Victorian pub, some scary folk who lived in maisonettes with small, overgrown front gardens covered in litter and household rubbish and my three-storey municipal-style flats that resembled a care home. There were some small semi-detached houses full of folk who'd bought them a long time before, when houses were cheap. Lastly, there were the large Victorian terraced houses with their posh cars plugged into their brown kerbs. The screech and squeal of music lessons poured out of their windows.

I'd already told my confidante about one of the occasions when we'd spread our wings and gone to Westfield. A whole gang of us had sneaked into the cinema with stolen 3D five-channel goggles. I flicked between the five films on offer, but mainly watched the newly released *Tsunami*. Once the films had finished, we made our way back to the more familiar territory of our industrial estates. As we walked around the low-rise buildings, we were surrounded by litter tossed about in the wind as it raced through our empty streets on its way to the more glamorous skyscrapers that encircled our concrete valley. Finding a suitable wall to shelter behind, we sat down, opened a big bottle of synthetic cider and began discussing the film. Simmone talked over the top of us all, venting her disgust at the film's bias against a group of drug-addled students who hadn't understood that when the warning came, they needed to run. She explained how political propaganda, fuelled by powerful lobbyists, portrayed any illegal drug as evil, because it wasn't a source of income for the government or the corporations. The others started to poke fun at her for taking a film so seriously, which only made her all the more determined to argue her point. Gradually, the others got bored and one by one drifted away until it was just the two of us. I really liked the way she saw the world and that she was prepared to be hassled for caring.

'Aled?' she said.

'Yes?' I answered, wondering what was coming next. She had a habit of throwing curve balls when you least expected it. She was prolific at challenging my beliefs with extremely well-constructed arguments and I enjoyed practising the art of withstanding the hostile scrutiny.

'Have you ever had sex? Boy or girl?' she asked, with a mischievous grin on her face.

'What's that about?' I batted back.

'Well…I'm ready,' she said.

'Yeah, right,' I replied quietly, in case she was winding me up.

'Seriously. And I'd like it to be with you.'

She'd hit a nerve. I wasn't too sure how I felt sexually. I'd been attracted to boys and girls over the previous couple of years, but had suppressed it all because I knew that sex, outside of marriage, was wrong. At church they'd made it clear that even if you looked at someone lustfully you'd committed a sin, a sin that would eat away your soul.

'Simmone? Are you really serious? You know how my Church feels about that, don't you?' I asked.

'Sure, but they're wrong. As they are about so much, Aled. If only you could see that.'

She kissed me on the lips and it felt so good. For the first time I smelt the perfume in her short dyed-black hair and noticed that her smile was a bit crooked. As we kissed, the desolation of our surroundings evaporated, replaced by an exhilarating happiness welling up inside me. Although I couldn't help thinking she tasted of popcorn. As she moved her hand to undo my trouser belt, I panicked.

'No.' I pushed her away. 'You're great, but I can't. Not yet.'

I stood up and, turning my back, quickly walked away.

'I'll be waiting,' she shouted.

Nothing happened again between us until a few months later when we were sitting in Victory Park having a heated debate. We'd been talking about oppression. How on one side of us lay London's financial powerhouses – the predatory centres of capitalism, dripping in luxury but choking the lifeblood from our community. On the other, and in stark contrast to our own local Olympic legacy of semi-built buildings, abandoned once it was obvious they wouldn't be finished in time for the games, lay the luxurious 2012 Olympic village. Somehow, Simmone moved on to arguing that the Church oppressed women, particularly keeping them from any meaningful leadership. I counter-argued that we're all equal in the eyes of God, whatever role we have.

As we sat there, I couldn't help but fancy her. She was so fired up and alive, touching me every time she wanted to stress a point. I leant over and kissed her on the lips, partly because she was so fanciable, but also because I was losing the argument and couldn't think of any other way to win. She pulled back, held my gaze and, with the most sensual twinkle in her eyes, grasped the back of my head and drew it to hers, kissing me as if her hunger had to be satiated immediately. She pushed her hand inside my shirt. I was burning with so much passion that, although her eagerness freaked me out a bit, I responded by shoving my hand up her t-shirt. The shock of touching her breast made me pull my hand out quickly, as if I'd burnt my fingers. I burst into tears. She stood up and walked off without saying anything. I sat there alone, feeling deeply ashamed and embarrassed. I'd broken my spiritual vows and I'd cried in front of Simmone. Over the next few weeks, we met a couple of times and it was awkward between us. We never mentioned it and she didn't try to persuade me again.

It was this second encounter that had prompted the 'sex' conversation with my confidante, but no matter how much I tried to explain the turmoil inside me, she couldn't understand and so we ended our session with her praying that God would help me find the good and true path of righteousness. The next few weeks were torture because I couldn't talk to anyone about it. I knew the Church would simply condemn me and I knew that my friends would just laugh. I was caught between my two worlds; alone and confused.

A couple of months later, my dad told me he'd come into a bit of money and would like to take me to the old-fashioned shops of London's West End to buy some new clothes. He'd never done this before, so I jumped at the chance.

On the day of our shopping trip, he was sharply dressed. He seemed to be in a thoughtful mood and as we approached the underground station to catch a tube train to central London, he broke his silence.

'Aled, son. What is it that you want from life?'

'Dunno,' I answered.

'You must have some idea? Don't you and your mates talk about it?'

'Nope.'

'Go on, you're coming up to fourteen. You're almost a man.'

'I want to be a pastor,' I said, hoping that's what he wanted to hear.

I checked the busking-plugs were in my pocket. They were banned on the tube, but I was sure they'd pick up some interesting DJs plying Oxford Street with their tunes, trying to get enough recommendations for a slot in the major clubs. His interest in my future was uncomfortable and I was dreading him trying to continue, making ours the only conversation that could be overheard on the train as everyone else followed convention and kept silent. Thankfully, he stayed quiet. As we came up to the surface at Tottenham Court Road, he held on to my shoulder and pointed down the length of Oxford Street stretching out in front of us.

'Come on then, son. Let's find some clothes.'

I only popped a busking-plug into one ear, so I could still hear what was going on around me. I found a DJ that was playing a fusion of Blip and Country. I gave my dad the other plug and we dived into the first shop. I was surprised at how big and spacious it was. It had loads of little nooks and crannies with tiny, neat piles of clothes stacked in them. This was more like exploring than shopping. Every shop seemed to want to entice you with their secret alcoves of merchandise and, as the shops were all of different shapes and sizes, their individuality leapt out as soon as you entered. I now understood what Simmone meant about Westfield's small and regimented shops being a concentrated consumerist pill. It took us seven hours to explore the entire mile and a half, making sure I'd investigated every single shelf and alcove it had to offer. Eventually, I chose some trainers, trousers and a t-shirt, all in a revolutionary fabric that never got dirty so never had to be washed. In the days when I'd hung out with Simmone at Westfield she'd said how cool and sexy it was for men to wear this new fabric, 'designed for those who care about the world's environment'.

'Fancy something to eat?' he asked, as we left the Japanese clothes shop with my precious purchases.

'Yeah, a burger would be great.'

'I'm sure we can do better than that,' he said, with a big grin on his face. 'Come on, let's go to Chinatown. We just cut through here, down through Soho and we're there.'

We crossed Oxford Street and as we wound our way through the back streets, the swagger of his walk became more and more pronounced. He obviously knew his way around, nodding to the occasional drunk, stepping nimbly round kissing couples – mainly men – and acknowledging beggars without parting with his money. But it was the semi-naked women, trying to persuade us to follow them through narrow doors for a 'glass of fizz' that intrigued me most.

As we walked through the tall gate of Chinatown, with a mini pagoda crowning its narrow red pillars, I was bombarded by the smell of half-rotten food in the alleyways behind the restaurants. It was mixed in with the sweet sticky smell of cooking wafting through the crowds of loud-and-fast-speaking Chinese tourists. We picked up a paper-thin microcapsule street-guide and, as we strolled past the myriad of red-and-yellow restaurant fronts, their menus and today's specials appeared on the screen. They beckoned us to enter and enjoy the exotic delights they offered; this was nothing like the comparatively bland Chinese takeaway next to the pub on our street.

'This one's the best,' he said, stopping outside a particular restaurant and holding the door open for me as if he owned it. A traditionally dressed doorman ushered us into a long room with ornately carved dragons around the edge of the ceiling and large round tables at one end. The street-guide led us to a small table, already laid out with chopsticks and napkins.

'We'll have the meal for two, please,' said my dad to the guide, as he put it down on the table.

Egg-fried rice, shredded duck, spring rolls, beef in black bean sauce and some slimy green vegetables that I didn't recognise all arrived and were placed on the candle-powered hotplate. Just as we were about to start, a waitress with a sizzling iron skillet on a wooden tray hurried across the room and put it down on our table.

'What do you think then?' he asked me.

'I like it. Not sure about the slimy veg, though,' I replied.

'Me neither. Wash it down with some sake?'

We ate in silence, occasionally commenting on the food and sipping at the sake. At the end of the meal, as we ate quarters of orange and drank our final glass, he started to talk.

'Son, I don't need to tell you about all that girl stuff, do I?

'Of course not, Dad. I know all there is to know. Don't worry.'

'Good. Whatever happened to that geeky girl – Simmone, wasn't it?'

'Yeah. We sort of fell out.'

'Really? Why? Not over sex, surely?'

'She wanted to…but I knew I shouldn't.'

'Son. There'll be plenty of times when you're tempted, what red-blooded male wouldn't be? Lean on God in those times. It's the only way,' he said, taking a large slug. 'You just have to find ways of dealing with it.'

He shuffled the bowls and cups around the table and then looked up. 'While we're on the subject of growing up…'

'Yes?'

'Well. You're almost fourteen now and nearly a man. I might not be around as much, so you're going to have to look after yourself. You okay with that?'

'Sure. Of course.'

The bill came, interrupting us, and as we left the restaurant I felt a sense of finality. That night, as I lay in bed listening to Sean snoring, I tried to work out exactly what he'd meant. I had an overwhelming feeling that he'd washed his hands of me. On the Monday morning he went out as usual but the following Saturday, as we sat there waiting in the pristine kitchen, I realised he'd left us. After waiting for a couple of hours, Ma stood up and simply said, 'Good riddance.'

I turned fourteen in August 2027 and the world seemed to take another seismic shift.

In the eyes of my Church I became an adult and was therefore no longer eligible for a confidante. Ma had become intensely introspective, spending hour after hour reading her holy texts, and had no time for me or Sean; we stopped functioning as a family.

A political coalition, dedicated to total liberalisation, came to power and counter-coalitions soon formed. The first act of the political coalition was to liberalise the state education system by funding parents directly. Many religious and scientific groups responded by setting up their own schools, taking advantage of their new-found freedoms. The space widened between those who believed in the existence of absolute truth and those that didn't.

For me, this new Liberalism meant it was difficult to talk openly at school about my beliefs and, especially without my confidante, I was all alone. I had to choose my path carefully – whether to follow the destructive Liberalists or the Absolutists who protected the right to believe in truth.

I chose truth.

4

Grey

2029 – 2031

I was no longer Kate. I had become Grey. Cleo gave me the nickname because I didn't see the world in the same black and white way as her. I was sixteen, was ready to leave Narberth and to save the world.

These were good times. The coalition government had made quite a few changes when it came to power. They liberalised cyberspace, deliberately breaking the stranglehold of the Cloud, and the rival Cumulus soon became top dog. They freed up the health service, in the same way they had schools a couple of years before. They still collected taxes, but rather than spending it inefficiently themselves, you now got your own annual health payments and could choose whether to save them, buy insurance or spend them and hope. I saved all the money the government had given me since I stopped going to school and now had enough for the down payment on my university degree – the career mortgage. I wanted to study physics and was confident that I could pass the entrance exams. I was deciding which university to go to when all the Russell Group universities merged into one single University UK and the rest, including Mum's, closed. She was furious and adamant that I should protest by refusing to go to university. I did what she wanted.

One of the great things about this new era of politics was that it prompted all sorts of creative eruptions that previously would've been accidentally suffocated by the overbearing state. I wanted to live in the heartland of one of these eruptions. A group of displaced academics, scientists, engineers, philosophers and Green Party activists, who didn't agree with their party's support for the Eco-absolutists, had all come together to form the Alternative Centre for Alternative Technology in South Wales. When I heard about this fantastic Centre, I talked it through with Mum, Aunt G and Cleo and we all agreed that this would be the best place for my talent to thrive. I packed my bag with essentials – two sets of good practical clothes, Barbie, *Madonna* and *The Silver Chair* – and set off on my big adventure. I was following in the footsteps of my gran who, sixty-two years before, at the age of nineteen, had left home and travelled across the world to San Francisco. The summer of love had started her profound life of free love and political activism. Here I was, a bright sixteen-year-old, determined to follow in her footsteps and make my mark on the world.

I put my rucksack down on a pile of brown leaves that had started to turn to mush, took a deep breath and studied the old farmhouse. It was three storeys tall and pleasingly symmetrical. The three upstairs windows were surrounded by vibrant red ivy and the middle one was placed exactly above a black front door. Built on a steep hill, it appeared to slope down to the right, to a small, octagonal summer-house attached to its side. I'd found out, through looking it up on the Cumulus, that in the eleven acres of land there were cottages, outbuildings and four acres of woodland. It was perfect.

The front door opened and a young woman, about my age, called across.

'Hey, girl. Can we help? Or you just gawping for no reason?'

'I've come to join you,' I said.

She stood there, like some throwback to a bygone era. A white girl, with the tips of her dreadlocks touching the top of her low-slung jeans. Slowly, she walked down the front steps, picked up my bag, turned and carried it back to the house. 'I'll follow then?' I asked.

'Up to you really. No one's gonna be bothered either way.'

I followed her up the steep stone stairs, unable to take my eyes off a spider tattoo that poked its head from the top of her knickers and wriggled with every sullen step she took. She dropped my rucksack to the floor and I followed her as she unceremoniously dragged it into the kitchen. A tall, rugged-looking man wearing brown corduroy trousers, a checked shirt, Peruvian knitted socks and with his sleeves rolled up, was standing next to a cast-iron oven kneading a large ball of dough. He had long, blond, curly hair and when he turned round, I saw that he had the most dreamy turquoise eyes. He was clean-shaven and his face was streaked with flour.

'Hi. So what brings you here then?' he asked, as if it was the most natural thing in the world for a stranger to walk into the house.

'Came to save the world.'

'Really? That's interesting. How you figure on doing that then?'

The dreadlocked girl chipped in as she left the room. 'Father. Behave,' she said.

'Sure, Honey,' he called after her.

I was standing in a kitchen with the most handsome man I'd ever seen, desperately trying to think of a smart comment to clinch his attention. 'What you making?' I stuttered, metaphorically kicking myself for being so awkward and clumsy.

'Daily bread-making duties,' he replied, as he carried on kneading, pulling and stretching the dough with his big, firm hands. For the first time ever, I was tongue-tied and I loved the feeling.

'She's your daughter?' I asked.

'Yup. Honey by name, even if not by nature.' He chuckled.

'So, if I want to stay – how does that work?'

'People come here all the time, for a short break. We've got some spare holiday cottages. You either help out with the chores or pay us some money. It's up to you really.'

'No. You don't get it. I want to come and live here. Learn all about what's going on. Become a physicist. Do something worthwhile, rather than lining the pockets of that corrupt elite University.'

'Interesting,' he said, rubbing his face and leaving another floury camouflage stripe across his chin. 'Have you read Keith Skene's seminal work, *Shadows on the Cave Wall?*' he asked.

'Of course. My Aunt G – she's a biochemist – bought it for my fourteenth birthday,' I replied, feeling calmer now I was on more secure ground.

'Impressive,' was all he said, before turning his attention back to the dough.

I stood there wondering what to do next, when Honey came strolling back in. 'Guess you want to be shown where to put your things then, if you're staying?' she said.

'Please. Bye…um…I don't know your name,' I said, in his general direction.

'Clive. But we call him Boss – to take the piss,' replied Honey.

'I'm Grey,' I said to the back of his head.

'Grey, you're bunking up with me,' said Honey.

A few months after I arrived, the Centre reached its full complement of twenty-five – crammed together in ten bedrooms. We were a tight-knit group of extremely bright people, determined to find the best future for mankind, focussing almost all of our attention on the efficient generation and consumption of energy. We struggled with loads of ideas, but they all seemed to require national or global structures which, as Liberalists, we couldn't endorse. However, we quickly solved how to grow food using Aeroponics for vertical city-farms, finding a way to make the environmental cost of creating artificial environments far less than the transport costs of centralised farming. We were buzzing, but our Holy Grail – understanding photosynthesis to find a way of tapping into quantum mechanics to produce super-efficient energy – was proving elusive.

I was having the time of my life, though, surrounded by clever, creative people who took the world seriously. Those of us who lived in the main house gathered every evening, to eat and listen to the BBC radio news. It helped us keep our feet on the ground, a particular problem when you've got so many big brains future-gazing. Clive was insistent that we didn't watch the television, or get our news from the Cumulus, because radio was a less manipulative medium. He cared so much for what we were doing and was so switched on; it was hard to imagine that he had a daughter who was my age.

We were all sitting around after supper and, because it was the one-year anniversary of my arrival, I was allowed to choose the topic for the evening. I posed the question, 'If God's outside of time, how come there's no evidence of Her time travelling?'

This prompted all sorts of interesting debate about whether God existed, what exactly did we mean by time travel and what sort of evidence might we expect to see. I was the only one convinced that God existed. I didn't have a problem with believing in Her and Science, but the others insisted that the two were mutually exclusive. We were just getting into the swing of the debate, when Clive turned on the news. It was December 5 2030, the day of the Chancellor's Autumn Statement. The newsreader was going mental. It had all started at about 3pm as an organised march of bankers protesting against laws to curb their excesses had dissolved into disparate groups, shouting and chanting as they aimlessly wandered the City of London streets.

It had been a long time coming; in the first few days of power, the coalition had promised to treat everyone as equal and had committed to applying the same regime to the private sector that previous governments had applied to the public sector. Essentially, they were going to introduce a link between high and low wages, so that no one could earn more than ten times the amount of the lowest paid worker. The coalition believed that this was the single piece of legislation they needed to make a free and happy society. It had taken them a couple of years to get the legislation in place, all the while being threatened by banks saying they'd leave the UK. After decades of ducking the issue, the politicians had stuck to their guns; this was the day it would become law. But it had become apparent, over the past few months, that the banks were doing everything in their power to subvert the move. They'd been paying themselves even bigger bonuses than before and siphoning off money into secret bank accounts. The government had got wise and the next day was going to take back all the money and redistribute it through their two main channels of tax payments – the education and health funds. Once the bankers realised that the game was up, they reacted in the same way that many of the public sector workers had previously, by protesting on the streets. The bankers' equivalent of an activist wing was spending as much of the money as it could, rather than let the government get their hands on it. They'd been on a spending rampage for forty-eight hours and, fired up by a heady mix of drugs, alcohol and testosterone, they'd been causing havoc all night long, smashing up restaurants to shouts of "Viva la Bullingdon!" In the last few hours there had been a more serious contingent of hardcore protesters out on the streets. The financial Absolutists, who believed in the absolute purity of money, were whipping up a maelstrom of anger and disbelief amongst the already edgy crowd, urging them to show what happens when you try to dismantle capitalism. Already, there were reports of the City of London on fire; the rioting bankers were laying waste to their home as they retreated and left the country.

The atmosphere in our kitchen was one of stunned silence. Clive eventually spoke. 'Good. It makes our job a lot easier,' he said, standing up.

We all agreed.

'It's great that it's flushing out yet another set of Absos, isn't it?' I asked him.

He didn't answer.

I spent a lot of time with Clive, learning all about physics and quantum mechanics. I soaked up everything he had to say, but I was never sure if he truly liked me; in our world there was no such thing as absolute truth and so we only talked in theoretical terms, even about our relationships. I started to care about my appearance, and had even begun wearing some of Honey's make-up. I thought I looked great, but it seemed to have no effect on him. I was lonely, and without Cleo I was desperate for a friend. Honey was so moody it was impossible to get close to her. One night in our bedroom, as she was going on and on and on about a lad from the nearby farm and how cute he was, I decided to confide in her.

'Clive is so cool,' I said.

'Grey! Stop!'

'No, seriously. I know he's your dad and all that, but he is fantastic. And sexy,' I carried on, oblivious, in the dark room, of the effect I was having on her.

'I'm warning you, Grey!'

'I know. I know,' I replied, trying to back-pedal quickly. 'But can't you see it?' I said, unable to stop myself.

'You're creepy, you weirdo!' she spat out across the room.

'Honey, you don't understand. Would it bother you if…'

'Fuck you.' She gathered up her bedclothes and slammed the door behind her.

In the morning, I was sitting at the kitchen table eating my breakfast when Clive walked into the room, turned around and walked out, without saying a word. This happened time and time again throughout the day – I'd walk into a room and he'd leave or he'd come into a room, see me there and turn around. It was obvious that she'd said something. I stopped trying to spend any time with him at all; Mum had warned me that unrequited love erodes your self-esteem.

A few weeks later, I was almost speechless when he asked me to join him in his own private outbuilding. He never let anyone into that room – his refuge – so I was flabbergasted. It's what I'd wanted for months and, to be honest, I'd been thinking of leaving the Centre because it was so hard to be near him but not with him. We walked across the courtyard – me an over keen, but very confident seventeen-year-old and him, a worldly thirty-four-year old. I knew this was it, the moment I'd been waiting for. As we entered, I couldn't believe my eyes. There was the most amazing model railway taking up the whole space. I gasped in awe as he took me by the arm and led me into the room.

'I thought you'd like it,' he said, still holding my arm.

'It's amazing,' was all I could I could think of to say. 'How long have you been…'

'Oh, about six years. I had to be very careful not to damage it when I moved it here.'

'I didn't know about this at all. Honey never mentioned it once.'

'It's my secret. You're the only one who's seen it.'

'Why me?' I asked, hoping I already knew the answer.

'Come on. Look at this broken-down barn I'm in the middle of modelling,' he said, ignoring my question. He took me down to the other end of the workshop where there was a bench, scattered with all sorts of intriguing tools. On it was a tiny model of an old railway-yard barn, with a photo of the real thing propped up next to it. We both leaned in closer to have a look. 'Do you like it?' he asked. His hair was brushing my cheek, tickling my face. I turned my head and kissed his mouth. He stood up abruptly.

'Grey. What? Oh…' he stuttered, 'you thought?'

'No. No. Yuk. Can't a girl show some affection?'

'Sure…Sure…Sorry, I misunderstood,' he said, concentrating on the photo.

I was confused. I was sure I knew what had just happened, but it was only my perception of the truth, so I kept quiet.

Feeling insecure about the reality of a situation was a particularly difficult Liberalist pill to swallow. It was made a little sweeter because I knew the alternative to supporting these Liberalist ways was worse. The Absolutists were trying force their truths on all of us and they were on the rise.

5

Aled

2031

Four years after I'd left my dysfunctional blood-family – Ma and Sean – and moved to a new church, I was standing on a makeshift stage, looking out into the old school hall that we hired every Sunday. From the fold-up chairs we lovingly set out every week, four hundred familiar and smiling faces looked back at me. Then, as Reverend Osborne started to pray, all four hundred heads bowed in one smooth movement, as if they were connected by a single, unseen force. Which I guess they were.

'Goodbye, Aled. The time has come when we must send you away, into the wilderness. You must face your own temptations; forty months alone in the world. Dear God, Aled has been with us now for four years and we have grown to respect his honesty and his ability to love you, come what may. And now, at the age of eighteen, we send him out in the world to discover for himself that he can rely on you, even if his community, his fellowship of believers, is not close at hand. We pray that you will keep him safe and that he will return to us of his own choice, to serve you and your Church, as the great leader that we all know he can become.'

Echoes of 'Amen' could be heard around the room as my spiritual-family of four hundred blessed the journey I was about to embark upon. I'd been preparing for this for the last six months; the Church believed that to really embrace the life that God intended for us, particularly those of us who were destined for great things, we needed to test our loyalty to God and the Church. I was about to leave the comfortable embrace of the family that had nurtured me since I was fourteen, and spend the next three and a bit years alone.

Reverend Osborne continued. 'Brothers and Sisters, Aled has been with us since we started our church and our school. He is the first of our flock to undertake this wilderness test. And, although we know him as a strong believer, wiser than most his age, it is with some trepidation that we ask this of him. At school, he has been a model pupil. In my classes, he has been a model disciple. We know he will stay true to the path of righteousness and we pray that he will be back among us in 2035, to celebrate the New Year. As many of you know, he will continue to do God's work at the charity, Tourism Aid, as head of the campaign to stop space tourism. An industry that we know panders to the vanity of the rich, causes irreparable environmental damage and is decimating the emerging tourist industries of China and Brazil, which cannot compete with the lure of outer space. Many will die from poverty because of this unholy industry. We wish him well.'

The reverend raised his hands in the air. 'Aled. Go in peace.'

The entire fellowship stood up and turned their backs to me. I was now, officially, alone.

I walked down the steps at the front of the stage and through the middle of the hall to the sound of four hundred people speaking under their breath, blessing my departure. As I got to the doors and pushed them open, I turned to see the place where I belonged, carrying on without me. I ached inside with an emptiness that was so profound it felt as if my stomach had been removed, leaving a hole in the centre of my body. I held my head up high and went to find my new home.

As I walked along my new street for the first time, counting the house numbers until I reached number twenty-six, I was playing over-and-over in my head what this new life would be like. Would I be able to cope without the structures my church had provided over the previous four years? I was worried that I'd return to the acute loneliness I'd experienced as a young lad, unable to connect with my peers. So it was with some hesitation that I climbed the stone steps of the end-of-terrace house, turned the key in the lock and stepped into my new life.

'Hi, anyone at home?' I called as I banged the door shut behind me. The charity had found me somewhere to live and the church had paid for the whole forty months rent up-front – we were a generous fellowship and money was never a problem. I had the estate agent's microcapsule leaflet which could give me a tour of the house if I wanted. I'd read the description on the way over. I knew that the house was in a 'Lovely residential street,' had been 'Beautifully refurbished in the early 2010s' and offered 'Traditional character with contemporary styling'. It had four bedrooms 'Finished with wooden flooring, original fireplaces and double-glazed sash windows', and two bathrooms. At below-street level there was a kitchen and dining area with parquet flooring. And finally, 'A manicured, landscaped garden with integrated lighting' and 'A purpose-built shed ideal for extra storage'.

But it was the people I'd be sharing with that I was most interested in. I could hear noise coming from the room to the right of the hallway, so I knocked on the door and shouted once again, 'Hi, anyone home?'

'Yeah, what d'ya want?' came the reply.

I stuck my head round the door and sitting there on his bed was a guy, about my age, with a shock of red hair and a six-inch beard, tied with a knot at the bottom. On the eWall was Stan Laurel with a light bulb in his mouth, trying to shave.

'Hey, that's *Great Guns*, isn't it?' I asked.

'Yeah, that's right. There's not a lot of people would know that. Impressed you know it well enough to recognise it without lenses. You a Laurel and Hardy fan then?' he asked.

'Absolutely. And Lee Evans – they're my favourites,' I said.

'Well, I'll be…me too. I'm Zak, ' he said, holding his hand out.

'I'm Aled. Nice to meet you. I'm moving in.'

'Wanna sit down and see it to the end? And then I can show you your room.'

'Please. Got any lenses?' I replied, realising that I'd struck gold and this wasn't going to be so bad after all.

'Here,' he said, chucking me a pair of 3D contact lenses.

I took to the charity work easily and had great success in bringing the issue to the world's attention, but less in actually stopping the onslaught of space-tourism. The economies that had set themselves up to depend on tourism from the richer countries were being destroyed and the Liberalist mood of the time did nothing to help reverse the trend because, as far as they were concerned, all choices were moral-free. My life was quite ordered. I threw all my effort into work, Monday to Friday, and then at the weekends I hung out with Zak. We were close friends and, as well as the obligatory partying, we confided in each other about our dreams, our fears and our experiences of growing up. Zak had been affected deeply by his gran. She was the only one allowed to call him by his real name, Patrick, and now lived on her own in a flat in Kentish Town, but kept a room ready for him, whenever he wanted to stay. He'd had a secure upbringing compared to mine. His family all got on well – a brother and a sister, a mum and a dad and his gran and grandpa. And yet, despite all that, he had a temper that he found hard to control; he reckoned that his gran and I were the only two people in the world that could get through to him when he lost it. She sounded formidable. Zak would often refer to the time she made him come and say goodbye to his grandpa and, while he lay dying next to them, she gave Zak a lecture about mortality, how we all die and that we shouldn't be afraid. He'd grown up with a mum and dad who were madly in love and shared everything. More than anything else in the world, he ached for a serious girlfriend but he was awkward around girls. In fact, he was awkward in almost all one-to-one situations. Instead, he thrived on large groups of people. He could bring a party to life in a way that few people can, but he confided in me that he could only do it when his mates were with him, otherwise he would lose his confidence and shy away from talking to anyone at all.

Every Friday evening, Zak and I went out to meet up with a load of other friends over in Brick Lane and, after eating our favourite lamb curry, we moved from one club to another, dancing and drinking the night away until the early hours. For me, the sheer happiness of these nights out was only slightly blighted by the guilt of such hedonistic escapades. I spent every Saturday morning, until the stroke of midday, locked in my room praying. Zak didn't understand this part of my life and would tease me if I left a club early to spend more time with God the next morning. But he was not a great one for deep thinking, so it never really got in the way of our friendship.

His Saturday routine was to spend from eleven o'clock in the morning until three o'clock in the afternoon experimenting with technology, trying to hack into systems. He was secretive about how he managed to pay the high rent for his room, but friends had hinted that he made a good living from putting his technical expertise to use in ways that were not entirely legal or ethical. His skills did occasionally come in useful, though. I'd had no contact with either Ma or my dad since I left home and, as neither of them had tried to contact me, I asked Zak to track them down. In case I wanted to get in touch with them. He found an address in Cardiff for my dad, but couldn't trace Ma.

6

Grey

2031

On a late summer's afternoon in 2031, a few months after the incident with Clive, I was sitting in the backyard of the house. The sun was gorgeous, warming my face just enough to make it worth staying outside. I was having a glorious, well-earned break from my work. The rhythm of the day had been so relaxing – reading some William Blake, drifting into sleep, waking up, reading some more and then drifting off again; the world was peaceful and it was a luxury to let my mind wander. I'd just finished reading *The Schoolboy* and I was pondering whether it's cruel to make children go to school in the summer. A little yellow-breasted bird with a green head and white belly – probably a wood warbler from the Ynyshir reserve – was showing great interest in the lichen layer of our vertical farm. We used the lichen extensively in our photosynthesis experiments and there was something exceptionally magical about seeing this composite organism of a mycobiont and a photobiont in its natural habitat.

The bubble of my idyllic afternoon was burst by a helicopter landing in the back field. This was the first time I'd seen one in real life and its brutal arrival shocked me into action. I jumped up and ran across the yard. A well-groomed man with swept-back, grey-speckled brown hair stepped down and walked towards Clive, who was already half-way across the field. Our mysterious visitor walked with confidence and although his clothes were plain – a pair of nondescript blue jeans, a plain blue shirt and deck shoes – he wore them in a way that made them seem like badges of authority. He shook hands with Clive and patted him on the back; apparently they already knew each other. Clive guided the visitor into his private outbuilding. I was curious, so I crept up close and listened through one of the cracks in the old door.

The stranger's voice was smooth, as if the edges of each word had been rounded off before they left his mouth. His was the voice of one of my mum's pet hates – an Oxford graduate.

'Can you?' asked the stranger.

'You know I can. You know I'm the best. That's why you're here, isn't it?' replied Clive.

'Partly, but not the only reason,' said the stranger. 'Will you?'

'Fifty per cent of the profit will come to the Centre?'

'If that's what you want, then yes. As soon as prohibition is repealed,' said the stranger, nodding as he spoke.

'And you're happy with the sample?'

'You know we are. I'm told it's the best MDMA on the market,' said the stranger, a little quieter than before.

'Douglas, it's a deal,' said Clive.

'Good. Now that is agreed…can I ask, do you have a Katherine Davies here?'

'Not that I know of,' said Clive. 'Why do you ask?'

'No reason.'

At the mention of my name, I knocked and entered without waiting for permission. Clive's face flashed with anger but he regained his composure immediately.

'I'm Katherine, Kate, Grey – known by all three – who wants to know?' I asked.

'Grey,' said Clive. 'Meet Douglas DeSouza. He's from University College London – UCL – and he's going to fund the Centre.'

I put my hand out towards Douglas and he took it, giving it a vigorous shake. 'Pleased to meet you,' he said.

'What makes you think they'll end prohibition?' I asked.

'We've told them to,' he said, not flinching as I revealed that I'd been listening to their private conversation. Clive coughed and was obviously uncomfortable.

'Grey, I've told Douglas a lot about your work and your theories,' he said. 'And, Douglas, as I mentioned before, she'd be a great asset to your project.'

Douglas tensed at the mention of the project but remained charming, nonetheless. He switched his attention to me. 'Clive is quite right. He has told me all about your incredible aptitude. Did you say your name was Grey?'

'Nickname,' I replied.

'If Clive is coming with me, and we are going to fund the Centre, I'll need a point of contact. Is that you?' he asked, staring at me with his piercing grey eyes. I glanced over to Clive, who nodded.

'Yes. I'm the one to contact,' I said.

'Well, I'll be in touch. Do feel free to get in touch with me first, won't you?' said Douglas, as he transferred his details to my uWatch. 'We need to depart,' he said, turning away from me and focussing all of his attention on Clive.

'Sure. Grey, the model's yours to complete, ' said Clive, picking up a small cloth-bag. 'And can you tell Honey that I love her.'

Without looking back, they strode across the yard to the helicopter. And they were gone.

7

Aled

2032 – 2034

It was a few months after I met Zak that prohibition was abolished. The Liberalists, who were keen to show how easy going and youth friendly they were – and to try and rescue the economy – decided to legalise all drugs. For those of us that wanted to try drugs but believed in obeying the law, this was great. The night of the repeal, every club in London was hosting a party and we'd been deciding where to celebrate for some time. Zak was only interested in being where Tess would be. He had a massive crush on her. She was nice enough and attracted a lot of attention because she was a barrister and rode a unicycle. I didn't understand how she could attract so much attention because, although she was fun and quirky, she didn't really have a lot to say for herself. But Zak was smitten.

We were sitting in his room having a drink before heading out to the party at Loose. 'I know you reckon she's outta my league,' Zak said, starting yet another conversation about her.

'Not true. But, I don't get why you're so obsessed,' I replied.

'She's gorgeous and witty and pretty.'

'Pretty vacant,' I replied, but making sure I smiled at the same time, so he wouldn't take me too seriously.

'Well, I'm gonna make a move tonight.' He playfully prodded me in the ribs.

'Okay. I won't hang around and cramp your style…if that's

what you're trying to ask, in some roundabout way.'

'Mate, that's exactly what I'm getting at. It's going to be one banging night out, so you'll probably have to come home early to leave yourself enough time for all your Saturday morning repentances,' he said, chuckling at his own joke.

He'd hit a bit of a nail on the head, though, because deep down I already knew that I was going to do far more than take drugs; the temptations of such a momentous night were too enticing to miss out on. I was sure that God would understand.

We left the house and walked up to our local high street, which had been transformed over the previous few years into a pleasure area for locals and tourists alike. Cars had been banned because, although you could personalise them to have any engine sound you wanted, not everyone did. Some were still, as manufactured, silent. Pleasure areas and silent cars didn't mix well.

The boards that had been covering up the bars along the street for the previous few weeks had been taken down to reveal the new post-prohibition offer. This wasn't only about stopping prohibition, it was welcoming in an age of Liberalism which put the choice of leisure activity well and truly in the hands of the consumer, not the government. The street was vibrant with every kind of pleasure you could imagine. It was early so there weren't a lot of people there. A few tourists walked cautiously along the street, keeping their distance from the occasional body slumped in the gutter, bleeding, shaking or puking.

We walked past a self-harming bar called the Heal Bar which had old-fashioned razor blades hanging in the window, a laser flashing across the arm of a mannequin and an advert for cigarette burning.

Zak was enthralled. 'Look. You can cut yourself with a laser.'

'I heard they're nowhere near as good as the old-fashioned cutting,' I replied.

'Didn't realise you were the expert,' he challenged.

'I'm not. Look at this one – is that piles of heroin on those scales?' I asked, as we passed by the Skag Bar.

'Reckon all those different-sized syringes give the game away, don't you?'

We walked past the Skag Bar queue of nervous-looking people and then six shops in a row with vaporisers and huge lumps of hash in their windows. On the opposite side of the street was Sherlock's Delight – an underground bar guarded by two doormen dressed in long black coats, half-size top hats, and motorcycle goggles. The bar's only branding was a bronze nameplate set in the pavement. Every time the dark wooden door was opened, to let in an eager visitor or to let out a satiated customer, the doormen would check their Victorian fob-watches, make a note of the time and close the door with an air of extravagance.

The woman on the door at Loose gave us a bag of powder, encouraged us to test a little in the machine in the foyer and told us to 'Enjoy'. It tested purple-black which, according to the graphic on the side of the machine, was pure MDMA.

Inside, the music was pumping, the sweat was running and the smiles were as big as Jim Carrey's in *The Mask*. It turned out that Zak was right, though. Almost as soon as we arrived he hooked up with Tess and left me to my own devices and I did some stuff that took a lot of repentance.

Tess and Zak became an item and I didn't see as much of him. But every Thursday, rather than at the weekend, we still met up at the local pub. We were comfortable together and were such close friends because of these few months; we learnt things about each other, helped each other and saw each other in such embarrassing and compromising situations that we couldn't shock or disappoint one another.

And then it happened: on the 1 April 2033, the Liberalists declared a War on Absolutism.

At first nothing changed, but once they declared that they would stamp out any belief in absolute truth, whatever form it took, their acidic campaign of lies began. To voice a strong opinion was seen as tantamount to blocking the progress of the human race, to be dragging it back to an age when it was thought that the elite knew best – an age where everyone knew their place. This was predominately a war of propaganda in the same way that the previous War on Drugs had been. Its aim was to kill all trust in anything other than self. Scientists, Christians, Muslims, Humanists and Atheists formed the Coalition of Believers in Absolute Truth – to protect the right to believe that absolute truths exist, even if you don't know what they are. I publicly sided with them; I was unsure about a lot of things, but I knew deep down that the truth was there, waiting to be found.

I'd been an outsider for much of my childhood, so a campaign against my beliefs didn't bother me too much. I carried on as before, but my friends found it harder and harder to associate with me. One Thursday night it all came to a head. Zak and I were arguing again.

'The CCTV's to make us obey, to oppress us,' he said, looking at Jon and Dave for approval.

'It's there for the protection of everyone. It reduces crime and, more importantly, it stops people being afraid,' I counter-argued. These were well-worn arguments that we'd had many, many times before. This time Zak was different and started to get really wound up.

'You Absos…all you want is to be watched over, to obey the rules so you don't have to think for yourselves,' he continued.

I got upset. I knew he was being disingenuous because a few days before he'd confided in me that he'd been out in his car for no other reason than to feel the excitement of driving. He was panicking that he'd been picked up by CCTV and the authorities had worked out that he'd been nowhere, that he'd been joyriding. He'd asked me to keep it to myself, which I'd no problem with until that evening when he kept on at me, while evading his own issue.

'It's the principle. We're all responsible for ourselves, not a set of rules. And you've got to consider the context,' he said, using the usual Liberalist excuses.

I started to provoke him by asking what he'd been up to that he was so reluctant for us to know about and hinting that he should own up to the fact that he was only anti-CCTV because he'd broken the law. Anger built up inside me. The hypocrite was trying to destroy my faith in order to protect his own guilt.

I used my belief in the purity of truth as a weapon and called his bluff. 'He's been joyriding…he's shit scared of being caught… that's the truth,' I told Jon and Dave.

They went silent and changed the subject. I felt a rift open up between us.

It wasn't long before the funding for my charity dried up; it had become illegal to financially support any specific campaign. I watched the War from the sidelines, desperate to fight for the Absolutists, but it was eighteen months before I could return to my church. I'd lost my friends and my job. I was totally alone and spent most of my waking hours on my uCumulus, searching for others on their wilderness test, but I couldn't find any.

Early one morning there was a knock at the house door and, as it was never for me, I waited for someone else to answer. They didn't, so when the knock came again, this time more vigorously, I went down and opened the door. A short man, wearing trainers, jogging pants and a grey duffle coat with its hood up so you could hardly see his face, stood there, looking furtively from side to side.

'Aled?' he asked.

'Who wants to know?'

'It's crucial I get to talk to Aled, please,' he said, quietly.

'Come in then,' I said, desperate for some company – any company, no matter how strange.

He walked through the door, hunched up as if he was expecting to be set upon by a host of demons straight from hell. His head was hung so low that he had to look up at me, through his eyebrows.

'I have something of extreme value for Aled Griffen,' he said.

'That's me.'

'This is a very dangerous artefact to be in possession of. Please, only take it if you are truly Aled Griffen.'

'I am,' I replied, nervous, but intrigued all the same.

'This is from the New Natural Philosophers. It's documented proof of the existence of God,' he said as he placed a uWatch into my hand.

'Who are the New Natural Philosophers?' I asked, irritated and embarrassed that I didn't know what he was talking about.

'I presume you've heard of Newton?' he said, raising his eyebrows.

'Yes. But I don't see the connection.'

'He was an early Natural Philosopher. I'll keep it very simple for you – it's the study of Physics, mainly. But philosophically… without the experiments.'

'Oh. I see. And why should I believe that this has any credibility?' I asked, rolling the uWatch around in my hand.

'Take a look inside at the eminent names that have put their weight behind it.'

I plugged the watch into the uCumulus and it loaded on to the display. I stroked the front cover of the manuscript slowly, as if I was opening the most precious present in the world. Inside there were three signatures that would have impressed the most sceptical person imaginable. This certainly seemed to have the credibility he'd promised.

'And what does this conclude that's so dangerous?' I asked.

'It proves, through theoretical physics, that not only does God exist, but that it would be impossible for there not to be God – God as an intelligent non-human consciousness that we're connected to in some way.'

'You've got to give me a bit more than that.'

'Okay, but I'll simplify it for you. Quantum physics tells us that an event has multiple possible outcomes and it's only when it's observed that the event becomes fixed. This is all very well, but that means that each observation also needs to be observed. Following this logic, you have an infinite number of observations with no apparent end. There needs to be an ultimate observer who can choose one of the multiple realities, without the need to be observed. Their decision then cascades down a particular route and reality settles into one of its many possibilities. The difficulty with the theory of the omnipresent observer is that they would observe everything, including the experiments we don't. But, we've formed our understanding of quantum physics on the basis that some experiments aren't observed – the two theories cannot stand alongside each other. Until now. This theoretical proof shows you can be aware of what's happened without observing – to be conscious of an event and yet not interact with it. This is the proof of an omnipresent observer. Or God, to me and you.'

'This could win us the War then.'

'No.'

'What do you mean, 'no'?'

'Exactly that.'

'If this proves beyond doubt that there is a God. And these people are prepared to back it. We've won.'

'You're not strong enough. Yet.'

'This would make us strong. I don't get why you're so negative. You want me to accept this gift that could save Humanity, and then put it away in a cupboard somewhere?'

'What you need to understand, and you must promise to take my word for it, is that, if this was to get out at the moment, the Liberalists would start a ferocious campaign of propaganda against those names in the front of that book. It's unlikely that Science would survive. The cost to humanity and to the individuals is indescribable. I implore you to treat this with the utmost care. You must promise.'

'And if I don't?'

'I can't stop you. But, and I can't emphasise this enough, you'd regret releasing it now. Believe me.'

He moved his head closer to mine, as if he was about to tell an even greater secret. 'Create a Cumulus-Museum to hold it safe. You'll know when it's the right time to release it to the world, but watch out – we've had hints of a secret organisation that'll go to any length to destroy this. They will lie to discredit it and then destroy it and you with it,' he said.

'Why have you chosen me?' I asked.

'Believe me, you're the right choice for the future,' he said.

'Why should I trust you?'

He opened up his uCumulus. 'Database of Influence. Top-influencer,' he said, passing it to me.

On the screen was the database which ranked everyone's sphere of influence and where they sat in the world's pecking order. It did this by analysing the data on every individual's friends and links in their virtual social-networks, their profession, their net-worth, their grandparents' schools, and where they grew up.

A man in a duffle coat, with his face hidden and labelled unknown, appeared on the screen as that moment's most influential person in the world-wide database.

'Why a Cumulus-Museum?' I asked, still reeling from the discovery that I was in the presence of such an important person.

'We can keep an eye on it for you,' he said. 'And, it is God's will. I must go before it's too late,' he added.

I was frozen to the spot, completely convinced that this had been the most significant moment of my life. As soon as I heard the door close, I began to think about what to do.

I contacted the elders to ask them to take me back before my wilderness test was complete and they welcomed me back with open arms.

Back in the community I studied the techniques of the Liberalist propaganda machine and the way it latched on to a half-truth and then twisted it into a preposterous but believable lie. Once a week I spent an evening with the elders unpicking the lies so we could defend ourselves. I was good at it and I enjoyed it. But then the Liberalists killed my dad.

I became a front-line activist and an elder. I swore I'd destroy every last trace of their evil doctrines.

8

Grey

2032 – 2035

Douglas was an impressive man. Without him, it would have been impossible to pursue a scientific approach to our experiments, because in a world where it is illegal to believe something is true, it's also impossible to apply strict scientific approaches to problem solving. But, with Douglas's protection, we carried on searching for our Holy Grail – the use of quantum mechanics to produce clean, efficient energy. We managed to retain our environmental credentials by refusing to travel around the world, investing instead in the latest communications devices. Douglas seemed to be able to put us in contact with anyone, anywhere and, no matter who they were, he would set them up with the top-of-the-range uConference technology, so we could work together easily.

Whenever I questioned Douglas about the effect the War would have on The Project, he assured me that we were above all that petty squabbling about whether truth existed. He said that whoever controlled the world's energy would control the truth.

A few days before my twenty-first birthday, after the War had been running for almost eighteen months, I was busy working on the model railway. Putting the finishing touches to a hidden sound system that would give real life noise to the model. I'd spent a week building speakers into various bridges around the track and, finally, I was downloading sound files of twentieth-century railways to my sound console. Working on the model made me feel close to Clive and because The Project was such an integral part of my life and paying for whatever I wanted, it was becoming increasingly important to me to retain some independence. It was a relief to have a hobby that had nothing to do with Douglas.

There was a knock on the door. 'Come in,' I called.

In strolled the man I'd been wanting to see for the past thirteen years – my dad. Over the years, he'd sent me photos of himself tucked inside Christmas and birthday cards; cards full of promises to come and visit, but he'd never materialised and eventually I'd stopped believing he ever would. I recognised him instantly, even though he'd lost a lot of weight and walked with a slight limp.

'Happy Twenty-First,' he said, as if we saw each other every day. I stroked the web of fine cuts on my arm that, as a teenager, I'd carefully etched with a laser I'd bought when it was still illegal. Cuts that had eased the pain of being fatherless.

I was so pleased to see him, so pleased he'd remembered my birthday but I didn't know what to say, so I just looked at him.

'Kate,' he said.

'Grey,' I corrected.

'Kate. I have something for you. A sort of birthday present.'

In the corner of the building were a couple of rickety wooden chairs. My dad slowly walked over to them and sat down.

'What gives you the right to waltz in here as if it's the most natural thing in the world?' I snapped.

'Nothing. Except…well…it's important.'

So…have you brought me another family heirloom then?' I said, putting as much spite into the question as I could.

'Sort of.'

'What does that mean?'

'I'm giving you a flat in London.'

'A flat in London? How come?'

'It's complicated, but to cut a long story short – I have another family and it was their home. But they've all gone their separate ways now and I've lost contact. So you're the rightful heir.'

'Does my mum know about this "other" family?'

'Yes,' he replied solemnly, 'She was great about it…I sometimes wish…but I made my choice,' he muttered, barely audible.

'So. You're giving me someone else's flat?'

'Not really. You've got two half-brothers but they're not interested in it. And their Ma has been living in a nunnery for some time now and refuses to acknowledge me or her sons. It's rightfully yours.'

'Do they know about me?'

'No. And I know them well enough to know that they wouldn't be at all interested. They're totally caught up in their own world. Their ma kept them at arm's length from me so they're not going to welcome my other daughter, are they? Drop it…please.'

'I want to know more about your secret life,' I hissed, feeling stupid to be jealous. Like his other family, he wasn't part of my life either, but somehow he'd always been there, just under the surface.

'My secret life? There's nothing to know, there's no point,' he said.

We sat and talked. He talked about Cardiff, where he now lived, and asked me about my work – although I could tell from his expressions that he didn't really understand what I was saying. I knew from Aunt G that he'd been one of my mum's theology students so I steered the conversation towards God, testing to see whether he would clam up like everyone else or whether he was better than that. It was wonderful to hear his stories, to be able to talk about God openly and, most of all, to get to know this mysterious man. But it became obvious, as the afternoon progressed, that we had extremely different views.

He told his favourite story sitting forward in his chair with his hands clenched tightly in his lap. 'Grey. You wouldn't believe it. There was a young lad who'd been injured in a cycle accident, with head injuries that the doctors didn't think he'd recover from. The lad's parents set up a round-the-clock prayer vigil for the first week and he recovered much better than the doctors predicted; we all knew that this could only be as a result of prayer.'

This unswerving belief that there could be no other explanation and that this was the pinnacle of God's involvement with Her creation made me sad. With every other story, I prodded a little to try and see if his understanding went any deeper, but it didn't. His perception of God was childlike. It was a strange feeling to have affection for someone with such limited horizons. I think he realised how different we were and, after a couple of hours of talking, he stood up and, with tears in his eyes, he gave me a big hug, kissed me on the forehead and said, 'Girl, be the best you can – it's all a dad can ask.'

I cried as I watched him walk away into the dark night, knowing that we could never be equals. All my hopes of a dad I could look up to vanished. And knowing that I had half-brothers that I couldn't contact made the intensity of my loneliness, especially my lack of close males, more acute. The next time I spoke to Douglas, I asked him if he would be able to trace my half-brothers, if I wanted. He assured me that I only had to ask and that it would be easy for The Project, with its vast resources, to trace anyone I wished.

A month later, a message from Aunt G flashed up on my watch. 'I'm really sorry but I don't know how to tell you, so I've sent you her note. Call me as soon as you want, G.'

I fired up my uCumulus to see what Aunt G was talking about. The message was simply a link to a Cumulus site but I recognised it straight away. It was a suicide site that had become more and more popular over the last year or so. People who were struggling to cope with the uncertainties that the War propaganda was creating registered their suicides to declare that they'd taken control of their lives and claimed their own truth. I slumped to the floor, hoping that it wasn't what I thought it was, and asked the uCumulus to link me through.

'Dear Katherine and Geraldine, this is my choice and I'm proud of myself for having made it. This War has eroded all the trust I had in anything good. The Liberalists have left me no option but to take this ultimate, positive step. I'm taking control of my life. They've destroyed my beliefs in God and in human nature and, while I agree that the Absolutists are dangerous and must be stopped, I weep over the way we are going about it. I see no future for the world, it can only get worse and I don't want to be a part of it. I'm relieved to have made this choice, so don't be sad for me and don't let it affect the way you live. I had a choice and I took it. I'm proud of myself and you should be proud of me, too. I will always love you.'

I was proud of her. I knew that she would not have done this lightly and if that's what she wanted as her legacy, then who was I to disagree? But I was devastated and hated the world that had led her to kill herself. I knew it was no longer disgraceful, or even sad, to commit suicide because that would be judging another human being's choice, but this was yet another occasion when the bitter Liberalist pill was hard to swallow.

There was also a message from Douglas, asking me to call him and so, through the veil of despair, I called, determined to do as she'd asked and carry on.

'Douglas. You wanted me to contact you,' I said, as his face came into focus on the uCumulus.

'Thank you, Grey,' he replied in those soft rounded tones of his, 'I've some more bad news for you, I'm afraid.'

I chose not to ask how he already knew about Mum, focussing on the reason for his call instead. 'Is it Clive?' I asked, hoping to God that it wasn't.

'No. I'm sorry, but I traced your half-brothers and your dad.'

'I didn't ask you to, but that's not bad news.'

'I'm afraid it is,' he said. 'Last night, your dad died of a brain tumour.'

'No one has to die of a brain tumour. Why didn't they save him? I don't understand,' I said, with tears welling up, again.

'Bit of confusion over the treatment, I'm afraid. Your half-brothers couldn't agree and so he wasn't treated in time.'

I hung up. I didn't understand how that could happen. How could they be so stupid or so callous? It just didn't make sense.

It was shit. I was mourning for both of my parents at the same time and although I hardly knew my dad, it was his death that I felt most deeply. It wasn't just that I'd not had a chance to get to know him, it was the utter waste of someone dying accidentally, not of their choice.

It wasn't long before I wanted to move on from the Centre and to start another chapter of my life and, with Clive, my mum and my dad all gone, there was nothing to keep me there any longer. I moved to my flat in London, which made me feel closer to my dad and half-brothers, and contacted Douglas to ask if I could join The Project at UCL. He agreed immediately.

I'm not sure if Aunt G forgave me. She didn't like the sound of Douglas and his project, but then she was biased – she wanted me to stay in Wales.

Once I was in London, I was aware of the War, but it was still having little effect on me. In fact, I was having a ball.

Douglas put me in contact with Professor Staples at UCL. She was well-connected and agreed to take me on as her PhD student. I began my research into incidents in Holy Texts that might be explained by quantum physics. I focussed on the various apparitions in the Old Testament, the *Koran* and the *Torah* – investigating if they were in fact glimpses into alternative parallel universes. The story of Elijah – who appears in all of the main Holy Texts – being taken up into Heaven and not leaving any physical trace behind was intriguing. I was completely absorbed. The more I worked on it, the more I thought it might be possible that, every now and again, God swaps our universe for a different, parallel one.

Douglas also insisted that I work with his Neuroscience Project, developing ways to help people manipulate their brain patterns to change their instinctive behaviours.

One evening, in February 2035, another patient was brought to us in our basement lab.

'This little nuisance interrupted a classic piece of theatre to broadcast his own filthy propaganda,' said Douglas. Next to him was a sheepish-looking boy, a little younger than me.

'What's your name?' asked Douglas.

'You can call me Thomas,' he said, shuffling his feet as if he wanted to run away.

'And, we're going to help you. Aren't we?' said Douglas, looking him straight in the eye.

The boy sagged and nodded. 'Yes please,' he said.

A girl, who'd been brought in a few weeks before, was already sitting on a chair, hooked up to the FMRI brain-scanner. We sat him down next to her.

'This is Sarah. Watch her blue patterns and at the same time compare them to your own. We're going to help you change yours to match hers. That way you'll be cured. Okay?' I asked. He nodded again.

'Okay. Roll,' I called across to the control booth.

Up flashed images of the police, politicians, religious figures and popular scientists. We also vStreamed short loops of Absolutist propaganda and scientific documentaries. And, all the time we encouraged him to watch his blue patterns, compare them to Sarah's and try to change his to match hers.

Over the next few weeks, we gradually helped him change his deepest instinctive beliefs.

I was now focussing all of my energy and effort on devising the next quantum leap for humankind, and on rehabilitating the Absolutists who came to be cured.

9

Aled

February 2035

One of the first big battlegrounds of the War was the subject of love. The Liberalists ran a two-month long campaign to destroy the idea that there was any such thing as pure love. As usual they started with viral vStreams. One that became particularly popular was of a mother and her grown-up daughter on holiday together. They were walking along side by side, discussing the art in a gallery. Overlaid were cartoon bubbles of what was really going on inside their heads. The mother was gushing about how she was so close to her daughter, thanking her lucky stars that they loved each other so much and enjoyed being together. The daughter's bubbles consisted mostly of thoughts such as, 'She never stops talking,' and, 'Why isn't she more like Corrine's mum?'

Off the back of this viral sensation, they released increasingly serious documentaries and debates. The culmination of these was a popular-science documentary by Paul Boston – a neuroscientist. He studied and explained the brain-patterns of a couple that spoke of their shared love for each other. Once the media became interested and wanted to generate some controversy around it, our political wing finally managed to get some air-time. Daphne Hicksworth – one of our elders, despite being only thirty years old – was invited to take part in a snap-debate.

I joined the elders in the basement cinema of our church, to watch it live. Standing at a lectern, in front of an image of coloured pulses firing around a brain, was Paul Boston. Daphne confidently walked on to the stage in her signature sky-blue trouser suit and smiled. The backdrop to Daphne's lectern was an image of a candle next to a Holy Text, its fluttering pages giving the impression of a fragile moth that was a little too close to the flame. She stood and waved.

The screen behind Paul changed to the pulsating patterns of two brains and the soundtrack of a couple talking.

'We love each other. Have done for years, before we even became an item,' said a male voice.

'It's true. I loved him from the moment I met him,' said a female voice.

'It's amazing how much we have in common. We spend every possible moment together,' he said.

'I don't see us ever splitting up or falling out.'

Paul cut the air with his hand and the soundtrack stopped.

He leaned forward on his lectern in an authoritative manner. 'Watch the difference in brain activity between the two as they speak. They appear to be agreeing with each other, but in reality they are experiencing very different things.'

He left a dramatic pause and then continued. 'The activity in the woman's brain matches the same patterns we see in the man when he's scolding his children. What does that tell us about the inadequacy of language?' He pointed at Daphne. 'And no matter what she would have us believe about absolute and pure love, we know that it's a different experience for each person. We all have our own internal view of the world. You'll never truly know what is actually going on with somebody else.'

Daphne walked around to stand in front of her lectern. 'Paul. You know I respect your research. But, you're muddying the issues here. You're taking a little bit of knowledge about how the brain works and extrapolating it too far. It doesn't matter what someone's brain is doing when they talk about love. It's what's going on at a much deeper level that really counts. Just because, scientifically, you can't prove the existence of absolute pure love, doesn't mean it's not real. Truth is absolute, whether we can see it clearly or not.'

Paul had the final say. 'You can't prove it and you can't see it clearly. How on earth can you say it definitely exists? It's nonsense,' he said in a condescending tone.

The reaction on the Cumulus and in the media was heated. Initially, it was fairly evenly spread between support for Daphne and Paul, but quickly Daphne's supporters became silent. In the end, the talk was all about how soul-destroying it was to realise that you couldn't trust the feelings or motivations of those you loved and you thought loved you.

The newspapers were soon full of supposedly positive, but harrowing, stories of couples splitting up and of families being torn apart because they realised they couldn't trust each other. Soap operas were even more prolific in their portrayal of dysfunctional relationships, pushing the notion that you could trust nothing and no one.

I was convinced I needed to heed the advice of the duffle-coated man and build a protected place for the *Proof of Existence*. We didn't have the technical expertise and had to find someone from outside. Choosing the right person to build such a critical place was difficult because trust was in such short supply. I thought that, if he was willing, Zak was the ideal person. He was technically brilliant and, despite our falling out, I didn't think he would be taking any particular side in the War. He was more likely to be totally disinterested. I talked it over with the elders and they agreed.

I'd lost touch with him and trying to find him through the usual routes would be too public so I went back to our local pub and waited. I sat outside watching the comings and goings. I spotted a few of our old friends, but Zak wasn't with them. I kept watch night after night and, after three nights, I was on the point of giving up when he appeared with a large group of people. He was the same old Zak – the centre of attention, joking and laughing as they walked along the street and turned into the pub. He had to be alone when I made my approach, so I waited for an opportunity. After about an hour he reappeared, talking into his uWatch. I ran over to him, waving. He looked up and turned around, heading back towards the pub.

I shouted, 'Zak, please…hear me out.'

He let me catch him up. 'Surprised to see you, mister terrorist,' he said, with his characteristic grin spread across his face.

'Can we talk?' I asked.

'I never stopped.'

He did, but it wasn't the time to have an argument about who did, or didn't, do what. 'I need your help,' I said, offering to shake hands.

He stared at my outstretched offer and, after a few seconds, grinned and pulled me close in a big hug. 'Come on then, you look desperate. And a bit pathetic.' He pointed at the pub, 'Not in there, though – no one can know I've talked to you. You're definitely a persona non grata. I'm not on anyone's side in this stupid war of yours, but there's people in there that I get a load of dosh from. They'd cut me off without a second thought if they knew I was fraternising with you lot.'

'We'll need some tip-top technical stuff,' I said.

'Sure. Let's go to my workshop then,' he said, nodding in the direction of a side-street.

I followed a little way behind, so there was no danger of him being associated with me. We turned in to a small alleyway. Half-way down, he stopped and looked quickly from left to right. He took a small blue-glowing sphere out of his pocket and rolled it between his thumb and forefinger. A boarded-up doorway clicked and swung open.

'In you go,' he said.

'All a bit cloak and dagger, isn't it?' I asked.

'Can't be too careful. Let's chat inside,' he said, nervously checking left and right along the street.

The building was an old warehouse furnished from floor to ceiling with rack upon rack of machinery. The air was filled with the sound of a thousand computer fans whirring away.

'This is your workshop?'

'Yup. Fancy, eh?' he said, still grinning as if it was all a bit of a laugh.

'How come you didn't bring me here before?'

'You didn't ask.'

'We were best mates.'

'Yeah. Sorry about that. As soon as I'd told you to fuck off, I felt really guilty. But I can't afford to be seen with you – you understand, don't you?'

'Getting used to it,' I said.

He waved his arm around the room in a gesture of openness. 'My way of proving that I trust you. Now. What on earth's brought you out of the woodwork?'

'I need your help, badly. Things are not going great for us and I've got this document that could completely change the course of history. Let alone the War. But I can't publish it. I need to keep it secret and safe.'

'It's that important? And you've come looking for me?'

'Yes. It's the single most important thing that will ever occur in my life. I have to dedicate myself to its protection.'

'All a bit dramatic. But, hey…you're a best friend in need.'

'You'll help then?'

'Of course. Never any doubt about it. Let's chill and you can fill me in on the details. If my little buddy needs some help – he shall have it,' he said, in a mock-patronising voice.

As I got more used to the smell of the hot air coming out of the machines, I noticed a faint background smell of old food and stale alcohol. He pointed to a couple of lopsided armchairs surrounded by egg-stained plates, beer cans and pizza boxes. As we got closer, the background smell turned into a foreground smell.

'Bit stinky, mate,' I said.

'Complain and you're on your bike,' he said, gently punching me on the arm.

'Understood. Captain.'

We flopped down in the chairs. I declined a flat beer and a slice of stale pizza and began to explain.

'After you abandoned me…'

'No need for that,' he interrupted.

'True. Sorry.'

'No worries. Carry on.'

Gathering my thoughts, I took a piece of the pizza and a swig of his beer. 'Since I last saw you, a man came to visit me and gave me scientific proof of the existence of God. And, it's endorsed by the most eminent people in the field – it's the real deal.'

'No way. You sure?'

I nodded.

'Okay. Go on…' he said, looking less than convinced.

'Anyway. It's phenomenal. I've got no choice but to protect it, no matter what. Until we're told it's the right time to release it to the world.'

'You Absos do have a penchant for being dramatic megalomaniacs,' he said with more seriousness than I would have liked. 'And, you're telling me all this…because?' he continued.

'I need somewhere to keep it. Somewhere that's absolutely thief-proof. I want to create a virtual-museum to house all the religious artefacts of our movement. Inside it, I want a secret Holy of Holies for this *Proof of Existence*. I want you to help me build the museum and, more importantly, the Holy of Holies. Will you?'

'For old times' sake, although you sound like you've lost your marbles. But why a museum?'

'Please. Trust me.'

'Sure. Whatever,' he said, shrugging his shoulders.

'What do we need to do first then?' I asked.

He stroked his fingers across his computer screen for a few minutes. A couple of times he stopped to type something.

'Take a look at this,' he said, offering me his uCumulus. 'It's the specification for a downloadable museum. What do ya reckon?'

It seemed to have everything you'd expect from a top-of-the-range Cumulus-Museum. It even had optional extensions for Scent and 3D modules.

'Perfect. While I find all the artefacts and get the *Proof* ready for transfer, can you set it up?'

'Of course,' he said. 'So long as there's no trace of my involvement. Not good for business, if you get my drift.'

'Okay. Let's do it. And, by the way, thanks. I owe you.'

He picked up a black roll of material tied up with a fibre-optic cable from a pile in the corner and unrolled the mat on the floor next to his bench. He put on the visor and gloves that had been wrapped up inside it and stood on the mat. Moving between the computer on his bench and the mat, he was engrossed and only occasionally did he mutter something about the amateurishness of the template.

Equally, I was engrossed in finding all the artefacts, the hyperlinks to other museums and the explanatory commentary. I'd been collating them using uCurator for the past few months so it was fairly easy to get them ready for the museum.

'Ready when you are,' he said, holding his hand out for the uWatch. He plugged it in and transferred the curated files. 'There. The AGP Museum appears in the Cumulus.'

'AGP? What on earth does that stand for?' I asked.

'Aled Griffen's Paranoia,' he said, smirking from ear to ear.

'Very funny.' Zak always did have way of cheering me up and lightening the atmosphere. He'd done it again. 'Thanks. Appreciated. Any ideas about a secret, impossible-to-break-into Holy of Holies?' I asked.

'I've some technical thoughts, but what do you want it to look like?'

'How about I get the *Proof* document ready while you look up the Ark of the Covenant?'

'Oh, come on. You do make things hard for yourself, don't you?' he said.

'Meaning?'

'Someone's bound to have thought of it already. We can probably download one that's already constructed. Then we only have to alter the security. Okay with you?'

'In your hands,' I said. I was so pleased to be doing this with Zak; being with him again was great.

I turned my attention to the uWatch from the duffle-coated stranger, making sure that when the *Proof* was transferred, no trace was left behind. Leaving multiple copies floating around would not have been good.

After a little while, he passed me the uCumulus. 'This one looks good. I've checked it against that rather tedious description in Exodus – it's got the pretty curtains, the gold-coated ark with the gold mercy seat on top and some rather excellent cherubim with their regal faces, lion bodies and eagle wings. We can place the *Proof* inside the Ark. All looks spot on to me. I was wondering…as part of the security…could we use some of that funky stuff about burning the fat and internal organs of a young bullock?'

'Great idea. I'd love the security to be based on the original rituals. Do you think we can do it?' I asked.

'Don't see why not. We can hide the entrance so you'd only look for it if you knew it existed. Anyone trying to get inside will be subject to the usual identity checks. There can be extra layers of protection – a special set of clothes which can be specifically made to only fit particular avatars. If you give me a list of who you want to have access, I can create the necessary items. We can also make a limited number of the altar offerings; the sacred virtual-animals would have to be dissected by the avatar in exactly the way prescribed. Then, and only then, would the curtain open. Finally, only if you've done all of this perfectly would you survive entering the Holy of Holies and gain access to the *Proof.* Anyone getting anything wrong would explode in a cloud of smoke. How does all that sound?'

'Superb,' I said, completely in awe of his ability to grasp something and turn it into reality.

'Give me an hour and I'll have it done,' he said.

'Sure.' I passed him the uWatch, sat back and watched the master at work.

Code and algorithms that I didn't begin to understand flashed across the screen. Every now and again, Zak would lean back, twizzle his beard for a few minutes and then bash away at the keyboard with an energy that you'd expect from a top athlete rather than a tech-geek in a dark and smelly basement.

'Gotcha,' he announced, looking at me over his shoulder. He took a long swig from a fresh can of beer. 'I've also set up alerts to let me know if anyone's behaving oddly in your museum. I'll let you know if it happens. Do you wanna have a look?'

'Of course,' I replied.

'Get one of those,' he said, pointing to the pile of black rolled-up mats in the corner.

I unrolled my mat alongside his and put on the visor and gloves.

'How does this work?' I asked.

'Right. Never seen one then?' He grinned. 'The mat creates a ten-foot high grid of beams that registers your movements. The gloves allow you to touch and move things and the visor displays the virtual world. If I had the full helmet, you'd also have audio-ception and olfacoception – sound and smell. Sadly, I don't. Still, it'd take ages to get every sound and smell just right and we don't have the time. Anyway, a lot of them are generic and in the museum already. It's a shame I couldn't download the smell of burning bullocks organs, though. You okay?'

I nodded.

'Right. To move around, you drag your foot across the mat. Front to back to move forward and speed up. Back to front to slow down. Face left if you want to turn left and so on. If you want to freeze your position, just wave your foot over anyone of those silver discs around the edges.'

'No one's going to have this kind of equipment, though, are they?'

'Top-end cultural museums have them. And, you'd be surprised how many rich people have them. Hey, I thought you wanted to limit access?'

'I do. But, I need to be able to get in. Me and a few others.'

'Take a bunch of mats 'n stuff then. I got more than I need.'

His uWatch buzzed. 'Damn. Gotta dash. Money calls. You'll have to take a look later,' he said.

I took off the visor and gloves, rolled up the mat and picked up another six sets from the corner. 'I can't tell you how grateful I am. Does this mean we're mates again?' I asked.

'Like I said, we never weren't. But, I can't be seen with you. Once your bloody stupid war is over, we'll pick up where we left off. Yeah?'

'Yeah,' I said, wishing things could be different.

10

Aled

February 2035

As the leader of a direct-action wing, I was responsible for as many as twelve campaigns a day. The longest running of these was designed to spotlight the government hypocrisy at the heart of the Education Department's Arts Directorate. The wing was made up of eight cells, each of eight devotees. We were trained to take action, whereas other parts of the movement were focussed on political posturing. It was public knowledge that there were also Scientist, Muslim and Atheist wings and everyone suspected there were more. Each wing was deliberately kept in the dark about the others to avoid a security breach that might compromise our secret identities. I knew very little about the members of my cell – their real names, where they lived or even if they intended to take part in that day's action – it was safer that way. I contacted them by using coded messages, left in the forgotten corners of the Cumulus.

The Heiner Müller Theatre was staging a deconstructed remake of *Fragments* – the Hopkirk classic from the twenties – and we were going to take direct-action against it. We met at two o'clock in a pub sympathetic to our cause. We sat there, a crew of eight, drawn together by a common hatred of Liberalism.

'What's the target?' asked the most vocal member – I called him Peter.

'It's the Heiner Müller again,' I replied.

'I hate that underground monstrosity. All those dark caves and corridors,' he said.

There was a lot of nodding and profound sipping of beer, but no one else spoke.

'What crap are they pumping today then?' he asked.

'A new version of *Fragments*. And they'll be broadcasting it live across the Cumulus.'

I put my beer on the table and placed my hands either side. I was ready to give them their instructions.

'Six of us will go in and you two will keep guard outside. Any sign that we've been spotted, alert us with these,' I said, handing two of them a small black cube each. I gave dark-purple spheres and pay-as-you-go uWatches to the others.

'Your tickets are already loaded on to the watches. Right. Let's go. You know what to do,' I said as I waved them out of the door. One by one, they left the pub.

Outside the theatre, a group of activists were protesting, chanting and shouting at the embarrassed queue. 'Long live scientific truth! Kill propaganda!'

I didn't know them, but I guessed they were humanists. I crossed the picket-line and queued with the rest of the ticket-holders. I took a leaflet from a group on the opposite side of the queue to the protesters. It was advertising Elective Disability – 'Ever wondered what it's like to be blind? We offer you an experience you'll never forget.' On the flip-side it explained that they would remove your good eyes and replace them with eyes that only partially worked. After your disability experience, they put your original eyes back. The leaflet gave a Cumulus address for details of a wide variety of other disability swaps; preying on the guilt of not being able to experience the world from others' perspectives was big business.

We spread ourselves throughout the queue. I loved this part – taking action, going undercover and throwing a great big spanner in their works – exposing them for what they really were. I listened to the conversation in front of me.

'As editor of the newspaper, it's my job to make sure the masses understand there's nothing they can rely on. Not even so-called scientific truth.'

'Absolutely. Same here. When I write episodes for the soap operas, that's exactly what I'm aiming for.'

These were the movers and shakers of the propaganda machine. I was pleased we'd targeted this event.

The queue inched forward as people were let in through a ten-foot-tall steel door. When I got to the front, I held out my uWatch and a robot chameleon flicked its long tongue and licked it, checking my ticket. The door swung open of its own accord and I stepped inside.

There were four clerks, each sitting at the entrance to a corridor. Three of them had their heads slumped in their arms, apparently asleep at their desks. The fourth sat there licking a lollipop, beckoning me towards her. I walked over and she waved me past.

With each step on the luscious deep-pile moss-green carpet, the damp and salty smells grew stronger. After a few metres, I emerged into a cavern. About fifty people were standing around, talking in half-whispers as they waited for the spectacle to begin. Peter was standing on his own, so I stood nearby, but didn't acknowledge him. No one else from the cell was there and that worried me.

It went dark and we all fell silent.

A voice from out of the floor said quietly, 'Fragments. We all have them. We all make them.'

A blinding white flash filled the space and, once my eyes had focussed again, I could see a man and a woman standing on a slightly raised platform.

The man spoke and the audience turned to face him.

'So. You think it's okay, do you?' he said.

'I don't know what you're talking about,' replied the woman.

'You didn't even have the courtesy to ask. If he hadn't have told me, I'd never have known.'

'What is it you think I've done?' she said.

'You know what I'm talking about. Don't deny it.'

'I don't. What has Susan told you?'

'Don't lay it all on her.'

'Stop it. You're creeping me out,' she said.

The room went pitch black for a few seconds and then a faint red glow appeared. They were gone, but a sliding door in the wall had opened. A chameleon beckoned us through with its tongue. The audience hesitated until a couple near the door plucked up the courage and walked through the gap. The rest of us followed, in a hushed silence. As soon as we were all through, the door slid shut and there was another flash of white light. This time the platform was empty, but we dutifully turned to face it anyway.

A disembodied voice filled the chamber. 'Will someone tell me what's happening?'

We all looked around the room – at the ceilings, the floor and the walls – desperate not to catch anyone else's eye.

'You in the pink jumper. What happened back there?' asked the insistent voice.

A chameleon, which had been camouflaged against the wall, stepped out and handed a small flat red rectangle to a woman in a pink jumper standing next to the platform.

'Speak,' commanded the voice.

'Er…well there was an argument between two lovers because her friend had told him a secret and he was upset,' said the pink-clad woman.

'Thank you,' said the voice and another white flash temporarily blinded us.

When our sight returned, the same two actors were back on the platform.

'She had no right,' said the woman.

'She's my friend. She had every right.'

'She's my friend, too…You don't know. Do you?'

'Obviously not,' said the man angrily. 'Are you going to tell me?'

'How do you think she knows so much about my mistake?'

'Mistake. That's an interesting word for it. I'd call it betrayal, myself.'

The woman looked at the floor and in a stage-whisper said, 'She's as much to blame.'

The room went dark, a red glow appeared and another sliding door stood open. This time we all naturally moved into the next cavern. As the door slid shut behind us, the voice once again asked, 'What happened that time?'

The chameleon gave the flat red rectangle to a man standing near the door.

'She admitted to an affair with her best friend,' said the man from the audience.

A bright flash and the actors were back.

'How could she?' asked the man.

'She tried to tell you, but you wouldn't listen.'

'Tried to tell me what? When?' shouted the man.

'The other day when you came home,' she said quietly.

'Had she been…that day..?'

'Yes,' she replied and the lights were extinguished.

The room glowed red and the familiar sliding door appeared. We moved to the next cavern. The door slid behind us, but there was no white flash. This cavern had an eWall.

A live-feed of our cavern was showing in one quarter and there were three similar groups in the other quarters. I was pleased to see members of the cell in each of the audiences.

The screen faded and a replay of each group's first cavern experience was played back in the four quarters of the screen. I watched the one diagonally opposite ours.

All the same theatrics played out – the white flash, the dialogue between the man and the woman, the red-glow and the sliding door. Except this time, the audience had come to the conclusion that it was parents arguing because their daughter had confided in her mum but not her dad and the mum had admitted allowing her daughter to joyride in their car.

I pressed my thumb against the uWatch to send the "go" signal to the rest of the cell, hoping it would reach the other chambers. I was about to activate my own dark-purple sphere – my uInterrupter

– when the image on the eWall was replaced by a single green tick. Peter had got there first. The blue, yellow and green of the Brazilian flag replaced our single green tick. It slowly faded to an image of a young girl with long black hair carrying a battered pink and grey rucksack. Her lilac checked jacket and her light blue, slightly flared jeans were torn to such an extent you could see her starving flesh through them. She stooped down and picked through the rubbish of the vast dump that she'd been carefully and slowly crossing. She picked up a piece of rotting fruit and lovingly put it in her rucksack. A sombre voice broke the silence of the room. It spoke slowly. 'Truth is not relative. And, not everyone can afford the luxury of pretending it is.'

The uInterrupter had hacked into the theatre's system and vStreamed our message. The audience gasped, a few people fainted and a low hum of whispering filled the cavern.

A neon-blue beam swept the room, piercing the air around us, and settled on Peter. Six security guards, dressed in blue jeans and plain beige shirts, escorted him out through a door marked Emergency Exit. I quickly de-activated my sphere, hoping the others would have the good sense to do the same. We all knew the risks of these type of missions and sometimes one of us would get caught and never be seen again. But this was the first time we'd encountered this neon-blue tracker technology.

I mingled with the rest of the audience as they shuffled out. There was lots of mumbling about how shocked and angry they were to be caught up in an Absolutist attack.

One woman was asking her friend, 'Are they right? Shouldn't we be helping those starving kids?'

Her friend replied, 'Who knows what the reality is? For all we know, they're happier than us. Not having to strive the way we do. It's just not as simple as these Absolutists would have you believe. I hate them. They're just fucking with your head.'

I left them to it, hoping that we'd disrupted the status quo for at least a few of the audience.

All of us, except Peter, made it back to the pub, returned the equipment and left without discussion. I sent a simple message to the elders: 'Mission accomplished but lost a comrade.'

After filing my report, I carried on with my usual early-evening routine. I walked along the South Bank with my uInterrupter tuned in, ready to latch on to any passing uCumulus. As it homed in on someone, it would send a vCard announcing that 'The truth is out there if you want it – all you have to do is say *yes.*'

I strolled up and down for a couple of hours until the small black cube in my pocket alerted me to the presence of the Police. I left immediately and made my way back across Westminster Bridge.

I squeezed down the side-alley of the church and pressed my thumb on the nose of the stone angel that stood in an indented part of the wall. An opening in the wall appeared and I stepped through.

'How's your day been?' one of the other elders asked, as I checked my equipment back into the stores.

'We lost an operative at the Heiner Müller. They seem to have a new technology for locating our uInterrupters. We should get someone to look into it. Apart from that, fairly typical. Got some good connections on the South Bank. Was there much database activity as a result?'

'A little. It's not really happening, is it?' he said.

'Hard to tell. It all adds up, I guess. How's the other Absolutists doing?' I asked.

'Not faring much better, from what I hear.'

'I hate being on the same side as them. We don't believe in the same things.'

'We all signed up to the Coalition of Believers in Absolute Truth, though. Didn't we?'

'Guess so. It's so hard. No one's really interested. If only we could get the upper hand long enough so we could release the *Proof of Existence,*' I said, with the same level of despondency I'd felt for some months.

'If only, but we seem to be further away than ever,' he replied.

As I made my way back to my room, my uWatch buzzed with a message from the Council of Elders.

'Aled. Come quick. We've found a private conversation between the Pope and his Bishops. This is dynamite.'

I ran down the underground corridors, slipping occasionally on the wet floors, until I reached the elders' den. They were sitting in a circle in deathly silence.

'What is it?' I asked.

The most senior elder spoke. 'We've picked up a strange thread of conversation floating around the Cumulus. It registered in our daily trawl but, strangely, it wasn't part of the public data-web – someone must have deliberately led us to it. It seems to be a debate between the Pope and the Bishops that are trusted exclusively to interpret the word of God. We're stunned at how poorly secured it was.

'It centres on some early church manuscripts that the Pope has been studying. He feels these in particular should have been included in the Holy Text and because they've been kept out, he's calling its whole validity into question.'

'But we know that loads were kept out,' I said.

'True. For some reason he's agitated about these. In particular, he's talking about those written by the women of the early church. Phoebe, for instance. He doesn't describe in any detail what he's questioning, but it's apparent that he's starting to reconsider some of the basic foundations of the Catholic Church – such as women priests and sex without marriage. He wants to go public about these doubts. The Bishops are encouraging him to keep silent. They feel it would destroy the faith of his followers.'

For hours we debated what we should do with this knowledge and, after much deliberation, we decided to tell the Vatican that we had "stumbled" across it. We sent a message that included some extracts and made it clear that we agreed with the Bishops. We threatened to expose the Vatican's inability to keep its innermost thoughts secure if he didn't resign.

The Vatican responded, telling us that the Pope himself wished

to have an audience with us, immediately. The elders asked me to
be our representative. They wanted me to force the Pope to resign.
We all agreed that having the heart of the Catholic Church riddled
with doubt would play right into the hands of the Liberalists.

The next day, a Vatican helicopter collected me and took me
to see him. I made our demands clear.

'You must resign or we'll publish enough evidence to show
that you lead an antiquated and useless church that can't cope with
the modern world.'

'No one else will be prepared to be my successor and the
Catholic Church will become a headless body of one billion people,'
he explained.

'But this is not the moment to undermine their beliefs.'

'There is never a good time. Except for the one prompted
by God.'

'You can't.'

'I must.'

The discussion was over. It was obvious he wasn't going to
back down and nor were we.

Back home we discussed his reaction and, after a lot of
soul-searching, we decided it was a bluff. We published sufficient
to discredit him personally, but not enough to undermine his
followers' belief in the Holy Text.

As soon as we released it, he resigned and announced that no
one was taking his place.

We sat around in silence for hours, staring at the eWall.
Watching the Cumulus activity reporting the collapse of the Catholic
Church – country by country. Like a decapitated body, it crashed to
the ground, twitching but incapacitated.

We were still sitting there when the image on the eWall changed
and the duffle-coated man appeared. 'Aled. Let me in. I'm outside,'
he said.

'Aled, explain,' said one of the other elders.

'He's the man that gave me the *Proof*.'

'What do you want?' asked the elder.

'Let me in. Quickly. I don't have long.'

The elder nodded to me. I stood up and flicked a switch by the door. The outside door opened and he shuffled in.

'Bring him to us,' said the elder into his uWatch. He turned to me. 'Aled. Should we trust him?'

'I think so. Yes.'

The door to the den opened and he walked in, still with his hood up.

'What do you want from us?' asked the elder.

'Aled needs to leave. He's in danger. And so's the *Proof.*'

'I don't have anywhere to go,' I said.

He handed me another uWatch. 'Tickets on there to get you to a monastery in China. It's the safest place on earth, at the moment.'

'A monastery in China?' I asked.

'Yes. You'll need to travel a particular route, avoiding much of the social collapse brought on by the end of the Catholic Church.'

'Okay. Tell me where to go and I will,' I said. Having watched this disaster unfold, I knew we were in a dire situation and despite his rather secretive way of going about things, I trusted him.

'You'll need to cross Europe to Russia and then through Mongolia to China. Someone will pick you up when you reach Beijing. The worst-hit countries in Europe are Italy, Spain, Portugal and France, so heading east is your best bet. Poland's been hit really hard as well, so you'll have to be careful there. We'll try to get you an escort, but don't rely on it.'

'When do I go?'

'Today. Three-thirty-one this afternoon. From St. Pancras Station. Good luck.'

Just before he left the room, he shook my hand and for the first time I saw into his eyes. They looked sad and ancient and wise.

11

Grey

February 2035

'We've got one on the move,' said Carlos.

'Where?' asked Douglas.

'St Pancras Station. At the Eurostar. Trying to leave the country, by the look of it. We picked him up through that recog statue we installed a few weeks ago.'

'Which one is it?'

'I'll check,' said Carlos. 'It's a leader of a direct-action wing.'

'Doesn't tell us much,' said Douglas.

'Hold on. It's him. Look.' Carlos stroked his uCumulus to life and the feed from St. Pancras Station came up on the eWall. The recog software homed in on the back of a man with long black hair. He was wearing jeans, a blue t-shirt and boots and had a travel bag slung over his shoulder. He stood alone, with his head bowed slightly. Occasionally he looked around, giving the recog statue a chance to scan his face and match it against the database.

'Aled,' I said under my breath.

'Yes,' said Douglas.

'Should we stop him?' asked Carlos.

'Grey? Should we rehabilitate him?' asked Douglas.

I was torn. I'd spent the past few months helping Absolutists rewire their brains. It was what I did. Here was one of my half-brothers, an activist, and I was being offered the chance to heal him. It didn't feel right, though. The Absos we'd been working with seemed to lose something once we'd completed their treatment. Something deeper than the way their brains worked also seemed to be affected. It was if they lost their edge. As stupid as it was, I wasn't sure I wanted to do that to my own flesh and blood.

'I think we should let him go. Once he's cut off from his cell, he'll be pretty harmless,' I said, hoping Douglas would accept the logic.

'Or we bring him in and help him,' said Carlos.

'It's your call, Grey,' said Douglas. 'I'm sure you don't want to lose him, though. Do you?'

'No,' I said.

Douglas had been offering me the chance to meet Aled face-to-face for a while. Each time he'd offered, I'd turned him down. I couldn't be sure that it was the right thing to do. As much as I wanted to meet him, we were on opposing sides. It was his job to destroy our progress and my job to realign that sort of misguided thinking.

'We can keep track of him, though. Can't we?' I asked.

'I think we should. He might come in handy one day,' said Douglas. 'Carlos. Can you arrange to have him followed? I want updates every couple of days on where he is and what he's doing, please.'

'Of course. No problem,' said Carlos. He disconnected his uCumulus and left the room.

'Thanks,' I said and followed Carlos out.

I was sitting on a stool waiting for Douglas to arrive. We were going to get our first live report back from Carlos. Aled had been gone for a week. All I'd heard was that he was okay and still on the move.

Douglas came in and switched on the eWall.

Carlos, sitting in a train toilet, filled the screen. 'We're just arriving into Warsaw,' he said. 'Rumours are that it's a total nightmare. None of the public services are working. No police. No ambulances. No fire. All a bit chaotic.'

'Can we see?' asked Douglas.

'Sure. I'll show you Aled first. We're in the same sleeping compartment. And then once we've pulled up, I'll show you the city.'

His uWatch transmitted the view from his wrist as he walked along the corridor of the train. He opened a sliding door. There were four beds in two bunks. Aled was lying on the bottom-right with his eyes shut and his bag held tight to his chest. He looked as if he was patiently waiting, ready to leave at any moment. The image juddered as the train came to an abrupt halt.

'Friend,' said Carlos, shaking Aled. 'We've arrived in Warsaw.'

Aled opened his eyes and sat up. He leant over, opened the curtains and looked out of the window, scanning the platform as if he expected to see someone he knew.

'I'm getting some snacks,' said Carlos. 'Will you join me?'

'I'll stay put, thanks.' Aled pulled out some coins and handed them to Carlos. 'Could you get me something? Same as you.'

Carlos slid the door open, left the compartment and stepped down on to the platform. It was full of people stretching and walking up and down with money in their hands. The snack kiosks were closed. The platform was empty except for those that had got off the train. A scuffle broke out towards the front. No police arrived and no station officials were to be seen. The train conductor stepped in to calm the situation down. It was if they'd pulled up in a deserted town in the middle of nowhere.

'Seems the rumours are true then,' said Carlos into his uWatch.

'Seems so,' said Douglas. 'Better get back on the train. Do you know where he's going?'

'China. Trans-Siberian through Mongolia.'

'Check in again once you reach Beijing. Unless there's any problems along the way.'

'Okay. Talk again in a week or so,' said Carlos.

The screen went blank and Douglas turned to me. 'Back to work then. I'll let you know when Carlos contacts us again.'

'What do you think is going on in Poland?'

'It's a Catholic country. Probably lost its way when the church collapsed. They'll find a better way before too long. And, they'll be stronger for it.'

My uWatch buzzed with a message from Douglas. 'Seems Carlos has an emergency. Can you join me straight away.'

I put my microcapsule model railway magazine down and joined him in the next lab.

Carlos was on the screen. 'I've lost him. A man came into the compartment and Aled got up and left with him,' he said.

'What did this man look like?' asked Douglas.

'Mongolian. Dressed in a long black wrap-around coat with an orange sash, a baseball cap and walking boots.'

'Where are you?'

'Just arrived in Ulan Bator.'

'Get off and find him,' said Douglas. 'We can't afford to lose him after all this. Grey. Any ideas?'

'None. Sorry.'

Carlos kept his uWatch transmitting as he walked through the train. The restaurant car was empty, giving us a good glimpse of the ornate wooden carvings that formed the chairs, the tables and the ceiling.

'Mutton curry? Mongolian Beer?' said a hopeful waiter with a thick accent.

'No thanks,' said Carlos as he sped past.

Out on the platform, Carlos walked up and down. 'Can you connect this feed to the recog software?' he asked.

'Good idea,' said Douglas. 'Grey, can you get that sorted?'

I connected them up. The software scanned all the images coming through from Carlos. It didn't recognise any of them, except once when Carlos looked into the uWatch and the software immediately brought up his record on the Citizen's Database.

'Lost him,' said Carlos. 'Any luck your end?'

'No,' I said.

'Get after him. And don't come back until you've found him,' said Douglas. He switched off the eWall. 'Maybe we should have realigned him after all. What do you think?' he said and left the room without waiting for an answer.

Part 2

12

Aled

June 2037

The War was over. Three years of a global war changed me for ever; I had to grow up fast. I'd escaped its dying embers and found a sanctuary, of sorts, in south-west China. It was monotonous, but the best I could hope for. The blandness of my existence was strangely comforting, despite being tormented by the drip, drip, drip of failure.

The monks had been whispering behind my back, nudging one another like schoolchildren and giving me the personal space I had spent months longing for. Except, with all the whispering, it made me uneasy. I was afraid.

I lay on my bed contemplating this when the gong sounded, resonating perfectly around the old monastery. I dragged myself from the wooden bench in my cell. The moonlight streamed in through a tiny window high up in the wall, illuminating the smooth dark wood of the bench on which, night after night, I tried to sleep. Looking at the reflected glory of that celestial body, I fleetingly considered the hundreds of thousands of visitors that had slowly but surely worn the wood smooth with their restless attempts to get a comfortable night's sleep.

I was a speck on the face of the planet compared to this. And that night, as every night, I felt even less.

I picked up my Tibetan singing bowl, lifted the ancient latch and quietly left the room. Crossing the courtyard in my bare feet, my dark-brown robe dragging on the dusty floor, I looked up and saw the familiar line of monks moving towards the chapel. Like a brown-spotted, bright-yellow snake, they slithered elegantly across the floor. I fell in line, as I had five times a day for the previous twelve months. I took a deep breath and began to whisper my own chant, 'I'm a believer, I'm an Absolutist, I lost. I'm a believer, I'm an Absolutist…' I'd used this chant for three months, desperately trying to keep out uninvited and unwelcome thoughts.

We arrived and knelt in our places, each of us rolling a wooden mallet around the rim of our singing bowl until the ugly dissonant noise transformed into a perfect harmonic note. A beautifully ornate, six-foot high, Buddha sat at the front of the room, calmly surveying the spectacle in front of him. Their volume gradually increased and, being in such close proximity to the others, I didn't chant out loud but continued silently in my own head. Rocking back and forwards, I gave the impression of someone having a mental breakdown, which was not far from the truth.

The monks were probably Neo-Buddhists, but I couldn't be certain. I didn't speak Chinese and they didn't speak English, so I superimposed my own culture on theirs. I interpreted their world through my own eyes and imposed my fantasy, a silent one-man imperialism, on them.

As the gong kept resonating, making that deep hum, I could feel the pain of my mind, body and soul touching tentatively; they were dependent on, and yet afraid of, each other. The pain was vividly real and pierced the blandness of my existence, providing a tormenting comfort that confirmed my soul still existed.

After two and a half hours, the chanting died down and we rose to leave the room. The same beautiful snake formed and slithered out into the sun, which was rising from behind the mountain. I inhaled the invigorating fresh air, which was tinged with a hint of incense and dusty soil, and took my habitual look at the clouds below, reassuring myself that I was on the rooftop of the world, a long way from trouble. I paused. My life was now a monotonous cycle of working, sleeping and eating. Punctured five times a day with the deep pain that was necessary to keep my soul alive and just teetering on the right side of meltdown.

Each and every one of us was desperate for the one and only toilet – a suitably positioned hole to deposit our waste. It was housed in a precariously built shack over the edge of the mountain, with bamboo supports forming one side of a triangle. The other sides being the face of the mountain and the floor of the cubicle. The daily queue had formed and once again I waited in line for an experience I needed, but didn't want. I was convinced that one day this ramshackle bamboo hut would topple over the edge with one of us in it. I presumed that there was a monastic policy of taking every opportunity to practise self-control and the single toilet, open once a day, was therefore to be embraced.

After an hour of waiting I got to squat in full view of the queue, torn between a physical need to deposit my waste and the privacy I would have preferred to do so. There was a slight spring in my step, as I walked back along the remaining queue to collect my pieces of wood and carving knife from my cell. I was doubly relieved that the shack had remained intact and that I'd completed the required task.

Everyone, unless they were passing through, played their part and in return received food, clothes and shelter, which is all a man needs to preserve his physical life. My contribution was to carve and I had done my best to let the monks know that the solitary nature of this occupation was vital to my well-being.

Hitching up my robe, I squatted on the floor near to the kitchen to enjoy the cooking smells, accentuated by sizzling chillies, and the distant chatter and clatter that came through the open door. It was also a perfect spot to watch comings and goings. There were monks sweeping the floor, monks tending to the plants and monks practising Tai Chi. It probably wasn't Tai Chi and Tai Chi may not even exist in that part of the world, but I came from England and it was the best term I had to describe whatever it was they were doing.

Most days the monks would go about their daily business in a friendly and jolly way, albeit in efficient silence, but that day there was a tangible excitement that I'd only experienced once before. I sat and carved, letting my mind wander back to the last time – I remembered it clearly.

A few months before, a group of four people had arrived by car and with a translator. This immediately gave them a different status to the usual straggle of travellers that made their way there.

The man I took to be in charge, probably because he looked the oldest, spoke first. 'Good morning. I'm Douglas DeSouza and this is my partner, Linda. This is her daughter, Harmony, and Harmony's friend, Peace.' He paused for a moment and then carried on. 'We're tired and want to rest here for a few days. Is that possible?'

'We can pay for our board and lodging,' chipped in Linda.

Everyone knew, including Douglas and Linda, I suspected, that the only possible answer was yes and sure enough the reply, through the translator, was, 'Please be our guests for as long as you need.'

Douglas was dressed in shabby clothes – knee-length khaki shorts and the remnants of a blue-and-white striped polo shirt, similar to the ones that London city workers used to wear at weekends. He looked to be in his mid-fifties and had the air of someone who had strong opinions and was used to being listened to. Linda, who was of an indeterminate age and held herself with a composure that exuded English upper class, was dressed in brand-new clothes. She wore lots of Gore-Tex and lightweight materials that you would only find in a good European walking shop and which most people could no longer afford.

She announced loudly, to no one in particular but looking straight at me, 'We thought it would be such fun to bring the kids here. Hope you don't mind.'

I felt intimidated by her but said nothing. I was intrigued that, although I was thousands of miles from home and practically a hermit having a mental meltdown, I was still susceptible to my English class system. Peace and Harmony's names made me chuckle, which helped me relax and warm to them. I think this was the first time in a good while that a smile had found its way to my face. They were in their late twenties and their features were wholly androgynous. Harmony wore an inexpensive, but thoroughly stunning, pure white cheese-cloth shirt with a saffron-orange silk sarong. Her toenails, peeping out of brown leather sandals, were painted with the most exquisite shade of turquoise. Peace had the same uniform, but in reverse – he wore a turquoise sarong and had saffron-orange nails. They both had long straight hair, but shaved on one side and pierced noses, in a style that had been popular amongst some of the drop-out classes of the twentieth century. Their skin was very smooth, almost white, and for the first time in a long while, they both caused a stirring of lust in me, which was not something I enjoyed, or should allow. I was already so compromised by living amongst these Buddhist heathen that I was on a slippery slope anyway, with barely enough spiritual energy to keep temptation from bursting out into the physical world.

The empty room next to mine had two sets of bunk beds and, with no favouritism shown, no matter what earthly wealth you might possess, Douglas and his family became my neighbours. I remember thinking, spitefully, hard wooden beds for all.

As the sun set and the last gong of the day filled the air, they were shown to their room. The rest of us fell into line once more for another session of chanting. 'I'm a believer, I'm an Absolutist, I lost...'

That night I lay awake with a tornado of thoughts battering my brain and, although in itself a tornado wasn't unusual, that particular swirling debris of thoughts was. I was not convinced that the newly arrived group were simply sightseeing. Since the collapse of the world economy, manufactured goods and education were rare commodities and to be able to afford both, in the form of a vehicle and a translator, showed extreme wealth. To travel with such obvious badges of wealth without any protection was sheer naivety, a deliberately bold move, or a complete belief in one's own safety. They obviously had access to lots of money and, assuming that their apparent naivety was a pretence, because they couldn't have got that far alive and be that naïve, then travelling without protection must surely mean they were either well-known and feared, or worked for someone who was well-known and feared.

I tried to bring the tornado under control but I became more and more concerned for my own safety and my precious anonymity. Irritatingly, and true to form when stressed, I started to have vivid images in my head of Peace and Harmony naked and locked together in a sexual embrace, inviting me to join them. Thankfully, I knew myself well enough not to be too disturbed by this and just let the images come and go. More important was knowing who this group of four strangers were and why they were really there.

The gong once again called us. Before I rose from my bench, I had concluded that the difference in the quality of their clothes meant they were not a real family. Douglas's ragged attire was a sure sign that he was not rich and I presumed they were not locally powerful or they would have been recognised by someone at the monastery. They had to be working for someone who had lots of money but was strict about how it was spent and didn't pay well enough for Douglas to buy new clothes.

As the sun rose the next morning and we filed out from the first chants of the day, Douglas and Linda were already outside performing some sort of stretching exercises similar to the local Tai Chi. Douglas winced and grimaced as he attempted to replicate Linda's graceful movements. His was the face of someone who has not slept well, whose body has started to rebel with age, and is so far out of their comfort zone, it's physically hurting them.

Linda, on the other hand, didn't seem to be at all disturbed and, if anything, was even more graceful than the previous evening. As they completed their exercises, Linda called, 'Harmony, time you were up, darling,' and out lolloped two gazelles. The stuff of dreams, or nightmares, depending on your spiritual morals.

During the morning I caught glimpses of them being taken around the monastery by an old monk, explaining which parts had been built in which dynasty. Later on, I watched them from my carving spot having a lesson from the chefs on how to make perfect replica joints of roast meat from soya. And, during the afternoon as I sat carving a Buddha in the hope of selling it to our guests, they crossed the courtyard and, in what seemed like a set piece, I overheard Douglas saying, 'Do you have many other guests like him?'

I may have been paranoid but I'm sure Peace looked at me to see if I'd heard.

At the monastery, we eat in little indoor booths with formica tables. During the last meal of the day, they came and sat with me.

'What brings you here then, young fellow?'

I looked Douglas straight in the eyes, trying to unnerve him, to make him trip up, because there was definitely something unbelievable about him.

'I was looking around the world and I liked the pace and rhythm I found here, so I stayed,' I answered, repeating my well-practised lie.

'It is rather lovely, isn't it,' commented Linda absent-mindedly, as she looked out of the window.

I decided to get on the front foot with the questions. 'Are you from London?'

'Yeah we're from UCL,' drooled Peace, in a lazy, overly-sexy way.

'From University College, London. I'm the Head of Anthropology,' said Douglas.

'So, is that what really brings you here?' I asked. 'It's not the easiest of places to get to, even with a car and translator. Must be important.'

For the first time Harmony spoke. 'Just trekking around in the holidays, getting a feel for the world. Not really working.'

'You must be the idle rich to be able to afford this,' I said.

This time Linda took control. 'Douglas is being sponsored

by the University to study the effects of the War on remote indigenous religious groups. The rest of us are along for the ride,' she quipped.

'You would be a valuable source of data. Would you assist us?' asked Douglas.

'I keep myself very much to myself, I'm afraid,' I answered, as plainly as I could, trying to disguise the rising anxiety I was feeling.

'Shame,' said Harmony, smiling at me.

I could feel myself blushing as I suppressed thoughts that were not meant to be and then realised I'd been staring at Peace. This wasn't going well.

'I'm just here to get some peace,' I muttered, blushing once again as I realised the unintended double-meaning.

'Aren't we all,' said Harmony, picking up immediately on my mistake and my discomfort.

Douglas brought the teasing to an end by asking how long I'd been there.

'About two years,' I lied.

'And what did you say your name was?' asked Linda.

'David.' I lied again.

'And you observe all the religious paraphernalia of the monks, don't you?'

'Yes, it keeps me sane,' was my rather careless response.

And so the evening went on. Trading pleasantries with each other, not mentioning either their study or why I was there, until the gong echoed around the monastery and Linda asked, in her authoritative manner, 'Did you come here to escape the War?'

To which Harmony added, 'I bet you're quite famous in some circles, aren't you?'

Not knowing how to respond without revealing a little of my secret, I tried to look nonchalant and puzzled. But, as I got up to leave, Peace whispered under his breath, 'Fooling no one there, matey.'

Back in my room, I lay in bed with the moon streaming in, thinking about the day. It was clear that they were not ordinary guests and that there was far more to them than they'd admitted. They were probably quite dangerous.

I slept even less than usual that night and wasn't looking forward to another encounter, so it was with some relief that, as I walked back to my cell from prayers the next morning, I noticed that my mysterious neighbours had packed up and gone. Over the next couple of weeks, each day passed uneventfully and my anxiety gradually diminished.

13

Aled

I'd missed prayers for the first time ever, thinking about how that mysterious visit had disturbed me. I lay awake staring at the walls, trying to imagine what the monks were so excited about this time. In the morning, standing in the courtyard, was my answer. Talking to the old monk, were four people. I recognised Linda, Peace and the translator, but with them was a new woman who never stopped looking around. Like a lioness, she seemed alert, lithe and ready for action.

She was dressed in practical clothes – walking boots, combat trousers and a loose brown cotton shirt – and would have looked every bit the normal backpacker, if they still existed. Her red hair was in a single plait, the tip just touching the small of her back and, in contrast to Linda's rather brash style of authority, this woman radiated something far more intriguing. I was too far away to hear what was being said, but I could tell from the body language that Linda was speaking and things were getting quite heated. The monk was shaking his head and she was pointing towards the car.

A calm descended, as the new woman placed one hand on the monk's shoulder and the other on the translator's, and both men began nodding in agreement. She had my attention. I decided to say hello, hoping I could hide how nervous I was about them returning. I forced a smile for Linda and a nod for Peace. 'What brings you back then?' I asked.

'We're here to see you, of course,' joked Peace. 'But, Confucius here is being difficult about us staying.'

'I don't think he is, you know,' said the lioness, quietly but firmly. 'And now we've sorted out how to pay, I think everything's fine and dandy.'

'I offered to pay the man and he refused,' snapped Linda.

'Yes, but they don't take money,' said the lioness calmly. 'I've agreed to lend the car to the monks, as payment for board and lodging. Oh, and by the way, I'm Grey. Nice to meet you.'

I put out my hand and lied once again. 'David. Nice to meet you.'

'We're in the same room as last time. Next to you,' said Peace, still dressed as before but looking a bit over-the-top sexy, next to Grey's subtle charms.

'We'll meet for supper then,' ordered Linda.

I was surprised to hear myself agreeing. 'Yes, let's.'

I walked away with a sense of apprehension – a mixture of fear and excitement – deciding that I'd skip prayers and spend all day carving. I went to my cell to pick up my wood and knife, secretly hoping to bump into either Peace or Grey. They were nowhere to be seen, so I collected my things and headed out to the edge of the mountain – the most splendid place in the world.

I found a rock to lean against, sat down and stretched my legs. Down below, the tops of other mountains were peeping out above the cloud. It was as if a giant dinosaur was sleeping in the mist, her spiky backbone laying claim to the valley. As I breathed in this vast horizon, I could feel my brain expanding. The sheer majesty of the view made it easy to see how humans, struggling to explain their world, have come to so many wrong conclusions. If only they'd hear the truth.

The arrival of this gang of four prompted me to think about why I'd gone to China and what was at stake. And even though

I had such an important mission, each day was a struggle to stay the right side of despair. I made myself available to God, five times a day, trusting I'd hear when he called. Hoping and praying that he'd forgive me for carving idols and that He understood I was there to protect the proof of his existence.

There were all sorts of other Absolutists at the Monastery. All wearing brown refugee-robes whether they were Muslim or Scientist and, wrongly, they believed that they were on the same mission as me. Despite fighting alongside each other, we made no attempt at contact – they'd retreated back into their own entrenched worlds, desperate to save their misguided beliefs. I should have been converting them to the truth, but I didn't have the spiritual energy to even try.

A hand touched my arm, bringing me back from my day-dreaming. 'Hi, mind if I join you?' asked Grey.

'It's a free world,' I replied heavily.

'Is it now? That's good then, eh?' she teased.

She sat down next to me, tucking one leg under the other as she took off her sunglasses, and looked me in the eyes. I could feel myself relaxing a little – a tiny speck of humanity peaking its fragile head out into the world, like a newly-hatched chick.

'So. David.' She smiled and paused, as if she expected me to correct her. 'What's a nice guy like you doing in a place like this?'

Despite myself, I smiled back. 'Well, I came for the night life, mainly.'

'Monks on MDMA…mmm, sounds like a twentieth-century B-movie.' She grinned.

'It's all gone a bit Buddhist gong?'

She looked at me as if I was completely mad and, whilst that was a strong possibility, it was simply a bad joke.

'It's all gone a bit Pete Tong?' I tried to explain. Thankfully, she ignored my attempt at humour, inhaled deeply and stretched her arms out wide.

She continued, 'Seriously, I can see why you stay here; this view is to die for.'

'That's exactly what I might be doing here. Sorry, ignore me. Just feeling sorry for myself.'

'Go on, tell me more,' she urged, briefly placing her hand on my upper arm.

'I'm out of the habit of talking, I'm afraid. Tell me what brings you here. And what's with Linda? I'm surprised you two get on.'

'We're colleagues, nothing more, nothing less. And she's cool, in small doses.'

'I'll take your word for it. Seems a bit bossy to me.'

'That's her job. Now, back to you. Are you really here to die?'

'No, quite the opposite, I came here to protect and survive. But I'm not sure it's working.'

'How do you mean?'

'Nothing, really. It's just a bit out of the way and sometimes I feel like I'm just marking time. Doing nothing but eating, sleeping and chanting.'

'Not what you intended then?'

'Don't know really. Just the way it is, at the moment.'

'I'd have thought this was every Buddhist's dream.'

'I am not a Buddhist.'

Grey moved away from me slightly, visibly shaken by the anger in my voice.

'I'm sorry, I think I've had enough chit-chat for today,' I mumbled.

I got up and walked off without looking back, devastated at what a traitor I'd just been. How could I have revealed my doubts to an outsider, just because I was feeling a bit lonely?

As I walked back to my cell, the afternoon gong rang. I decided not to take the day off after all, and as the brown-spotted, bright-yellow snake appeared, I joined it and breathed a sigh of relief as I sank back into my routine. 'I'm a believer, I'm an Absolutist, I lost. I'm a believer, I'm an Absolutist…'

The Buddha looked down on us and I felt the familiar sensation of my body, mind and soul touching. Only this time it wasn't so tentative and the pain was so much more intense, as the three of them started to come back to life and fight each other for supremacy. I kept my eyes closed for the whole two and a half hours, despite the pain increasing each minute. It was as if I was on the verge of exploding, my body flying into a thousand disconnected pieces. My brain unable to focus and manically skittering between multiple trains of thought. My soul slowly torn apart – wanting to stay with my mind and body, but also wanting to be released and fly home to Heaven.

I shuffled out of the chapel, keeping my eyes fixed firmly on the feet in front of me and only looking up as we got to my cell. I peeled off and took to my bed. I'd promised to meet Linda and the others for the evening meal but I wasn't sure if I'd be able to. I lay still for a while, gradually recovering. At dinner time, the autopilot kicked in and I went to eat with them.

'Hi. Glad you could join us,' said Peace, smiling at me.

'I'm not much company, I'm afraid,' I said, trying to smile back.

'No worries.'

Thankfully, Peace was not a chatterer.

Grey and Linda looked at me and then at each other, as if they shared a secret.

'Hello,' Linda said, quite formally but softer than I'd come to expect.

Grey rested her hand on my arm. 'Hi, no need for any great speeches. Just enjoy the company and the food,' she said, radiating the same warmth as earlier. A monk placed bowls of noodle soup, roast duck and little cups of tea in front of us. He pointed at the duck and grinned, showing off his few remaining black teeth.

'Why is he pointing at the duck like that?' asked Grey.

Peace chuckled. 'Cos it's not meat, it's tofu.'

'Wow, that's cool,' she said, flashing me a smile.

We ate in silence, until Linda spoke. 'Do you remember when our translator left us and we had to get food from that gentleman by the side of the road?'

'Sure do, tell him about it,' encouraged Peace.

'I will. We were in a village on our way here, trying to purchase some food for the journey. But the translator had wandered off somewhere and we couldn't wait for him any longer. Actually, Grey, I seem to remember it was you that was being impatient. Anyway. We approached this man by the side of the road and I mimicked placing things in my mouth, explaining we wanted to buy food. But he didn't seem able to understand. In fact, he started moving around with his arms out like wings, making buzzing noises and pointing to a calendar on his wall. This motley crew stood and sniggered, behind my back. Eventually, I realised he was pretending to be an aeroplane and wanting to know when we'd arrived in China. I nodded, in that exaggerated manner one does when they can't speak your language, pointed to his calendar and showed him the day we'd arrived. But he got very anxious, repeating his buzzing, pointing and shaking his head vigorously. This carried on for ten minutes or so and, as you can imagine, I was getting very frustrated. He took me into his house – still buzzing and waving his arms around – to give me a jar of yellowy-orange stuff from his larder. I stood there totally confused. As he became more and more animated about giving me the jar, I became more and more forceful about refusing it. Finally, the penny dropped – the aeroplane was actually a bee, he was trying to give me a jar of honey and the calendar was to indicate how fresh it was. Having worked out what he was trying to communicate, I smiled like a village idiot and nodded my head in appreciation. At this point he typed 100 into his calculator and pushed it under my nose. I was so shocked I gave him a hundred yuan, took the honey and returned to the car.'

'It was so funny to watch.' Peace laughed.

'And so expensive,' said Grey.

I smiled. The casual normality of the meal was soothing, but as soon as I'd finished eating I stood up, made my excuses, and returned to the emotional comfort of my cell. I lay on the wooden bench exhausted, but the contrast of the meal's normality with the pain of afternoon prayers stopped me from sleeping. That night's tornado of thoughts started to form.

I must have dozed off because when I opened my eyes Peace was standing inside my cell, looking very beautiful in the moonlight. He put a finger to his lips and walked slowly over to my bed, confident and yet testing the water. I kept quiet, but moved slightly on the bench to allow him space to lie down. He came and lay next to me, putting his arm around my shoulders and pulling me closer. I felt groggy, wondering if this was just a lovely dream. He was so gentle and warm, and to feel another body was an experience I'd been craving for a long time. He kissed my forehead and we lay in each others arms, for what seemed like an eternity.

He whispered, 'I liked you the first time I saw you – your long, dark hair, your blue eyes, your olive skin.'

He ran his finger down my leg. 'So athletic and so hairy.'

He inhaled. 'And your smell.'

I couldn't reply, scared that I'd break the spell and he'd disappear.

He shifted on to his side and leant over me, kissing my forehead again and then my nose and then my lips. I held his hand and looked him in the eyes, desperately hoping he realised that he had to take the lead.

I took a sharp intake of breath as he began to untie my robe.

Bang. It was as if someone had turned on all the theatre lights and I was centre stage – the gong rang, jolting me out of the sensual cocoon. I jumped up, muttering, 'Prayers,' under my breath.

Pulling my robe back on, I clumsily bolted for the door. Banging it open and running into the fresh air, I stumbled into the snake. The monks, ever calm, gave no indication that they'd noticed anything. But, as I looked across at Peace, who was standing nonchalantly against the doorpost of my cell with an over-exaggerated look of smouldering sex on his face, I realised they must have a good idea of what just happened.

I was devastated. It went against all that I believed in but, thank God, it hadn't gone as far as it might. I found my place in the chapel and, rocking back and forwards on my knees, began to chant. Again, it tore me apart. It was as if my mind, body and soul were magnets that are meant to attract one other but are placed the wrong way round. They repel, no matter how hard you try to force them together.

After prayers, I walked back to my cell with my head bowed. I was so ashamed of what nearly happened, but I still had a longing for some physical contact. It was as if an old addiction had been brought back to life, my body remembering past pleasures. I lay down, racked with guilt, and aimlessly traced the web of little cracks that covered the walls of my cell. There was a knock at the door. I curled up and put my head in my hands.

'Hi, anyone home?' called Grey, through the door. I turned over and looked as it slowly creaked open. I said nothing. Grey's face appeared round the edge. 'Mind if I come in?' she asked gently.

'Sure. If you want.'

'Peace thought you might like some company,' she said.

'What the bloody hell would he know?'

'He told me about your "encounter" earlier and thinks he may have upset you. Did he? You can be honest with me.'

'He. Thinks he might have upset me? Ego or what? I upset me. I disgust me. I hate me. Honest enough for you?' I replied. 'And remind me again what you're fucking well doing here,' I said, through gritted teeth.

'Let's chat about that,' she said, putting her hand on my forearm.

With tears welling up inside and a lump in my throat, I managed to mumble, 'If you're going to try and seduce me too, you can forget it – once is enough.'

'I'm not,' she said.

I sat on my bed, tired, lonely and distressed. The more I struggled to hold it together, the harder it got. Grey's kindness, and her hand on my arm, was the final straw. The tears came and I couldn't stop them.

'Nothing to be ashamed of,' she said soothingly as she held my hand.

I cracked and started to weep, uncontrollably. She drew me

into her arms, letting me soak up the simple love of another human being. We stayed like this for half an hour, neither of us speaking, until Grey sat me up. I pulled myself together, still vulnerable and yet strangely calm. We both sat on the bed, facing each other. Grey smiled warmly and offered me some chocolate.

'More sensual bribery?' I asked, but with a smile, betraying how at ease I now felt with her.

'Of course,' she winked. 'But first, I owe you an explanation.'

I nodded and deliberately leant forward to show her that I was listening. At the same time I kept quiet, protecting myself from saying more than I should.

'Okay, I'm not sure where to begin. I'm Grey, as you know, and I've been called that since I was sixteen and, of course, it's not my real name. I'm a Physitheist. I study the awesome place where science and God meet. The intersection of theology, metaphysics and quantum physics. I believe God exists, that our understanding is flawed and that science can help us reach a deeper and more accurate knowledge of God.'

'Why are you called Grey?' I asked, trying to slow things down so I could take it all in.

'It was a silly nickname my best friend gave me because I'd refuse to accept black and white answers. I thought it was cool, so I kept it.'

'Yeah,' I said.

'I fought as a Liberalist and I believe that Absolutism stunts the exploration and understanding of the divine creator. You okay with this?' she asked, seriously.

'Yes, carry on, I'm listening.'

'Towards the end of the War I was approached by Douglas – you met him – to join a special project team at UCL and I accepted. He's a genius, you know. I've been there for the past year.'

'And where do the others fit in?' I asked, not feeling confident enough to comment on the revelation that she was a Liberalist, believed in God and was a scientist.

She fixed me with a challenging stare. 'Your turn for some

truths first,' she demanded firmly, but with a smile.

'Sure, what do you want to know?'

'Your name and why you're here would be a good start.'

I took a deep breath, not sure how much I needed to reveal about me to get her to reveal more about herself.

'My name is David.'

'Come on, I know your name's not David,' she interrupted, 'I looked you up on the Citizens' Database.'

I was surprised and even more cautious of revealing too much, but I needed to have answers. And I had a sense that God was with me on this.

'Aled. My name is Aled and I am a believer, an Absolutist and I know that we lost the War,' I blurted out. So used to my chant that I pretty much repeated it, word for word.

'Thank you. And why are you here?' she asked, softly.

'I came here to get away from the War and to find some peace with God,' I told her, wondering if she'd realise that I'd only told her part of the reason. 'And contrary to you, I don't think you can just make up a version of God that suits you best. God is God. You're wasting your time,' I added.

'Is She? Am I?' asked Grey, staring at the ceiling as if I wasn't there.

I knew it was fashionable to ascribe a female gender to God so, although it upset me, I didn't correct her.

'What's the others' role in this?' I asked. Again trying to move on to safer ground.

Grey focussed her attention back on me and smiled. 'Fair question. Linda's the project manager. She gets things done and looks after the finances – that sort of thing – she's very good at it, but it does make her a bit bossy.' She rubbed her face. 'Peace. Well. He's…bait,' she said, screwing up her face as if she'd got a bad taste in her mouth. 'Linda's idea. Not a very good one,' she added, absent-mindedly. 'Douglas knows how people tick and understands quite a lot of science. Harmony, you met. More bait, I'm ashamed to say.'

I wasn't sure if I was following what she was implying. 'Bait? So you can blackmail me?'

'No. To get you to follow them back to London. We need you.'

'Need me for what?'

'I can't tell you. Except to say that it could change your life and lots of others.'

'I can't leave here. I'm here for a reason.'

'I think I know what that is and this could be part of it. If you come back with us, you can ask us to bring you back here whenever you want, and we will. Straight away, no questions asked,' she promised.

'Aled, there's one more thing I need to tell you…'

'Enough, please.'

'Aled, please let me…'

'Grey. Stop.'

I rested my head in my hands to show her I was thinking about it. 'Do you mind leaving me alone? I'm a bit stunned by all this. I need some time to absorb it all. Please. I insist.'

She uncurled herself from my bed and walked towards the door. 'Please, please give it some thought…I beg you. Maybe we can talk more tomorrow?'

I nodded.

14

Grey

June 2037

I'd spent hours studying War footage of him and he wasn't at all what I'd expected. He was the leader of an Absolutist direct-action wing. He'd made the Pope resign. He'd sanctioned the killing of his chief diplomat. Douglas had painted a picture of a cold-hearted Abso – Aled, the arch-manipulator, dedicated to stopping the human race making its next evolutionary leap. I was biased, but he seemed okay to me and it was incredible to meet him at last, face-to-face. I desperately wanted to tell him my secret, tell him why I'd pushed for him to be the one, but I had to get to know him better first.

We were in a private room of the monastery that Linda had arranged for a debrief.

'He's so handsome. And a little bit vulnerable. Killer combination, eh?' Linda asked me.

'Bit hard for me to say,' I replied.

'I kinda like him,' said Peace.

'Don't give me that. We know exactly how you feel about him. And I want to talk to you about that later. It's not fair on him.' I said.

Douglas intervened. 'We agreed, did we not, that we need to push him to see where he might crack?'

'We did. But…'

'Grey. It's too late to change your mind. You wanted him.

You've got him. But under my terms. Agreed?' said Douglas, fixing me with his eyes as if I was the only one in the room.

'Agreed.'

'Good, because he belongs to The Project now,' said Douglas.

'So, Grey, how do you think it's going?' asked Linda.

'He knows a bit about me. He knows that the thing with Peace was a set-up.'

'Cheers,' muttered Peace.

'Peace, you're a mercenary, you're not paid to have feelings,' interrupted Douglas.

I continued. 'He knows we need him back in London but I've not told him why. Except that it could change his life and others.'

Douglas took control again. 'Ramp it up. Tell him whatever you have to, but get him on board. Tomorrow. This can't wait for your pussy-footing around.'

'Anyone else?' asked Linda, but nobody spoke.

'Right. Peace. Grey. Come with me,' said Douglas.

Back in our cell, I was hunched up in the corner setting up the equipment that Douglas had asked for. It connected us to any CCTV camera in the world and, with the top-of-the-range additions that Douglas had provided, we could use the cameras as speakers and project our image on to the floor in front of them. We could communicate with anyone in the world who was within sight and sound of a CCTV camera – this was awesome stuff. As soon as it connected, I called Peace and Douglas in.

'Where do you want to go then?' I asked.

Douglas pulled out his uCumulus and stroked it to life. 'We need to go to the Whitechapel area, to Bangla-Town. Direct access is blocked to anything close by, so try logging in a few streets away and then see if you can hop from one to the other, keeping under their radar.'

'Should work. Try location SE1 1TL A7' said Peace.

I punched in the code and Borough Market on London's South Bank came to life on the floor, in front of my projector.

Douglas nodded and patted Peace on the back, 'Good, well done. Grey, make a note of that location because, after we've done this, I want you to experiment on some of the people from around there. They're Survivors – not completely Disintegrated, but not fully functional like us or those in Bangla-Town. I want you to try and see what degree of trust they still have, deep down.'

I sent a quick message to my team back in London to be on stand-by for more experiments. I hopped from one camera to another and the streets, projected on to the floor, were like a boring set of holiday snaps, until we crossed the river and the beautiful, but ruined City of London came into view. It sparkled in the midday sun, shooting light in a zillion different directions – far superior to any sculpture.

After about thirty camera hops, Douglas stopped me. 'There. Grey, activate our feed to that CCTV camera and let's see what happens,' he said.

I plugged my uCumulus in and fired up the relevant uApp. We could now use the cameras in reverse and broadcast our own sound and images to the streets of London. 'All ready to go,' I said.

Douglas took my uCumulus, 'Good afternoon, Whitechapel,' he said to an empty street with a wall made from bits of old metal and concrete. Two figures came out of nowhere, wearing long black overcoats with scarves covering their faces.

'What do you want, stranger?' asked one of them.

'We want to chat to someone in charge,' said Douglas.

'Tough.'

'Come on, is Rahman there?' said Douglas. Turning to Peace, he added, 'Old college tutor of mine – best anthropological brain in the business when it comes to virtual social-networks. I heard he'd holed up here, as some sort of guru.'

Neither of the figures moved or spoke, but Douglas continued, 'Tell him DeSouza's here. He'll be interested, I can assure you.'

One of them put his wrist to his mouth, speaking into his watch. He moved it closer to his ear to listen, started to nod and then said something to his compatriot that I didn't catch. He looked up into the camera. 'You're honoured, he's on his way.'

Douglas relaxed a little and we sat and waited for this mystery guru to appear. After a few minutes, an old man wearing a dull, off-cream tunic and trousers emerged from a hidden gate in the wall and limped towards the camera. He looked like a battle-weary soldier from the old Chinese Communist Army.

'Prove who you are,' he said.

'How do you expect me to do that?' said Douglas, as he chuckled.

'Say her name,' Rahman spat at the camera.

'Direct,' said Douglas, sneering.

'Just say it,' said Rahman.

'Linda.'

'We're the only two who know. I guess you're DeSouza. I'm not pleased to see you.'

'Didn't think you would be. But times change and we have to move on, eh?'

Rahman waved his two sidekicks away and they slunk back into the shadows. He sat down on a piece of wall that was jutting out. 'Go on then, get it over with. Why are you here?'

'No time to reminisce then?' Douglas chuckled again.

Peace interrupted. 'Boss, it's more than likely they're trying to work out how to disconnect us. I reckon we've got about another five minutes, maybe less.'

'So. Rahman, do you think we can be civil to each other?'

'What do you want?'

'To encourage you back on to the grid. It's not good – some parts of the world declaring unilateral disengagement.'

'Is that it?' said Rahman.

'Not being on the grid must be difficult. Quite a big deal to the youngsters, isn't it?'

'Not really. We've been like this for years now. No big deal to anyone. But come on, why are you here? You didn't expect to turn up, ask once and we'd say "sure, if that's what you want", did you?'

'Let me put it another way. There's a lot of bother out here and I'm sure you've got some of your own. We could help each other,' said Douglas.

'We're fine, actually. We have food and clothes. We've had no crime for years and we get to choose who comes and goes. It's a damn fine way to live, compared to that hell the Liberalists peddle.'

'Forget them, they don't count. But you do know you're illegal, don't you?'

'We know. What is it you really want? Are you still embroiled with those people?'

'I'm running a project for them. They're not as bad as you remember.'

'If you say so.'

'Rahman. We need you back. I need your expertise to nudge the human race into its next phase. It's right up your street and you're the best.'

'Thanks. But no thanks.'

'You can't live like this forever,' said Douglas, raising his voice.

'Watch me,' replied Rahman, also raising his voice.

'They won't allow it. They will come and force you, if they have to,' said Douglas.

'Are you threatening me?' asked Rahman.

'Just telling it like it is. Much simpler and safer to come back on to the grid, let someone else run this shanty town and come and help us move things along.'

'No,' said Rahman.

'I can't guarantee your safety, or that of your community, if you don't,' snapped Douglas.

'Goodbye,' said Rahman as the CCTV feed switched off.

'Damn you, Peace,' said Douglas, spinning round.

'I warned you, Boss,' said Peace.

'Don't get smug with me,' said Douglas. 'Grey, pack that useless piece of kit away and let's get on with what we have to do here. Tomorrow, press Aled as far as you can and see if he starts to crack. I need to know his limit.'

Douglas stormed out of the room, slamming the door behind him. I'd never seen him so angry. 'Will he be okay?' I asked Peace.

'Sure. He's a bit uptight but don't worry, he'll find a way to get someone in there, undercover. Now, tell me exactly what you've said to Aled.'

'Nothing much. I told him that the only reason you came on to him was to make him fall for you so he'd follow you back to London.'

'Why'd you do that?'

'It's true, isn't it?'

'Not entirely. And anyway, just because he's your brother doesn't mean you can risk what we're doing here.'

'Half-brother. And how on earth do you know that?'

'I know loads. Bit of friendly advice – stay the right side of Douglas and Linda, if you know what's good for you,' he said as he walked away.

I called after him, 'Let me be the one to tell him, please.'

I didn't like the tone of Douglas's spat with Rahman or Peace's warning. And I certainly didn't like Peace knowing my secret – I thought only Douglas knew. But I had to see it through. I'd put all of my Physitheist knowledge at the disposal of The Project, in return for Aled.

I logged into the CCTV feed at our London Lab to check on the waiting area, the cage as some of my team had nicknamed it. This was where we held participants in our experiments. In each of the two waiting-rooms, there were six people sitting with their backs to the wall, watching each other with the intensity of newly-caged animals. The smell of stale piss, sweat and shit would have filled the room by now and I was glad I wasn't there.

These Survivors were generally hard-core Liberalists that hadn't fully Disintegrated, but were starving – victims of the collapsing infrastructure – and now foraged and stole to survive. They tended to gather around the old trendy food-markets of London, the chattering-class alleys, as Peace called them – Borough

Market, Marylebone High Street, Hackney's Broadway Market and Portobello Road. These farmers' markets in the heart of London had been promoted as modern-day versions of Thomas Hardy's England, with carrots caked in mud and off-the-shelf harvests of hog roasts and cloudy cider. These pinnacles of middle-class refinement were still inhabited by the same people, except now they were the feral middle-class.

We only had to promise a warm night's sleep to persuade them to be part of our experiments and we were as humane as we could be. Still, I hated treating fellow human beings like this. Ultimately, we were trying to save the human race and that was what we focussed on.

I switched to the lab's prep room. Jane, Carlos and Jinghua were busy setting out plates of fried potatoes and boiled eggs.

'Hi, Jane,' I said.

Jane looked up at the camera and waved. 'Hi, Grey.'

'Do we know what we're doing then?' I asked.

All three of them made the letter O, with their thumb and forefinger – our code for yes.

'Great, let's get this done then,' I said.

I connected my uCumulus to the two-way mirror in the lab, so I could see the experiment as clearly as if I was in the observation booth itself. Jane and Carlos came in with two women in their forties and offered them chairs, either side of the table. The first one to sit down had matted grey hair, hacked off at the shoulders. She was wearing ripped jeans made from dirt-resistant material that had reached saturation point, a pair of new-looking, sturdy boots and one of those ridiculous Korean hooded-tops in pink and with rabbit ears. If it hadn't been for the layer of grime that covered her face and clothes, she would have been attractive. The second woman, also with saturated dirt-resistant clothes, was wearing slightly-heeled blue shoes that were falling apart, black leggings with a rose-patterned skirt over the top and a thin black chiffon shirt, through which you could see her bra and her starving body. Her hair was short and newly cut. They both sat there, constantly scanning the room and each other, like cornered wolves.

Jane pressed the red button on the recording equipment and it made the familiar buzz, signalling that we were starting. She put a microcapsule leaflet in front of each woman. 'Read this, please,' she said. They both read for a couple of minutes, still scanning the room, and then sat back. 'Can you tell me what it said?' Jane asked the woman-in-jeans.

'Use the short-haired one as the lead,' I said, into Jane's earpiece.

The woman-in-jeans read the leaflet aloud. 'One of you will be in charge and will decide how much of the food in front of you to give to the other. The rule of the game is that if the other person doesn't accept the portion you give them, then neither of you get anything. The most logical thing to do, as the receiver, is to accept what you are given, because it is always going to be more than nothing. Likewise, it makes sense for the giver to keep as much as possible for themselves.'

We kept the rules simple because, after being on the verge of starving for so long, these souls were having trouble with their eyesight and their cognitive functions. We were going to compare our results with similar, but more complicated tests that had been done before the War. In these, altruism had been the most common outcome – almost never did the players display zero trust in each other.

Carlos came in and put a plate of four hard-boiled eggs and ten pieces of fried potato on the table in front of the short-haired woman. She didn't move a muscle, staring at the food as if it was from another planet. The receiver, the woman-in-jeans, said and did nothing. We waited fifteen minutes, hoping that hunger would override whatever was holding them back, but nothing happened.

'Ask them why,' I instructed Jane.

'You're starving. What's stopping you? As soon as you divide up the food, you can eat it,' said Jane.

The woman-in-jeans looked at her. 'I don't know what to believe, or who to trust. It could be a trap, poisoned or something.' And the short-haired woman nodded in agreement.

'I'm Jane, this is Carlos and this is Jinghua. Pick any one of us and tell us which egg and which potato to eat – we'll prove they're safe,' said Jane. The women sat rigid, furtively looking around the room and not touching the food.

We tried the same experiment with the other ten Survivors and there was no difference. They all sat and stared at the food, even when one of the project workers ate some in front of them. We now knew that the Survivors, those that hadn't Disintegrated, trusted nothing. I don't think they were even making a conscious choice, it was just the way they'd become.

When Douglas came back to the cell, I told him what we'd discovered and asked him why he thought that we, also Liberalists, had not gone the same way.

'Often, they only pretended to be as broad-minded as they appeared,' he said.

'But that can't be the only reason, can it?' I asked.

'No. It's also likely that you and I formed some very strong neural paths that give us the ability to both question and believe at the same time. To hold on to something as true, until we prove it isn't.'

'But that's Science, isn't it?'

'Yes, in its purest form. But most of the Survivors only had the rubbish that was fed to them through the media. That watered-down tabloid-shit they peddled as Science.'

'From what I know about neuroscience, I can buy that,' I said.

'Good. That's why you're The Project's lead scientist,' said Douglas. 'Now, tomorrow – I want you to unsettle Aled. Tell him as much as it takes. I want you to find out how stable he is and whether we're right that he can do this stuff without Disintegrating.'

'Sure. Can I ask? I've told him that we have the backing of the most powerful world governments but after your discussion with Rahman earlier, I'm not so sure I've got that right.'

'Don't worry. Governments or no governments, we're in charge,' said Douglas, as he lay down on his bunk to sleep.

15

Aled

June 2037

It occurred to me, as I walked back along the line having successfully endured another embarrassing episode over the side of the mountain, that it was only the men that had to expose themselves so thoroughly, once a day. With that thought in mind, I looked up and saw Grey strolling across the courtyard towards me.

'Morning!' She giggled, casting her eyes up and down the line of monks. 'Did I miss all the fun?'

I looked at her, smiled and raised my eyebrows. 'Strengthens the soul, not to mention the muscles,' I said, laughing.

I was glad to see her and pleased she was alone, because I'd decided to talk to her about returning to London. I'd spent morning prayers totally focussed on it and experienced a real sense of peace, the nearer I got to a decision. I glimpsed what it might be like to be whole again, with my mind, body and soul sitting comfortably alongside each other.

I pointed to where we'd sat the day before. 'Fancy a chat?' I asked her, as if it was the most natural thing in the world when, actually, my stomach was all churned up and I was terrified of what I was about to do.

'I'd like that. Shall I bring some tea over?' she replied, with a chirpy lilt to her voice. If you didn't know better, you'd have thought we were sitting in a café, a couple of old friends about to catch up on the latest gossip.

'I'll see you over there,' I shouted, glad for a few minutes to rehearse what I was going to say.

My chanting had led me to the place where I wanted to hear more about this special project. I also wanted to test her promise, that if I did go to London, but didn't want to stay, they would bring me back – no questions asked. I still felt a little cautious but, as if some miracle had occurred, I felt tuned into God and safe to follow my instincts. I sat down on the ground, with my back to the monastery, overlooking the sleeping dinosaur, and breathed deeply, letting my mind expand. I heard her footsteps and braced myself for what was to come. Half scared, half excited, and feeling more alive than I had for ages.

Grey placed the teapot and two miniature bowls on the ground and sat beside me, tucking one leg under the other. She sighed. 'Tea, on top of the world.'

We sat side by side in silence for a few minutes, just looking out across the clouds. I wasn't in any hurry to speak and, I guessed from her silence, neither was she. She changed the mood, carefully.

'So. Aled. Have you had enough time to think about what I said?'

'Tell me more,' I said, but then turned to confide in her. 'Actually, I feel better than I've felt for a long time. And most of that is down to you.'

'Maybe,' she said in a low voice, making a smacking noise by sucking her bottom lip. 'We'll see. How much do you know about the outside world? When did you leave it?' she asked.

'About a year ago. Assume I know very little of what it's like now – I can only guess.'

'Tell me what you know,' she said.

'When I left London, the War was still happening, but it was clear that we'd lost. We'd used every trick we knew – and copied most of yours – to try and discredit you, to destroy you. The propaganda from both sides had divided families. The economy was failing as bitterness and mistrust made it impossible for people to work together. Society was polarised, unable to function. As we tasted defeat, it was clear that we were slowly retreating into our separate Absolutist groups – mainly Christians, Muslims, Atheists, Humanists and Scientists. We'd come together to defend truth, to oppose you Liberalists, but ultimately we disagreed with each other and couldn't afford to water-down our own beliefs – we were doomed. Families were torn apart and, as our emotional and spiritual structures collapsed around us, we started to see our individual and communal collapse. I was asked to come here – the last remaining pure place on earth. Your witch hunts destroyed lives.'

'That sounds like a text book response,' she said. 'Tell me about you.'

'I can't, it's too painful. I lost everything. My friends, my family, my job. I wasn't able to function outside of the movement. And, inside, I had to work alongside people I thought were completely wrong. The toll it took on all of us was indescribable because, although we agreed that there was an absolute truth, each group believed that every one else's truth was wrong.'

Grey interrupted me. 'How did we let it get so bad?'

I was almost in tears as I talked about it for the first time in what seemed like a lifetime. 'Honestly, Grey, it got so hard and so ridiculous – the lies that were told in the media about how there was no truth, that it was all a matter of judgement and interpretation.'

'That's just healthy debate, surely?' Grey interrupted again.

I looked at her in disbelief. 'You are kidding, right?'

'No, I'm serious.'

I took a deep breath, letting her see my exasperation. 'Okay. Let me tell you a story.'

I shifted a little to make myself more comfortable, getting ready to talk about one of the most painful parts of my War.

'In November 2034, I received a message that my dad had to go into hospital for some tests. This was very early on in the War, so hospitals still appeared to be functioning. I took time out from the campaign and travelled across the country to Cardiff, where he lived, and went straight to the hospital. When I got there, the doctor was telling my brother that they suspected a level-five brain tumour, but they didn't want to be prescriptive about the treatment. I just caught the tail end of the doctor suggesting to my brother that he went home, checked out the options in the Cumulus, and came back the next day with the choice of treatment he preferred. To my absolute astonishment, my brother was agreeing to this ridiculous suggestion. I couldn't help but interrupt and, with a level of intensity that probably didn't help, I accused the doctor of not caring, of not being a doctor. I shouted at him – all I was asking was that he, the trained professional, tell us what was best for our dad, but he wouldn't. He just kept repeating that there was no definitive cure and they were not prepared to force a solution on us. I was livid and started screaming for him to put faith in his training and experience and tell us what to do, but he refused. To my horror, my brother sided with the doctor, explaining that we couldn't expect him to impose his version of the truth on us and it was our choice that mattered. The doctor said we should go, gather the facts and make a decision as quickly as possible. The argument escalated as we carried on shouting and screaming at each other, right there in the hospital. Finally, I realised that the only way we were going to get any treatment at all, let alone the right one, was to do as they asked and make our own choice, based on whatever WikiHealth could offer us.

We left the hospital and went back to my brother's house but he just wouldn't let it drop. We argued and argued, but not about the best treatment. We got so caught up in arguing about whether there was such a thing as truth that we didn't look at our options. We didn't even talk about buying any of the black-market advice that had become prevalent, since hospitals began refusing to help. Later the next day, the hospital called to remind us that if we didn't decide soon he would die. We didn't. And he did.'

I looked her in the eye and said very quietly, 'I never spoke to my brother again.'

She whispered, 'At least you knew him,' and then more confidently added, 'Anyway, that could have happened at any time. Arguments about treatment. Families not speaking after a parent has died.'

There was a brief silence and then she said, 'Aled, I need to talk to you about something…'

I interrupted. 'The point is, you demonised us to such an extent, that no one was prepared to show any signs of belief, not even in themselves. Everything had to be a "choice", no matter how dangerous. You killed my dad, as sure as if you put your hands round his neck and squeezed the life out of him.'

'Aled. Please don't say that.' She looked at the floor for quite a while and then, when she eventually looked up, she said, rather sheepishly, 'That's one incident out of a lifetime. You can't base a world-view on that.'

I stared at her for as long as I could, and then at the floor.

'Okay, let me tell you another story. I had a really good bunch of mates – known them since I was eighteen – and we'd meet down the local pub once a week, mull over the world and have a laugh. As your campaigns started to take effect, they challenged me on everything. Nothing profound, just ordinary everyday stuff and at first I thought it was tongue in cheek but it got nastier and nastier. We were in the pub, talking about holidays and who was going where, and I just happened to question the ethics of space tourism – it was crippling China by devastating its tourist industry. But, before I'd even finished my sentence, they were down my throat, going on about how Absos were creating bad feeling and how they could make their own minds up rather than being dictated to by the likes of me. They blamed me for the CCTV cameras and then – and I remember this quite clearly – my best friend Zak looked me calmly in the eyes and said very slowly, 'Aled, you're so perfect and always right, aren't you? Fuck off. Now! And don't even think about coming back'.

He meant it, because of something that had happened the week before and the really sad and insidious part is that all they could think about was that to have an opinion, a belief, was the root of everything that was wrong – climate change, space tourism, or, the one that really got them, the pervasive CCTV recording of everything we did or said. If it hadn't been so cruel and painful, it would have been laughable.

'Naturally, I retreated into my own group of believers and then, as you lot raised the ante, I was having to side with people I thought were right to believe that something can be absolutely true but whose actual beliefs I thought were totally wrong. Inside, it ripped me apart, and outside, it tore me away from my friends.'

'Oh Aled, that's awful,' she said, pouring herself a cup and offering to fill mine. I silently declined, by covering it with my hand.

'As I said, I retreated more and more into the Absolutist movement and, without any outside distractions, I worked my way up the ladder until I was a very trusted and senior member. So when we needed someone to protect the faith for the future, I volunteered to come here until I was asked to return.'

Exhausted, I paused and looked at Grey. 'Your turn now,' I muttered, hoping she'd stop asking me questions.

'Okay, that's fair enough. I want to show you London, so you can see why it's so important you come back and help us.'

She pulled out a small bag, about nine inches high and two inches wide, opened it up and took out a device that unfolded into a small satellite. She took out a tiny projector about six inches high and an inch wide, and finally a roll-out keyboard, which she connected to the satellite. 'Have you ever seen one of these in action?' she asked.

'No, what is it?'

'It's brilliant. It's a portable device for logging into any CCTV network in the world. And with the right codes, I can tap in and get a live feed from anywhere.'

She tampered with it for a few minutes until the device projected an image of an empty street on to the floor. As the camera panned, I could see it was Savile Row in London. Once a bustling street, attracting the rich and famous to buy tailor-made clothes, it now looked faded. As if the very life had been withdrawn. Nothing was boarded up or destroyed, it was just empty and you could sense that no one had been there for some time. As Grey hopped cameras, the scene remained the same until Sackville Street, where occasionally someone was dragging themselves along like a zombie walking the dead streets of this once thriving metropolis – they looked lost to the world and lost to themselves. Grey had a tear in her eye. I raised my eyebrows questioningly. She stretched, inhaled and sighed.

'Masses and masses of people just gave up trying to live. We think that we deconstructed the world so much, we took away all security and hope. Only those that could cope with this total ambiguity survived. It was horrible and as the scale of the problem became clear, we were shocked at how many people had only been pretending to cope. After a while, everything gradually stopped working. It was as if the life of the planet had dried up. It's worse in the cities or where there's a disconnect from nature, but it's not great in the countryside either.'

She paused for a few moments and then carried on. 'You need to know more about me before we can go much further.'

I nodded.

'Picture this – it's early evening and it's raining. I've walked through the streets towards Piccadilly, gradually meditating into a tightly focussed and insular world. Yearning to find new quantum theories. I believe I owe the world some solutions. That has been my routine for a month. I've reached the right state of mind at exactly the moment I arrive at St James's Church – timed to perfection. I cross my legs and, as usual, settle amongst the hundreds of Disintegrates, who simply sit and stare. I wasn't a Disintegrate but that place, with its complete and utter lack of soul, is the only place I can truly let go and wander the fascinating landscapes of my mind.

'It's a yucky evening, so I'm wrapped in a space blanket with the rain pouring down my hair and streaming across my face and into my lap. I close my eyes and retreat deep into my soul, dredging around for inspiration, for that spark of divine intervention that I can then slowly, but surely, form into a nugget of physitheist theory. I'm aching to change the world. That's the night Douglas told me how I could help reverse all this. That's the night this fantastic quest began.'

'Sounds as if you were having your own breakdown,' I commented, sympathetically.

She shrugged. 'Look, let me show you St James's – it's incredible and horrible and disgusting.' She flicked the hand control with her thumb until the church on Piccadilly came into view and there, sitting like a painting of lifeless corpses propped up against the wall and each other, were at least a thousand people, just staring into space. 'It's like this every day,' she said. 'This is what it means to be a Disintegrate.'

I had to look away. I hadn't realised how bad things had become since I'd left. I looked out over the clouds and began to realise that this was the same edge of despair that I'd been teetering on. This feeling of my body, mind and soul rejecting each other – of no stable place to hold on to – was the abyss of the Disintegrate.

Grey rested her hand on my arm, 'Look. Let me show you some other places.' She skipped around the cameras of the world, and each and every one showed either empty lifeless streets or gatherings of Disintegrates. 'We can't feed them all. The infrastructure's crumbling. People are dying and they have no motivation to survive. We've sucked the soul out of the human race.'

I got up and walked off in disgust at what she'd admitted. She sat, fiddling with the teapot and staring into space. I walked around the mountain top for a while, unable to focus my mind. Haunted by what she'd shown me. I could hear her calling, but I couldn't respond. I sat down and tried to absorb what I'd just learned. This could so easily have been me. Could still so easily be me. I couldn't go back to London, no matter how important Grey might think it was.

I was sitting there drawing circles in the dust of the mountain, when she approached from behind. 'Can I talk to you, Aled?' she asked cautiously.

'I don't know, Grey – that's some mess you've just shown me,' I whispered.

'I know,' she said. 'That's why we need you so desperately.'

'I can't go back there!' I snapped. 'You know exactly what will happen to me. I'm right on the edge as it is. It's not going to take much for me to Disintegrate, is it?'

'From what we've seen, we think you'll hold it together – you've still got such a massive desire to live.'

We sat in silence, looking at the clouds drifting across the sky beneath us, until the gong rang.

'I need to pray,' I mumbled.

'Please…please…please…' I heard from behind me as I walked slowly back to the monastery.

16

Grey

June 2037

'He's right on the edge,' I said, sitting in our cell, talking about Aled with Douglas, Linda and Peace.

'Grey, I'm sure you could have pushed harder. Couldn't you? We need him to make his mind up,' said Douglas.

'I've been wondering if we should use one of the other Absolutists. There's a few here that might work,' said Linda.

'Exactly what I was thinking. Why don't we do as Linda suggests?' asked Peace.

'Not a chance. Grey, you'll see this through with Aled. Get him on board and back to London. If you could see the bigger picture, you wouldn't even suggest we changed plans,' said Douglas, 'Not that they're ours to change anyway,' he added, almost to himself.

'Maybe you could let me in on the big secret?' I asked with a touch of sarcasm.

'Grey…' he started.

'Anyone wanna come down to the village with me?' asked Peace, breaking the tension.

It was the chance I was looking for. I wanted to put some space between me and Aled, to give him time to think about what I'd said. I didn't want to push him too much. Pushing him to the point of Disintegrating wouldn't help and, anyway, I was responsible for him.

'I'll come,' I said, giving Peace the thumbs-up.

'Great. Anyone else?'

'I was already going, so I'll come with you,' said Douglas.

'And to keep an eye on me?' I asked.

'No. But you have until the end of tomorrow to sort it out. I trust you know what you're doing. I know that pushing too hard will only make him run away. But don't forget he's a resilient chap. You only have to look at some of that War footage to see that,' said Douglas.

'Okay,' I said, pleased that Douglas seemed to have calmed down.

As we reached the edge of the village, Douglas headed off on his own. It was the first time I'd been outside of the monastery since we'd arrived and, after all the intensity of the last couple of days, it was a welcome relief.

We took a leisurely stroll. As we passed groups of villagers, busy going about their daily lives, they stopped to look. Among the multitude of food stalls by the side of the street was a woman with long straight black hair and great skin. She had a lovely smile that drew you into her stall and a twinkle in her eyes that made you feel she was having a private laugh, but not at anyone's expense. It was no surprise that this was where Peace chose to stop. She beckoned us closer and, lifting the lid on what looked like an old oil drum, she showed us what she had on offer. There, sitting in the drum, was a pile of one-inch cubes of crispy, pale-yellow tofu. Peace caught my elbow and steered me towards her. He said something in Chinese that didn't sound particularly appealing and she nodded in response.

'Fancy some?' asked Peace.

'Not really. But, what is it?'

'This is Lanlin, she's from Shanghai. And this is her *Lovers' Tofu*. It's packed full of all sorts of stuff – each cook has their own special recipe. But it's always complex. Like love,' said Peace as he winked at me. He turned to Lanlin, said something in Chinese and she opened up one of the cubes with her chopsticks. A whole load of red, green and orange stuff spilled out, as if she was a pathologist examining the stomach contents of a recently deceased body. 'Looks like chilli, ginger, bit of green pepper and that magic ingredient – mala sauce,' said Peace, grinning from ear to ear.

'Go on then, I'll have one, if you are,' I said.

Peace bought four cubes for eight yuan and gave me two. They were fantastic; inside the crispy skin was the milky tofu that I was more familiar with. In stark contrast, the filling was bursting with heat, spice and flavour making the bland tofu a welcome relief.

We strolled down the street like a couple on holiday, taking in the sights and bantering with each other, enjoying each other's company. Peace was so cool, knowing exactly how to behave – calling out 'Ni hao' to each street vendor as we passed. 'Hey, fancy a bit of afternoon gambling, Chinese style?' he asked me.

'Sure,' I said, feeling completely safe with this fascinating man. He was at ease with himself and seemed to be at home, wherever he was.

We took a left turn into a bustling market. Peace talked, in whispers, to the first half-dozen stalls and after talking to a seller of pots and pans, he turned to me. 'Now. You are sure, aren't you? It can get a bit boisterous, but if you just follow my lead it'll be fine.'

'This is brilliant. You're in charge – I'll follow. Thanks for this,' I said, squeezing his hand.

'We have to be serious, though. There's nothing more serious around here than an afternoon card game,' he said, taking the edge off my enthusiasm.

As we continued, I noticed a lot of activity. People pointed at us and, leaving their stalls unattended, they disappeared into the alleyways that led away from the body of the market. 'Seems to be a lot going on here. Are we safe?' I asked.

'I've told them how much I'm prepared to gamble. They're pooling the resources of the whole market to take me on. They'll put up their best players but use their communal pot as the stake.'

'Bloody Hell, Peace. How much are you planning on playing for?'

'I've got a few thousand. Should make it an interesting afternoon.'

At the end of the market, Peace stopped and sat down on an up-turned box and I followed. He sat and waited but never stopped looking around, as if he was expecting something to creep up on us.

'You seem nervous,' I said.

'Nah. Just used to being careful of those around me. A habit I learned here actually. But some time ago.'

'Tell me?'

'I worked for the Chinese government during the War. It was grim. The economy was going pear-shaped and the locals weren't happy – but then when have the Chinese been happy with their leaders? I led a group of mercenaries travelling around the countryside, bringing the warlords into line. I've a few enemies as a result.'

'Sounds scary.'

'Not really. It's what I got paid for. But, I'm not stupid enough to think they've forgotten.'

'Any more action-hero stories?' I said, as I smiled. I was loving sitting there and shooting the breeze with this gorgeous man. He was about to speak when four guys carrying machetes and openly flashing a large amount of cash came over and said something to him.

'This is it then. Last chance to back out,' he said.

'As if,' I said. But I was a little apprehensive and moved closer to him. We were flanked by two escorts in front and two behind and shown through a gate. On the other side, we were greeted by a wall of sound and a large arena, packed full of Chinese men. On three sides were rows of weather-worn plastic seats, eight tiers high. On a raised platform in the middle of the arena sat three straight-backed Chinese men at a square wooden table. Every inch of their faces, and a bird's eye view of the tabletop, could be seen on a large screen that filled the fourth side of the arena. A square had been drawn on the top of the table with each side numbered – one, two, three and four. Next to the square was a large pile of dried beans and a metal bowl.

'Fan – Tan. Fantastic,' said Peace, as the four escorts prodded me in the back and pointed to a chair in the front row, opposite the screen. 'Best place in the house,' said Peace.

The escorts turned towards Peace, but he was already climbing the wooden steps to the platform. The crowd roared as he took his seat. Dramatically, an old man hobbled from the side of the platform and grabbed two handfuls of the dried beans and turned his back to the table. He put the beans in the metal bowl, casting a few over the edge of the platform. He turned around, placed the bowl upside-down covering the beans and stepped back. Peace waved a huge amount of cash at the crowd and put three of his hundred-yuan notes next to the number two. Matching Peace, the other three placed their bets and sat back. The man next to me was frantically pressing numbers into a pocket-sized calculator. I pointed at it, raising my shoulders to show that I wanted to know what it was. He bashed some numbers in and pointed to the big screen, then his calculator and again to the screen. There were constantly changing numbers flashing up on the screen against each side of a replica of the painted square. As the totals increased, the odds changed. These calculators connected the crowd to a central betting system. The roar of the crowd and the cloud of dust created by their shuffling feet charged the atmosphere.

After a few minutes the old man stepped forward and raised his arm. The crowd fell silent, the screen zoomed in on the table and the old man took a small bamboo stick from out of his back pocket. He lifted the bowl and carefully removed four beans from the pile with his stick. He carried on removing four beans until he had three beans left on the table. The crowd roared, Peace threw his hands in the air with an over-exaggerated gesture of defeat and all the money was scooped up by the player that had bet on number three. The volume of the crowd increased again and the man next to me showed me the amount in the top right-hand corner of his calculator increasing – the excitement in the air was electric. For the next two hours, this was the ritual – dried beans covered by the bowl, bets placed, bamboo stick removing beans in multiples of four and a winner. Whenever Peace won, he'd stand and take a bow, prompting jeers from the crowd.

He had won five games in a row when a dozen men, wearing camouflage and holding rocket launchers, marched into the arena. Peace immediately jumped down and grabbed my hand as he ran past me. He pushed money into the top-pocket of a man holding a motorbike, leapt on it and signalled for me to get on the back. He fired it up and we roared out behind one of the stands, into the fields and away from the arena. We bumped and bounced across the fields towards a wood where Peace stopped the bike and got off, grinning.

'What the…' I said, laughing with relief.

'Bit close, I'll grant you.'

'Bit close?'

'Local warlord. He's got a thing about me. And not a particularly nice thing, at that,' said Peace.

My pulse was racing but Aunt G's well-used warning came to mind – "another unsuitable man".

On the way back, Peace asked me not to mention anything to Douglas. 'He tends not to understand. If he asks, say we were checking out the warlords to ensure our safe passage home.'

'Okay,' I said, still in awe. 'Any idea why Douglas came with us?'

'I was asking in the market. Seems he's been having a secret meeting with five men in suits. No idea what it's about and why I'm not there. Best not to say anything to him, though.'

'Okay. If we're sharing secrets…you know I'm desperate to be Aled's sister and to get my dad back?'

'You try to hide it, but it shows,' he said, patting me on the back.

When we arrived, we propped the motorbike up against a side wall and entered through the front gate, as if nothing unusual had taken place. I was about to open the door to our little cell when I overheard Douglas speaking into his uWatch. 'Almost bagged him, sir…No not yet…I guess it's in the Holy of Holies…But I need to win his trust…Yes, I know…Okay, I understand…Of course.'

Tentatively, I pushed the door open. 'Hi, am I interrupting?'

'No. Come in. We need to talk. When Aled agrees to be part of the experiment, you'll need to know where Zak is. At all times. Right now, he's at his grandmother's and she's the only one he trusts,' said Douglas.

'Should be easy, if he's already tagged.'

'He's not. I happen to know where he is, that's all. Can I leave it with you?'

'Sure,' I said as he left the room.

Straight away, I fired up my uCumulus and got on to Jane, back at The Project. 'You're going to have to go out and find some-one and tag them. They're important to us,' I said, before she'd even said hello.

'I don't like going out, if I can avoid it,' she said.

'I know. But this is vital. He's in Kentish Town, I'll send you the details. You'll need to go slowly, though, to keep an eye out for him in case he's already left.'

'I'm not walking,' she said.

'That's fine. Why not get Carlos to take you in one of the pedicabs? Take the facial-recognition gear and I'll log in as well.'

A few minutes later, my uCumulus screen came to life and I could see the back of Carlos, pedalling for dear life. Jane had the facial-recognition gear strapped to the side of her head. The streets were completely empty, until they reached the old temperance hospital – a derelict brick building that now housed hundreds of Disintegrates. 'He won't be in there. Carry on,' I said.

They carried on up the hill into Kentish Town. Jane swung her head round to capture a woman's face as it peered out from a window. The recog-app kicked in and, after automatically scrolling through different faces for a few seconds, it announced, 'Vera Marsh. Twenty-eight years old. Nurse and mother. No criminal record but suspected of running a neighbourhood watch. Unproven.'

'Not interested. Thank you,' said Jane, and Vera's record dis-appeared from the screen.

The only sound was Carlos wheezing as he carried on pedalling through Kentish Town. They turned into a block of flats that was identical to countless other blocks across London – five storeys high and built around a central quadrangle overlooked by walkways that ran past every front door and led to a stairwell at each of the corners. Jane scanned the quadrangle, looking behind the few cars parked in their allocated parking slots, their flat tyres confirming that they were abandoned. She walked to the base of the North-East stairwell, stepped over a pile of rotting cardboard boxes and climbed up two floors. As she was turning into the walkway that ran past the front of Zak's grandmother's flat, she stepped over three young children who were sitting staring into space, eating from a pile of bread rolls on the floor in front of them.

Jane knocked on the door. A dirty and haunted face with a straggly red beard appeared briefly at the window. As Jane lifted the letterbox to look inside, the sound of cupboard doors being slammed grew louder. She knocked again. The slamming stopped and an eerie silence fell. The door opened a crack and Zak's dirty face appeared. Jane took a step back to give him some space and he opened the door. He stood there, shifting from one foot to the other, looking from side to side as if he expected to be pounced on at any moment.

'Who the fuck are you?' he asked.

'Zak, can we come in?' Jane asked as she tried to push past, expertly brushing her hand across his hair and leaving a nano-tag behind.

'No. No, you bloody well can't,' he replied, pushing her back out on to the walkway. 'How do you know who I am? Who told you I was here?' he asked.

'Does it matter?'

'Of course it matters,' he said, shifting his body from side to side as he tried to look past her.

'Be careful, Jane. As far as he's concerned, his grandmother's the only one he can still trust,' I said into her earpiece.

'Who told you?' he repeated.

'Who do you think? Your grandmother,' said Jane.

Zak's whole body slumped as if his life-force had instantly

evaporated. He shuffled past and on to the walkway, staring straight through her and Carlos. We had pulled the last piece of trust from underneath him. He was Disintegrating.

'Jane. What the hell gives you the right to do that?' I asked, shocked that she could have been so cruel and for no apparent reason.

'He pushed me,' she scoffed.

I was confused about what had really made her punish him so completely because there'd been no need. She had been on The Project a lot longer than me and was closer to Douglas, so I kept silent. I didn't want to ruin my chances with Aled.

'Jane, check his tag's working and then trace his friends – Jon and Dave. We'll need all three in a few days time,' I said, and logged off.

I stepped outside and there was Aled, in the middle of the yellow-brown snake working its way to the Buddha. He didn't belong here and, even with Jane's display of cruelty, I wanted to get him back to London and get on with the task.

As the last monk of the snake passed by, Douglas and Peace appeared. 'Douglas. Can we talk?' I asked.

'Inside,' he replied. 'Peace, can you join us, please,' he added.

Peace closed the door behind us and I sat down on my bunk. 'I'm not happy with Jane,' I said.

'Tell me why,' said Douglas.

'She deliberately made Zak Disintegrate. She knew exactly what was going on. It was as if she took delight in it.'

'I find that hard to believe; you're all so professional,' he said, moving towards the door.

'Seriously, she was cruel,' I said.

'Peace. Talk to her,' he said and closed the door behind him.

Peace came and sat down next to me. 'I'm sure she had a good reason. It's best not to get too involved unless you want to put your place in The Project at risk.'

I knew, from being with Clive, that you had to be strong and focussed on the end goal to succeed, so I let it go.

17

Aled

June 2037

I didn't know what to do. I'd spent all day walking in the mountains, trying to get my head around the state of the world and all those Disintegrates. They were like a room of discarded toys, unable to think or move for themselves. As if they were waiting for someone to bring them to life, or discard them for ever.

It was a desperate situation, but I didn't think I could risk going back to London in case it happened to me. I had a job to do and, unless God really wanted me to, I didn't see how I could justify putting myself at risk. And it was unfair of Grey to ask. I couldn't risk falling victim to my demons and sinking into the pit of Disintegration. And, I couldn't dismiss the possibility that Grey, as nice as she appeared, was actually an attempt by the Liberalists to put Absolutism to death, once and for all.

The implications were huge and might be more than I could bear, but I had to make a decision. After all, the foundation of my beliefs was that you don't sit on the fence. I felt crushed by the enormity of the situation and as each nugget of information was placed on top of me, it was as if I was being slowly squashed. Without the mountain, the air and the horizon I couldn't think clearly. The hard wood of the bed kept me connected to reality as I allowed myself to drift into a dream state – not really sleeping, but resting nonetheless.

As the sun came up, I was already sitting in my favourite place, anticipating the relief that would come with the clarity of a fresh new day. I recapped all the things I'd learned – Grey was a strange mix of Scientist, Liberalist and Believer, the state of the world seemed to be dire and getting worse and I could feel inklings of life returning to my soul. But the big question was still, 'Could I trust Grey? Could I trust myself?'

I sat there, resting my chin in the palm of my hand, with the wide open space and the tips of mountains glimmering in the red glow of the sunrise. I was behaving like an ancient benign God, idly sitting above the world, detached from the human race. This was not the God I believed in. I must take the risk and get my hands dirty. I allowed my body time to reach a low rhythmic state. I could feel my resolve to act crystallising in the core of my being. The *Proof of Existence* was in the back of my mind as I pondered whether to trust Grey and return to London. At last, I felt in control of my own destiny and as I let the decision settle within me, I felt ten feet tall.

I'd been sitting there for a couple of hours and the monks' chants were about to end. If I hurried I'd be first in the queue for the toilet. I arrived just as the cubicle was being unlocked and made ready for use. I did my thing and then went in search of Grey, to find out more about the project. She was talking to an old monk, in the spot where I carved. I walked over slowly, giving her time to see me coming. She looked up and waved me over.

'Grey, I'm just going to get my wood and knife so I can carve while we talk. Wait here for me,' I said, asserting my control.

'Of course,' she replied.

I returned with my props, sat down next to her and started to carve. 'Grey. I've been thinking about coming with you, but I want to know more about The Project. Can you explain it to me?'

'I can try,' she said, biting her bottom lip as if she was contemplating where to start. Her hand touched my arm – in that now familiar gesture – creating a bridge of physical contact. Picking up a stick, she started to doodle in the dust. 'Aled, I'll try to explain what we think we've worked out. How much do you know about quantum physics and neuroscience?' she asked.

'Nothing at all.'

'Well. Where do I start? We're looking at change here, Aled. The potential to change the world, to fix it, and we think the answer lies in that incredible space where quantum physics, neuroscience and God come together.

'In essence, we know that very very small things – quanta – can be in more than one place at a time, which creates the potential for multiple worlds. You've heard of parallel universes? What happens to these we're not sure, but we think that something causes all but one of these universes to collapse, leaving the one and only truth remaining. Some people think that there's an ever increasing number of parallel universes. But if that was the case, we believe they'd eventually collapse into one.' She opened her eyes a little wider and made small, rapid nodding movements.

'Okay. Got that,' I assured her.

'Some neuroscientists think that brain activity around an action, such as moving an arm, occurs after the event – as if the brain is being informed of, rather than causing, the action. They believe this is the unconscious mind, that we can't observe, informing the consciousness mind, that we can. Informing it of decisions it's already taken. It's more likely that we're observing quantum biology at work, where multiple worlds in the unconscious mind collapse, leaving our version – the one we've just experienced – intact. That would explain why the brain activity seems to happen after the event.

'It's also been proved that the make-up of your brain – your personality, instincts and desires – can be changed. Neuroscientists have helped people control, and hence alter, some of their most basic instincts. And we know that people can change dramatically through prayer.

'The final piece of this jigsaw is the prophecies in holy texts – it appears that God is outside of time, as we know it.'

She paused again. 'Still with me?'

I nodded, calming myself by carving a crucifixion – the first since I'd been there.

She continued, 'If you accept that God exists, is actively involved and not bound by sequential time, then you can create the hypothesis that, through God, we can reach back in time to pull a different reality into existence.'

I was intrigued, and a little stunned, by what Grey has just explained. 'Are you suggesting that we might be able to reverse the affects of the War?'

'Yes, that's exactly what I'm suggesting – fantastic, eh?'

I carved in silence for a few minutes, grateful to Grey for allowing me the space to try and digest what she'd suggested. She was describing something similar to the explanation the duffle-coated man had given me of the *Proof.* It unnerved me.

'This sounds like wishful thinking to me – are you sure this isn't just the fantasy of someone who chooses to hang out with the lunatics?'

She didn't respond to the sarcasm but enthusiastically carried on with further explanation. 'In some ways it's very simple. God holds everyone's multiple universes in the palm of Her hand – like one big net of possibilities – and, with the right set of circumstances in place, She can pull whichever reality She wants into existence. Imagine Her drawing the net together into a single rope of reality – the one remaining universe – that's the quantum physics. In order for this to work we have to be prepared, able and actively looking for the fundamental change to the wiring of our minds – that's the neuroscience.

'So in a nutshell, our theory is that if someone can tune into God with a mind that is correctly wired for change and focussed on the historic event they want to alter, then God can pull a different version of reality into being.'

Grey was getting carried away, obviously excited and over-explaining, but I was happy to listen and take in as much as I could. She smiled, drawing her legs up to hold her knees tight to her body. 'Let me give you some examples to support what I'm saying.'

'In quantum biology we have deduced that the speed of energy transfer in photosynthesis is so efficient that energy must travel multiple routes at the same time. It works out which is the most efficient, settles on it, and collapses the other alternative realities.' She held up her thumb to signify one example.

'Before the War there were people working in neuroscience that used FMRI scanners with real-time feedback, to produce neural imaging. They realised that our brains are made up of different centres that compete to control us – such as the short time desire for chocolate versus the long term desire to lose weight. They used this, as part of a criminal rehabilitation programme, to teach inmates to exercise certain parts of their brain and learn to control and change their instinctive behaviour. These no-hope criminals changed their own neural signatures and hence their personalities.' She held up her forefinger indicating two examples.

'Time travel used to be considered an impossibility because it relied on the existence of tachyon particles, which travel faster than the speed of light. But the OPERA Neutrino kicked off a host of related experiments that proved beyond doubt the existence of these particles. God being outside of time no longer appears to contravene the laws of nature.' She held up her middle finger – three examples.

'The holy texts imply that whatever we focus on, we change. For example, there are passages that refer to *being transformed by the renewing of your mind*. And, did you know that Metanoia – the New Testament Greek word for repentance – can be interpreted as changing your mind and expanding your thought patterns?' Grey was now holding up a thumb and three fingers.

Tilting her head to one side, she grinned. 'Do I need to go on?'

'No, I get that you're not just some fantasist,' I said.

I stood up and held out my hand, offering to help her up. 'Shall we go for a wander and carry on talking?' I asked.

She smiled, grabbed my hand, pointed towards the garden and asked me to show her around.

We walked, side by side and in silence, along the corridors of ancient pillars and out to the sparse garden. The barrenness reminded me how dependent the monks were on the local villagers for food. Grey stood still for a while, looking around and commenting on the exotic nature of the buildings behind us, especially the ornate silver spires that flanked the golden dragons scanning the horizon like ships' figureheads. She pointed at the floor, where a cornucopia of purple and yellow flowers was intertwined with rows of prayer-candles that flickered as they tried to grab the attention of Buddha. We walked out to the front of the monastery and sat down on the top step of the long stone stairway that led down to the village.

'Aled, this is so beautiful. Doesn't it make you want to become a Buddhist?'

'No, but I agree it's lovely and peaceful. Thank goodness China got distracted by economic collapse and left it alone to flourish.'

'What sort of world have we created?' she pondered.

We sat there, lost in our own thoughts. Peace and Linda were climbing the steps. As they got nearer I could see, as if in slow motion, our bubble of contentment popping. I put my hand on Grey's knee. 'I am thinking about your project very seriously,' I said, quietly.

'I know,' she replied.

'Hi there,' called Peace, waving his arms as if he'd seen a long lost friend.

Linda complained, 'We've had to walk to the village thanks to that stupid deal you did with the monks.'

The peace and tranquillity Grey and I had created vanished. But not before I got a chance to wink at her, acknowledging the increasing friendship we seemed to feel for each other.

'So. What have you guys been up to in the last couple of days?' probed Linda.

'This and that,' I replied, not really wishing to be obscure or obstructive but, with my growing confidence, I no longer felt compelled to give in to Linda's demands.

Peace laughed out loud. 'In your dreams,' he said and sniggered. Grey gave him such a stern look of distaste that his laughing was cut short and he sat down like a scolded boy.

'Linda, I was wondering if you could help me get something straight?'

'Fire,' she replied, opening the palm of her hand in my direction, inviting the question.

'Wasn't it a bit risky to rely on me to save the world?'

Linda shifted her body sideways, so she could look straight at me. 'Yes, that would have been very stupid, if that's what we had done – but it wasn't.' She looked over to Grey, 'Do you want to tell him or shall I?'

My immediate thought was, 'Not again! What else haven't they told me?'

Grey nodded in Linda's direction, 'You can fill him in on this one,' she said nonchalantly.

Linda started, 'Aled, you were not – are not – our only hope, but you are our best hope. We looked all over the world for people we thought might be suitable. Do you remember when I first came here with Douglas? Although you didn't realise it, that was the third time The Project had visited the monastery. We set up scouting parties that trawled the world for people who had an unshakeable belief in God, but were not narrow-minded as a result. We had to find someone who, having heard all of this, would not pull down the shutters or Disintegrate on us.'

'Was Peace bait or a trial?' I asked bitterly.

'Both,' she said. 'Once the scouting parties had identified the potential candidates we, Douglas and I, visited them personally to see how they'd react if they were pulled in two directions. In your case, it was obvious you liked Peace, so we figured he was the best way to test your stability. It would have been a bonus if you had liked him enough to follow him back to London, but we weren't relying on it.'

I looked at Grey as if to say, 'you betrayed me,' and she held my hand, which calmed me down but made me feel stupid. 'Carry on,' I prompted.

'Sure. We found quite a few people who were candidates.

Actually, some of them are here and, once Douglas and I had seen for ourselves and talked at length to the monks, we decided that Grey should come and see how you got on with each other. If these experiments are to work there will need to be a high degree of trust between you. I also wanted Grey to assess whether she felt you would Disintegrate if we brought you back to London. She'd been insistent from the start that you were her preference and, once she met you, she wouldn't be persuaded otherwise.' Linda sat back, still looking in my direction, as if she expected me to say something.

I thought back to when they first arrived and how they'd caused such a stir amongst the monks, how they seemed so "other worldly" and how, over such a short period of time, they'd turned my life upside down. Strangely, the fact that I wasn't their only chance made me trust them more. Maybe because it reduced the pressure to perform and it was easier to believe they'd let me leave if things didn't go well.

Linda interrupted my thoughts. 'I'll keep quiet now and let you think, but please ask whatever questions you want,' she said.

I closed my eyes to consider my next steps. I thought back a few days, when I felt as if I was on the brink of Disintegration – mind, body and soul being shoved apart like badly aligned magnets. 'Can you guarantee that I won't Disintegrate if I come back with you?'

'We are convinced that there is no danger…' began Linda, but Grey interrupted.

'Aled, we really don't know. We're pretty sure that we can spot when someone starts to Disintegrate and if that happened we'd stop the experiments, but there's no guarantee. It's also possible that we'll need you to go right to the brink in order to really tap into this – you need to be prepared for that.'

I whispered, 'Thanks for the honesty,' and thinking aloud, I added, 'So no guarantees and, by the sound of it, a good possibility that I might, at least partly, Disintegrate.'

I paused to gather my thoughts. I was confused about what they thought would happen if the experiment worked in the way they hoped. 'Do you think that we'll do this thing once and the whole world will right itself?' I asked.

Grey sat forward. 'Again, Aled, we just don't know. It could be that, if it works, it will only affect the individual. But there is a possibility that, by pulling a different reality through, we actually ruin the very fabric of the world. We hope it might be somewhere in-between and that a different reality for the individual will have a knock-on effect for the rest of the world.'

'A sort of domino effect via the six degrees of separation?' I asked.

'Yes, although it might not be as simple and traceable as that. But the honest truth is, we don't know. We don't even know if the theory will work.' Grey sat back with a sigh, visibly exhausted.

After sitting in silence and thinking for a little while, I spoke. 'I've got two options, haven't I?'

I took a deep breath.

'I can come to London and take part in some sort of weird experiment, where I persuade God to bring a parallel universe into being and hence save the world. That may or may not work and I might Disintegrate in the process of finding out. Or, I can stay here and bide my time until one day I might get called into action but I might just gradually fade away.'

I folded my arms and raised my eyebrows. 'Does that sum it up?' I asked, pointedly.

'Very succinct,' said Linda.

'Perfectly,' said Grey.

18

Aled

June 2037

I looked around at the mountains, the clouds, the stone stairway, the rooftops of the village and the monastery. The fact was – I'd been living in unfamiliar territory for a long time, whether back in London during the War or China for the previous few months, and I was still in one piece. I looked at Grey, at Peace and at Linda and walked away from them, back towards the monastery.

I thought I was there for one purpose, but another was emerging and making a decision was difficult. Although I was drawn to London, I was worried it was a trap. That I'd regret my decision, in this life and the next, and that the *Proof of Existence* would be lost to mankind for ever. I thought about the parable where God is more pleased with the man who used a gift of gold and doubled it, than with the man who buried it to keep it safe but only returned the same amount as he was given. I made the decision. A well of excitement exploded inside me. I went back to the stone stairway, hoping to find Grey alone. She was.

'Okay. I'm in. What next? What do we do? How do we get back? How do I get ready? What's your role? Do I need to see Peace and Linda again?' I blurted out this series of random thoughts quickly, so there was no chance of changing my mind, pumping them at Grey as if a dam had burst and waves of curiosity were gushing out, forcing their way through my thin veneer of uncertainty and reservation.

Grey twisted the face of her uWatch and spoke briefly. 'MMS for Linda – he's on. I'll be in touch soon.' Carefully, she put her bag on the ground. 'Come here and give me a big hug,' she insisted.

I couldn't resist and, as a stupid grin appeared across my face, I wrapped my arms around her, lifted her off the ground and spun her round.

'Woah, steady, tiger!' she screamed, laughing and crying all at once.

'I. Feel. Alive!' I shouted, as loud as I could and then breathlessly, 'Grey, I'm so, so happy.'

'Me, too,' she said.

As my breathing returned to normal and the euphoria began to evaporate, reality started to creep into my consciousness and some of my previous anxiety returned with it. But the anxiety didn't outweigh the utter joy of deciding to give it a go.

'Calm enough to talk?' asked Grey.

'I think so, let's try,' I answered, feeling like a kid in a sweetshop.

'Actually, do you need to know anything else before we leave, or can we talk on the journey?' she asked.

'Let's just get on with it. I can still bail out if I want to, can't I? No questions asked?'

'Of course you can. You have my word.'

'Give me a couple of hours to pack and say some goodbyes. I'll meet you back here.'

'Sure, the car's in the village being serviced for the journey. Bring some of your carvings with you. Please?' she said over her shoulder as she walked away. At long last I felt like an equal.

I went back to my room, taking a detour past the kitchen to say goodbye to the cooks, giving them the thumbs up. They must have thought I'd finally flipped. I walked across the courtyard, relishing every single step, smiling and winking at everyone, even people I'd passed without so much as a 'Hello' since I'd been there. I opened the creaky door to my cell and started to put my meagre belongings into my Fabrication bag – my one luxury. In went my battered but beloved bible, a handful of Absolutist tracts, my carvings, knife and a few pieces of wood. Under the bed were the remnants of the clothes I'd arrived in – a pair of jeans that I'd cut off at the knee when it was really hot on the journey, a couple of plain blue t-shirts and a pair of seriously worn-out boots. I put them on and stuffed the brown monk's robe into my bag, in case I needed a spare set of clothes. Lastly, I moved the loose stone in the corner of the room, carefully lifting out my secret uCumulus. It'd been a while since I'd uploaded anything to the AGP Museum, but if ever there was a right time, this was it.

To protect our physical locations, we'd all agreed to only communicate via the museum. I recorded a ten-minute artefact explaining that I was returning to London and described, as best I could, everything that Grey had told me about The Project. I ended by making it clear that it was what God wanted and prayed that the museum was still being monitored. Using a uCumulus interface that Zak had given me, I connected via a back door to upload the artefact. An automated message from one of the other elders appeared. 'Be careful, Aled, and trust no one.' Another victim of Disintegration, I presumed.

I got up from the wooden bench that had been my bed for so long and looked around the room. The excitement of being active, rather than passive, was sending surges of oxygen around my blood stream. The elation was overriding all my misgivings; it was as if I was falling madly in love and having Christmas and Easter all at the same time. I swung the bag over my shoulder, giving it time to mould to my back, touched my lips and pressed my fingers on the door as it closed behind me. Blessing it, for what I hoped would be the last time. I ran through the courtyard, through the flowers and the candles, taking a last look at the golden dragons and giving them a wave. I was on my way.

Grey was stooped over her projector, concentrating on an image displayed on the ground.

'What's up?' I asked, apprehensively.

She quickly shut down the projector, stood up and said in a slightly irritated voice, 'Nothing – just looking at home, checking it's still there.'

I was a little suspicious but too caught up in the moment to bother worrying. If it was important, she'd tell me.

She put her arm through mine, and with a skip in her step, she dragged me down two steps at a time.

It took us thirty minutes to reach the edge of the village and as we walked through the gate in the wall, I felt anxious. Grey must have sensed it because she kept her arm interlocked with mine, giving me a little squeeze of encouragement every now and again. The villagers stared at us, as if we'd just landed from another planet: Grey in her chic but practical clothes and me in my cut-off jeans and t-shirt. Sitting outside a rickety bamboo garage was an old, wiry and toothless woman. Linda popped her head out of the door and beckoned us in.

'Hi, great to see you at last,' she said more to me than to Grey. 'Can we make a move? The vehicle is ready and charged to run. The sooner we move, the sooner we'll be able to pick up the plane back to England.'

I'd assumed we'd be travelling by train, but the mention of a plane reminded me that I was in the company of vast wealth.

'How come you're able to afford to travel by plane?' I quizzed Linda.

'One of the upsides of this mess is that academia has risen to the top of the "fixers" pile and our project has funding from a few major governments.'

'Do you mind me asking, is China one of those?'

'Do you think we'd be allowed to travel around so freely if we weren't endorsed and protected by the Chinese state?' she scoffed.

'I did wonder,' I replied nonchalantly, hiding my embarrassment as best I could.

The car was not the one I'd seen up at the monastery, but a four-wheel-drive Jeep. Complete with camouflage-netting and metal shutters over the windows. It reminded me of a pre-war anti-riot vehicle. 'That's some car you got there,' I said, to no one in particular.

Peace's voice echoed from within. 'We'll need it if we're to survive this trip.'

I looked at Grey, who shrugged, put her arm round my shoulder and elaborated. 'This whole thing is littered with dangers, Aled. I can't pretend that it isn't. But we've made this journey four times now without any significant issues, so I really don't think this part is the one to be worrying about. Not, when, as you put it, we're going to try and persuade God to bring a parallel universe into being and save the world.'

'Right, let's go then,' I suggested with a hint of amusement.

'All aboard,' commanded Linda in a mock pirate voice.

I'm not sure what was most comforting – Peace's worrying, Linda's boldness or Grey's realism. I prayed, just loud enough for the others to hear, 'God. Please protect us.'

I got into the Jeep and settled down in the back, resting on my Fabrication bag which, as ever, moulded itself to the purpose in hand. In this case, to the metal shell of the Jeep on one side and my back on the other. I was surprised to see Peace sitting in the driver's seat and turned to Grey.

'Is Peace driving?'

She smiled at me and in a conspiratorial stage whisper announced, 'Ex-British army. SAS – Strong And Sexy. You missed out there.'

I kicked her playfully. 'So not my type,' I corrected her.

Peace turned round, completely nonplussed, and barked, 'Until we get to London, I'm in charge. You'll do exactly what I say, when I say it. No arguing and no pontificating. For once in your lives, believe that someone knows best. And at this moment that someone is me. Aled, you okay with that?'

I was impressed. That was the most I'd heard Peace speak in one go and he obviously knew what he was doing. 'Peace, I'm fine and completely want someone in charge who knows what they are doing.' I added, possibly a bit unnecessarily, 'It's what I fought for, after all.'

He was busy checking all the instruments, but he fascinated me and I couldn't help interrupting him. 'Peace, I really like your name but where did it come from? Are you some sort of peace-warrior then? Fighting for the common good like Robin Hood? Or is the name some sort of in-joke?'

'Not really,' he said, back to his old chatty self.

A glass window rose between the front seats and the rear space, cutting Linda and Peace off from me and Grey. As soon as it was shut, Peace's voice came through the intercom, 'Right, brace yourselves. Here we go.'

I pointed to the glass divide. 'A bit over the top, isn't it?'

Grey shrugged. 'Depends on how you view protecting the saviour of the world. Sorry didn't mean to offend…but you are. I don't think it's over the top and I certainly feel safer behind bullet-proof glass. Peace knows what he's doing and reckons the best way not to be attacked is to look as if we can hold our own. To be more scary than the attackers. I don't know if you noticed the flags painted on to the roof. They send a very strong signal that if you mess with us, you mess with some of the most powerful governments in the world. And not necessarily ones that abide by any Sentient Beings conventions – if you get my meaning.'

With a mock cockney accent and clenching my fist in a boxer's stance, I said, 'Don't mess with us, geezer?'

Grey looked at me sternly. 'I wouldn't joke about this if I were you. It's very real.'

I dropped the joking and in a genuinely serious tone asked, 'What if the local warlords don't realise we have powerful friends? Or just don't care?'

Grey smiled. 'Then they're fucked, Aled,' she said, with quite a worrying glint in her eye.

'Really, are you sure? I've heard they're well armed and organised.'

'This thing is a weapon first and a vehicle second. And Peace is the best there is. This little beauty is almost an extension of his body.'

We both fell silent, too exhausted to speak. The metal shutters closed, the engines fired up and we crawled out from the garage. Out of the back window I could see the villagers self-consciously ignoring us as we trundled through their streets like a modern dragon, rumbling deep in its throat and flexing its muscles ready for flight. As we got to the edge of the village, the roar of the motors increased and, as if someone had hit a turbo button, we shot out on to the dirt tracks, kicking up a trail of dust and debris behind us.

'Here goes then,' whispered Grey, as if speaking any louder would attract too much attention.

We raced through the countryside. Tea plantations littered the hillsides, locals walked beside the road with their livestock and every now and again a group of cyclists stopped to let us pass. I hoped Peace was right that fear would stop any attack, because we weren't going to slip by unnoticed.

I tried to snooze as we bumped along the road but, just as I was dropping off, I heard an almighty racket that sounded like bombs exploding around us. I woke Grey, who seemed to be able to sleep through anything. 'What on earth is that?' I asked, in a voice that was a pitch higher than normal.

'Look out of the back window, Aled. Can you see the forest to the right there?' she asked, rather too calmly for my liking. 'Look back far enough. Can you see the smoke rising from the trees?'

'Yes, I can see it. What of it?'

She took hold of my hand, treating me like a small child that needed some re-assurance. 'That's the home of the most notorious local warlord. Every time we pass, Peace fires a volley of rockets at him. Attack is our best form of defence. It's the most effective way of signalling our strength. I have to say, so far we've not had any trouble, so I'm guessing Peace knows what he's doing. He was a mercenary for the Chinese government when the economy was collapsing and they had to suppress quite a few uprisings. He has a lot of experience. He's some guy.'

I shrugged. 'Okay. If you're not scared then I guess I won't be either. But it all feels a bit too much to me.'

As we bumped and swerved for another couple of hours, being thrown around like rag dolls in a careless child's suitcase, I wasn't really thinking about anything in particular except how weird and wonderful this whole experience was turning out to be. Suddenly the Jeep stopped bouncing and sped up. The road was now tarmacked, with concrete buildings on either side. I shook Grey from her drowsing. 'Is this the airport? Do you think we're in time to catch the plane?'

Lazily, she opened her eyes and smiled her mischievous smile. 'Aled,' she said, with a chuckle, 'We have our very own plane, it'll wait for us.' She stretched her arms. 'They're very rich.' She giggled.

'Oh,' was all I managed in response.

Peace and Linda were being extremely animated in the front, but because of the glass I couldn't hear what they were saying. Peace turned around, while driving, and signalled us to get down. I was frightened and wanted to see what was happening, but crouched down on the floor as commanded.

'No no no!' exclaimed Grey. 'Put these on,' she said, as she grabbed some straps from out of the side of the Jeep. I pulled them over my shoulders and as soon as I let go they clasped me close to the wall. They were made of the same intelligent fabric as my bag.

'I love this bit,' shouted Grey, over the escalating noise of the engines. 'Look out the back there – can you see the soldiers chasing us?' she shouted.

I could see a hundred or so camouflaged men riding on motorbikes and pointing rocket launchers at us, like some modern-day wild-west film. 'Grey, what the hell is that?' I shouted back.

'Always happens, don't worry,' she shouted, almost laughing. We hit a massive bump and the Jeep seemed to lift six feet off the ground and then it went dark.

I squealed in terror. 'Grey! Talk to me!'

'Aled, we're fine. We're in the back of the plane and safe,' she said calmly. And sure enough I felt the pull of jet engines and a little lurch in my stomach as we rose off the ground.

The window between us and the front lowered and Peace, verbose as ever, said, 'Sorted.'

19

Aled

June 2037

Linda opened the back door and invited us to sit in the lounge area, next to the vehicle. I followed Grey over to a large leather chair, sat down and let out an expansive sigh. 'Phew, that was close,' I said, hiding how unnerved I was, not being able to see out of the plane.

'Nothing to worry about,' replied Linda.

'So…what now?' I asked.

'Let's catch our breath and celebrate with a glass of wine. Then we can talk about London,' she suggested.

'Sounds good to me,' Peace called out, from behind the vehicle. He appeared carrying plates of little cheese sandwiches with a glass of wine attached to their side, as if we were at some seatless corporate event.

Linda raised her glass. 'I'm sorry the cheese is pretty ropey and the wine tastes a bit home made, but it is our way of celebrating being on the way home. Safely. And with you on board. Here's to Aled. It has been a long time coming.'

'I'm flattered. Cheers and here's to God and time travel.'

As I took my first drink of wine, I was thrown back in the seat with a tremendous force. 'What on earth?'

Grey chuckled. 'Not quite on earth, actually, Aled. They're testing the engines ready for when we accelerate out of the atmosphere. We're on one of the old space tourist planes, on a sub-

156

orbital flight so…better drink up, eat up, and strap yourself in 'cos when we've left the atmosphere we'll be weightless for about fifteen minutes. Then we descend into London.'

I drank my wine rapidly but only took one bite of the plastic cheese sandwich. Grey drank and ate everything, but the others only made a token gesture of enjoying the celebration "meal". They strapped themselves into harnesses that pulled down from the roof of the plane – like baby bouncers with oxygen masks – and I quickly did the same. The familiar feel of Fabrication was comforting as it gripped itself to my body and, although I was a bit apprehensive, I felt very excited. I pulled on the oxygen mask. I was about to go into space for the first time and it reminded me of how optimistic the human race used to be about its future.

The noise of the engines firing was horrendously loud and I was pushed back against the seat, which had swivelled into place to catch me. Abruptly, it went deathly quiet and windows opened. The black sky was twinkling with stars and nobody spoke except Grey, who captured our sense of wonder perfectly. 'Never ceases to amaze,' she said.

Peace unstrapped himself and informed us that we could all follow suit, which I did without hesitating. I was floating, weightless and in awe of God. 'Worth coming just for this,' I chuckled through a wide grin of happiness.

Grey looked over to me and winked. 'Welcome aboard The Project.'

'Linda, I'm really surprised that the infrastructure still exists to allow us to do this,' I said, as more of a question than a statement.

'There is no traffic control anywhere in the world, but there are virtually no planes either, so it's not a big deal. You have to keep your eyes open when taking off and landing, but apart from that we are pretty much alone up here.'

We all gathered at one of the windows, looking out into space. 'Is it okay if I float around?' I asked.

'Go ahead,' said Peace, 'you can't damage anything.'

I pushed myself off, drifting from one side of the plane to the other, as happy as a young boy at his first fairground. I was really enjoying it, but Peace soon ordered us to get strapped back into the harnesses.

Grey was deeply engrossed in an image she'd projected on to a screen at the rear end of the plane. 'Aled, I'd like you to look at this. If you don't mind,' she said, in a no-nonsense but slightly distracted voice. 'Do you recognise him?' she asked, pointing to one of the Disintegrates outside of St James's Church. I looked carefully, and after a while I started to see something familiar in the heavily-bearded face which, despite its blank staring expression, did occasionally show glimpses of life.

I stumbled in my response – asking, but not really wanting the answers. 'Is it?.. no, surely not?.. maybe?.. no, can't be?.. I think?.. Oh my?.. do you know?..'

Grey opened her eyes wider in encouragement and I composed myself.

'Is that Zak?' I whispered.

'Yes, I think it is.'

She carried on. 'We need to start thinking about how to test this theory. We could experiment with the moment you and him stopped being friends. What do you think?'

I stared at the screen, unable to speak, but thinking, This is… was…is…my best friend and I love him dearly. I reckoned Grey was spot on and my first attempt should be Zak. Although it was risky, he had no future otherwise and I was sure it's what he would want. I was sure his Disintegration was linked to some dodgy stuff he'd done since I last saw him. If only he'd been able to talk to me, ask me for help. 'Grey, will it be safe to start with him? What could go wrong?'

With an expressionless face, she answered, 'Honestly? I don't know, but I figure that he's your closest human bond, so it's the most likely of any situation to work. And, hopefully, the least dangerous. Partly because you know him so well but also, and apologies for this, compared to some other attempts we might make, it's not as critical or far-reaching if it goes wrong. I hope you understand.'

I nodded, unable to utter the words of agreement.

Peace burst the tense atmosphere with instructions. 'All strapped in? We're ready to land.'

As soon as he said it, the braking system kicked in and the plane started to scream. We tilted to forty-five degrees and the windows closed. We were back in the same metal shell and deprived of all sense of the outside world. The plane bounced as it landed and I let out another sigh of relief.

Grey and Linda smiled, as they unbuckled their harnesses.

'Welcome to London City Airport,' said Grey.

A London black cab owned by The Project collected us from a deserted airport with no border control and only a handful of dodgy-looking mechanics – modern mercenaries, according to Peace. Not stopping at any junction, and paying no attention to the road signs, the car sped us along the desolate city streets. Occasionally, we passed through an area that still seemed to be functioning.

'Grey, how come some areas are okay?' I asked.

She explained, 'In some areas, like Whitechapel where we've just been through, we think the strong community that existed before the war has, to some extent, immunized them from outside influence and they carry on with the same way of life they've had for years. They still struggle with the infrastructure and they're poor, so they can't live like we do, but they seem to be surviving and with no visible sign of Disintegration. There may be something for us to learn from them but they are insular and violently hostile to outsiders.'

'This really is quite bad, isn't it?'

Grey squeezed my hand in agreement.

Within twenty minutes, we arrived at a square of Georgian houses built around a small park. The car pulled up at number 34 and as we crossed the pavement, the front door opened. It reminded me of being an important guest at a posh hotel.

'This house once belonged to the ex-husband of Madonna. You know – the pop icon of the 2D era?' Grey informed me, with a pleased look on her face. 'Let me show you to your room,' she offered, taking me by the hand and guiding me through the house.

She took me to a plush but tired room with high ceilings, large windows and period furniture. It was regal but worn-out – neglected, unclean and crumbling – and reminded me of London. It was the perfect bedroom for me.

'Aled, this house is The Project living quarters. Some of our technical equipment is in the old swimming pool in the basement and the rest of the time we'll be in the UCL buildings just along the street. I hope you're okay in here. I'm just along the corridor, in case you need me. It's great to have you here.'

'Looks great to me. When do we decide what to do about Zak?' I asked, impatient to get on with things.

'Let's go out tonight to a Disintegrate shelter – the old RSA building – and you can get a feel for things.'

I was nervous but agreed with no hesitation, 'Do you think we'll see Zak?'

'I think it's best there's no one you know – just for the first night. Is that okay?' she said, in a voice that only invited the answer, 'Yes.'

'Can it just be the two of us, please?' I asked, wanting some security and intimacy.

'Of course. Actually, from now on it will be mainly just you and me. I don't like the others around, except Douglas, of course. They've done their job now,' she said, reassuringly. 'Shall I come and collect you in an hour?'

'Yup, sounds perfect.'

I flopped down on the bed, letting my thoughts wander back across the previous few months and cautiously forward into the coming weeks.

I was woken up by Grey squeezing my hand and whispering in my ear, 'Aled, time to go.'

We left the house and started the walk south, towards Soho. The streets were as empty and desolate as I'd seen from the satellite link at the monastery. The sense of post-apocalypse was tangible; a deafening silence, where the only sign of life was an occasional cardboard box on a street corner. 'Grey, what's the cardboard boxes in aid of?' I asked as we casually strolled along, arm-in-arm.

'They're food parcels. Local councils, what's left of them, distribute them every day in the hope that people stuck in their homes, too frightened to come out, will at least make it to the corner of the street and retrieve some food. They're mainly just bread and vegetables, but they're always empty at the end of the day, so it seems to be working.'

Along the way she pointed out two places where the Disintegrates congregated – the old Oliver Twist Workhouse on Cleveland Street and a ramshackle village of tents in Soho Square. We walked for another fifteen minutes through this surreal world of desolation and Disintegration and I couldn't help thinking about the fifth trumpet in revelation – *men will seek death and will not find it; and they will long to die and death flees from them.* Was I about to try and stop the God of Revelation ending his world? 'Grey, what if this is all part of God's plan?' I asked tentatively.

'She's not like that,' Grey answered firmly.

'I'm not so sure,' I said, but left it at that.

The RSA had always been a place of curiosity, intelligent thinking and dedicated to "civic innovation and social progress". In the War, it was one of the few places that adopted a neutral stance. Hosting discussions between the two sides, it attempted to help us reach a settlement and, although we didn't succeed, they were right to try. Without the RSA and the Quakers, we wouldn't have been able to talk to the Liberalists at all and things may have been worse.

Grey led us past a rather sinister-looking security guard, who obviously knew Grey. He waved us through and up some narrow stairs into an old room with a mural around the walls. 'John Barry's vision of the Progress of Human Knowledge and Culture. And, the reality,' she said, pointing first to the mural and then to the Disintegrates. On the floor were hundreds of people, propped up against each other in the same way as they were outside St James's.

This mass grave of the living-dead had a smell I didn't recognise, but it was so overpowering I instinctively pinched my nose and screwed up my face. Grey was breathing deeply, as if she was inhaling the despair. She spoke very quietly. 'Aled, let's sit down amongst them. I want you to be as empathic as you can. Let it wash over you. Hold on to the sensation, because that memory will help you stop your own slide towards Disintegration. Are you up for that?'

'Nervous, but willing,' I whispered.

'Good. Now you must do as I say. Okay?'

'Sure.'

'Sit down on the floor and pull six people close, as if you're a soldier on a battlefield trying to hide amongst the dead. Then, let go and allow yourself to be subsumed into whatever comes but, and it's very important, whenever I ask, 'how do you feel,' you must answer by holding up your fingers. Five means very good. One means you want out. If you signal with one finger, I'll pull you out at once. If you don't respond, I'll pull you out, but I'd rather not wait for that. Do you understand?' Reassuringly, she had the most serious expression I'd ever seen on her face.

I sat down on the floor with my back against the wall and pulled the closest six people on top of me, making sure that my hand was free and that Grey could see it. 'How do you feel?' she asked.

I showed her my outstretched hand, all four fingers and a thumb. I let my imagination take me back to the monastery, to one of the long prayer sessions. I chanted under my breath, 'I'm a believer, I'm an Absolutist, I lost. I'm a believer, I'm an Absolutist…' I slowed my breathing, to get my body into the rhythm of the chant, until I could feel the familiar intense pain of body, mind and soul tearing apart.

'How do you feel?' she asked again. I held up four fingers, still fairly confident that I'd got this under control. It wasn't as bad as the monastery, but after a few minutes a different sensation emerged – one of absolute nothingness – and I felt a black void, hanging in the air just behind my head. It must have been emanating from the Disintegrates; it was very scary. I held up two fingers, without Grey even asking.

'I see them,' she said.

My mind, body and soul were no longer fighting each other but were being helplessly dragged into a whirlpool, down into the black void of nothingness. I was transfixed by the film, *Lord of the Rings*, that was on the big screen at the front and it became my whole world. I was being slowly hollowed out from the inside, from the very core of my soul. Gradually, it became harder and harder to think or feel anything. I tried to signal to Grey, but couldn't summon enough energy or desire. It was the most wonderful I'd ever felt. So warm and pleasant and without a care in the world – a foetus nurtured by the womb. I drifted for a while until I felt a sting across my face and heard in the distance, 'Aled, get back here now!' Then another, more painful, sting and Grey shouting, 'Aled, if you don't come back to me this instant!'

I opened my eyes and gradually focussed on her. She looked worried. 'Aled, how are you?' she asked tenderly.

I held up one finger but smiled at the same time. 'Did you just rescue me?' I asked, rather pitifully.

'Yes, you went faster than I thought you would. Thank God you're back. Are you okay?'

'Think so…but that was scary. I now know what it is to be a Disintegrate, though. It's no wonder you can't get through to them. It's beyond despair – a deep black hole of nothing – but it's actually incredibly liberating. No need to strive for anything, you can just stop. My mind, body and soul weren't functioning, but they were at peace with each other. It was as if I was lying back in a pool of narcotic treacle. It's wonderful.'

'Shall we go home and sleep?' she suggested.

'Yes, please. But we must get on with this first thing tomorrow. I don't want too much time to think, otherwise I might change my mind.'

Grey spoke into her watch. 'MMS for Fitzroy Square. Car from RSA please. Immediately. And six Ds to the lab.' I leant on Grey as we walked back down the stairs and passed the security guard.

'How long was I out for?' I asked.

In a matter-of-fact voice, she said, 'Only five minutes, but you stopped responding so I brought you round rather more sharply than I would have liked. What was it like to come back so fast?'

I mulled over her question for a while, partly lost in my own thoughts, and then replied in a similar matter-of-fact voice, conscious we had started the experiments. 'I wasn't aware of it. I heard you calling me back and felt you slap me twice. I was disconnecting. Nothing was important. It seemed as if no one cared about me and nor did I. Slapping me was harsh, but it made me feel wanted.'

She took out a stylus and started to write into her uWatch. I could see the empty streets out of the car window as it whisked us up Charing Cross road and back to Fitzroy Square.

It had begun.

I woke early and decided to have a look around the house. It was a strange mix of the old and the new. Its high-ceilinged rooms, with large ornate crystal chandeliers, were full of Georgian furniture that had been re-upholstered with Fabrication. All of the rooms had specially fitted screens that could be lowered so you could watch CCTV footage from anywhere in the world. When you requested your entertainment – music, documentary or film – the system interpreted the intonation in your voice and chose appropriately for your mood. It was a bit unreliable, though, because the Cumulus broadcasts it relied on weren't functioning properly. I wandered around for some time, soaking up the atmosphere of this grand old house – a fraying matriarch surrounded by her grand-children's new toys – until eventually I found my way down to the basement, to the laboratory Grey had mentioned the day before.

The swimming pool had seen better days. It still had its gold railings, although the velvet cushions that lined the walls were threadbare. It was now kitted out with a neural imaging helmet capable of simultaneously displaying live brain activity on a large screen, as well its own visor screen. An observation booth, built into the shell of the old sauna, allowed the recording and play-back of neural-control experiments. On the wall at the far end of the pool, the 2026 version of *Tsunami* was being shown. I remembered Simmone and her anger at the portrayal of the drug-addled students. To my surprise and disgust, the six Disintegrates from the evening before were sitting in the pool staring at the film.

I sat down with them in the pool. Without realising it, I drifted into that soothing nothingness that I'd experienced the night before. Slipping into a world where all my elements – mind, body and soul – fitted together, as neatly as they were created. It was a slow, comfortable drift and after a while – I've no idea how long – I heard someone in the distance speaking, telling me to, 'Come back this instant, you stupid, stupid man!' She held my hands. I'm sure I heard her say, 'I love you.' Enticing me back.

Once again, Grey had rescued me from the slippery slope and brought me back to the painful reality of a broken world. She was very upset with me and chastised me thoroughly, through gritted teeth. 'We have to do this in a controlled way, otherwise we'll lose you forever and I won't let that happen. To let yourself drift off like that with no one else around is not only foolish but irresponsible. You are meant to be here to save the world. I thought you understood and agreed?'

I may have looked at her stubbornly and refused to respond, but deep down I was sorry and inwardly agreed to obey whatever instructions she would give me in the coming weeks.

20

Grey

July 2037

'Fourteen million minutes of footage. Grey, we don't stand a chance,' said Jane.

The three of us – Douglas, Jane and I – were busy deep-mining vast amounts of data, using the state-of-the-art quantum computer that Douglas had bought for our new lab. We'd been so keen to crack on, that some of the long lab benches still had their plastic coating on and, despite the heady smells of fresh paint, leftover meals and half-drunk cups of coffee, we were engrossed.

Over the previous few days, we'd been running ten year's worth of footage from every camera in the world through the face recognition software. First, we'd pared it down to footage that contained Aled. Then, we'd reduced it even further by selecting only four views – front, behind, above and below. The trouble was, it still left us with about fourteen million minutes of footage. We decided to use the Database of Influence as a second level of filter.

We were searching for tiny nuggets of data-gold – events that, if we could change them, would have the greatest chance of creating an alternative world. We used the influence rating, in combination with the facial recognition software, to pinpoint where on Aled's time-line we should experiment.

Douglas, Jane and I sat at one of the lab benches, ready to watch Aled's most influential hour of the War. The eWall was

divided into four – one for each camera. A strip down the right
-hand side showed the three most influential people in Aled's
vicinity at the time.

'Start,' said Douglas.

The footage began – Aled was walking along a corridor. To his
left was an English sea-front visible through tall windows, and to
his right was a wall of flaking pea-green paint. He walked briskly
along a sticky red carpet peppered with bald patches. He was
surrounded by people, but alone. His face was clenched in
concentration, blocking out the quiet hum of intense discussion
from the tea and biscuit-carrying crowd. They made their way
through the swing doors and into an auditorium. Aled sat in one of
the faded-blue padded chairs, part of a thousand-strong crowd all
seated in neat rows facing a large screen displaying a big green tick
– the logo of the Absolutists. On every empty chair was a booklet,
with the same big green tick on the cover. Aled began to read his,
occasionally glancing up at the stage. To the side of the footage,
our algorithm displayed the profiles of the three most influential
people it had identified – Graham Browne, Daphne Hicksworth
and Pavinder Campbell.

Daphne came on to the stage in her blue suit and began to
address the conference. 'My fellow Absolutists. Why are we here?
We're here because we are at war and we won't simply surrender and
give up our right to free-thinking. We may differ with each other in
what we believe but, unlike the Liberalists, at least we can agree on
one core aspect of what it means to be Human – we know that the
world does have absolute truths.'

Douglas paused the footage. 'This can't be the most influential
moment of Aled's life,' he said.

'Seems a bit thin,' said Jane.

'We don't have to watch the whole hour. We can get the
algorithm to focus in on the highest rated minute, followed by
the second highest. And, so on,' I explained.

'Show me the highest rated five minutes then,' said Douglas.

'Fast-forward to the top five minutes, please,' I said. The

footage sped forward through the speech, the question and answers, and the applause. Aled, along with the other delegates, started to leave the room and the footage reverted to normal speed, following him through the crowd to the side exit. Linda Hemingford, Douglas DeSouza and Barak Rahman appeared as the three names on the strip down the side of the eWall.

'Show me the influencers,' I said. The cameras zoomed in on the three of them, huddled in a corner having an animated discussion with a group of five men in grey suits. One of the men said something into Douglas's ear and, after what seemed like a small salute, Douglas peeled away from the group to follow Aled at a discreet distance.

'This is not working at all. How can it think that the three of us are the most influential people in Aled's life? Try the next one,' said Douglas.

'I didn't know you were an Absolutist,' I said, cautiously.

'I'm an anthropologist. I hung around a lot of places,' said Douglas.

'Next event,' I said.

Aled was alone and sitting at a low table in the corner of a dark room. Oil lamps flickered, giving off an orange glow, but barely lighting the room beyond the two red-velvet daybeds that formed a V around one side of the table. I recognised the music that was playing – the seventy-year-old classic tune, *Flying Teapot* by Planet Gong – because it had been on an ancient iPod that Mum and I had found in the bottom of a box of Gran's possessions.

Aled picked up some dried seed-pods from a pure-white china bowl that was decorated on the inside with impressionist red poppies – subtly indicating which plant the seed-pods came from. He put them into a hand-grinder and slowly turned the handle, lost in thought. After a few minutes, he poured the ground contents into an old-fashioned stove-top espresso machine and placed it over a flame that occasionally poked its head above the lip of the small red-and-black lacquered bowl that contained it. While it was heating up, he plugged his uWatch into his uCumulus. The espresso machine started to steam and, after its gurgling had stopped, he poured a dark liquid into a jet-black teacup. He covered the flame with a wooden block and, sipping the tea, read his uCumulus. I was desperate to see what he was reading but there were no cameras behind him. Only once did we get a quick glance at the screen, as he put it down on the table while he topped up his cup – he was reading what looked like a scientific theory. Frustratingly, this wasn't enough to tell us why this had been singled out as one of his most important moments.

'Damn, if that's what I think it is, we need to get hold of it,' said Douglas, straining to see what Aled was so engrossed in. 'Oh, for crying out loud! Speed it up. Let's see what else is in this hour.'

'Ten times normal speed please,' I said, and the footage raced through.

After an uneventful hour, Aled paid the bill and left via a set of stairs whose walls were lined with a million pieces of broken mirror. He came out of a big wooden door at the top and, stepping over a paving stone with Sherlock's Delight embossed into it, walked away with a distant look on his face. The footage stopped.

'Grey, this really is not working at all. Go back to see if we can pick up any footage before he's in that bar,' said Douglas.

I tagged the beginning of the hour and then asked for the footage to play backwards at double speed.

'There,' said Douglas. A man, whose face was covered by the hood of his duffle coat, was leaving Aled's flat. 'Who on earth is that?' asked Douglas.

'Enhance. Who is that?' I asked, but it couldn't find a camera angle that showed the man's face. *Unknown* appeared on the screen as the top influencer – I'd never seen that before. 'Image of unknown top-influencer,' I said. A photo of the duffle-coated man replaced unknown.

'Next,' said Douglas, slumping down into his chair.

Footage of a blue, yellow and red-striped helicopter landing in St Peter's Square filled the screen. Ten Vatican guards, in striped uniforms that matched the helicopter, appeared out of nowhere and formed a semi-circle. The blades stopped spinning, the door opened and Aled stepped out. The guards closed their circle and escorted him to a gap in the Vatican City wall. The Pope appeared, shook Aled's hand, disappeared back through the wall and the gap closed as mysteriously as it had opened. The footage went blank but the three influential names on display were Pope Innocent IV, the Secretary of State of His Holiness The Pope and the Substitute for General Affairs to the Secretary of State. We sat and waited as the clock kept counting in the corner of the blank screen.

'There were no cameras in that damn Vatican City. I'm glad it's gone,' said Douglas. 'Speed it up until we get something.'

'Fifty times speed, please. Until there's a facial recognition.'

After a few seconds the clock was at fifty-eight minutes and the speed returned to normal. Aled was being escorted out of the same gap in the wall with a guard holding each arm, but no sign of the Pope. They pushed him towards the Vatican Helicopter which was still waiting for him. He got on board and off it went. The footage stopped at sixty minutes.

'What does all that tell us then?' asked Douglas.

'I'm not sure. We need to get a better insight than this, don't we?' I answered.

'I've an idea,' said Jane. 'We're looking for key moments that changed the order of our society. Right?'

'Yes…' said Douglas.

'Well. We have all this data on influencers. Who's ranked where. If we could find some large-scale shifts in the rankings, we'd know when a key world event had occurred. We only have to match these to key events in Aled's time-line and we'll know which ones are relevant to him. Then we know where he needs to focus. Agreed?'

'Jane, you're a genius,' said Douglas.

'No. I'm a data-mining anthropologist,' she replied.

Douglas turned to me. 'Grey. I know you have some issues with Jane, but you can see why she's so valuable. Will you two kiss and make up?'

We looked at each other for a few moments and then,

reluctantly, I held out my hand. She shook it without any enthusiasm, but at least we could carry on working together.

'Thank you,' said Douglas.

'Let's see if we can do this then,' said Jane.

She turned to her uCumulus. 'We need to find a significant number of people moving a significant amount within the rank order.'

'What's significant, though?' I asked.

'The algorithm can work out what's statistically significant. But how will we know if Aled's involved?'

'How about if we correlate it with Aled moving up the rank order of influence considerably faster than anyone else?' I suggested.

'Got it. Well done, that should work,' she said, typing fast. We smiled at each other and got down to business.

For a few minutes, as Jane's reworked algorithm processed the data, snapshots of footage flashed across the screen. Finally, it settled and there was Aled standing at the front of a school hall, addressing three people on the stage and surrounded by men with stun-guns. He looked so calm and in control – I loved it when he was like that. A woman, wearing a vintage 2020s designer suit and the most amazingly large pearls, spoke. She had the same crisp voice of authority as Linda.

'Fellow Liberalists. You've heard both sides of the argument in this trial. You've heard the defendants tell us that they had a right to make decisions on behalf of their children. You've heard about the consequences of those actions. And, most critically, you've heard Aled Griffen's rather strange views on sexual liberation. It's time to vote – do we or don't we change the law?'

The footage paused but the three top influencers kept changing, never settling on any one in particular. 'This is it. Look at the amount of flux in the database. And, look at Aled shooting up the rankings,' said Jane.

'What is it?' I asked.

'That's the *Frigid Five* trial. That's our key event. Grey. First experiment is Zak and this is second,' said Douglas.

'Fascinating. There's so much flux in this data. There must have been some big shifts in the underlying structure of society. There's whole networks of people dropping like stones down the rankings,' said Jane.

'Grey. Can we have a word, please?' asked Douglas.

I followed him into his office. The walls were covered in books stacked on floor-to-ceiling bookshelves and, although I'd never kept books, even when you could buy new ones easily, I liked the feeling of security that being surrounded by such luxurious antiquities gave me. A rope hammock was slung across one corner of the room, next to a window that overlooked an enclosed rose garden. A brown leather chair, the type that can swivel and lean back, sat next to a dark oak desk covered in piles of paper. Even the large industrial-sized shredder that stood next to the desk was made from wood and covered in leather. On the wall behind his desk was the largest eWall I'd ever seen. In the corner opposite the hammock were two leather armchairs, placed either side of an open fire. I loved this room. It reminded me of the village pub near ACAT. I'd spent my Sunday evenings there, drinking a couple of speciality real ales with the old guys from the village and mulling over the meaning of life. I'd once told them that when I was growing up I'd been fascinated by Aunt G wearing men's clothes – tweed suit and brogues. It didn't happen often, but she'd explained that it was her way of asserting her independence and testing whether a man found her attractive for herself rather than some frilly female fantasy. They said they liked the sound of her. When I left home, I persuaded her to give me her suit and shoes and I wore them to the pub every Sunday evening.

Douglas poured us a measure each of whisky. 'Forty-year-old Aberlour. Enjoy,' he said, leaning back in his armchair. I sipped in silence, waiting for him to reveal why he wanted to talk to me alone. 'So. How is Aled coming along?' he asked.

'He's a star. He's totally committed to working out how we do it. But, I'm concerned that we're not making the progress we should. I can't test my theories until he can control moving to and from the edge of Disintegration. To be honest, we've had quite a few scares where I thought we'd lost him. I'm nervous of pushing him too far, too fast.'

'But you didn't, so don't worry. We know he's the right person for the job. How long before he's ready, do you think?'

'Well, we've been at it for a week but I reckon we need about another week. He gets stronger every day.'

'Good. Is there anything else you want to talk through?'

'Yes. Actually, now you mention it, there is. I'm worried about his reaction to the RSA. He was quite angry about the way we experimented on those Ds. I think his words were, "A holding pen for lab-rats, not a sanctuary". I started to talk about it but he said he'd rather not know and anyway he could always return to China if he discovered too much cruelty here.'

'You need to focus on the experiments. Don't worry about Aled. This is all still a shock. He's bound to overreact. Oh, and stop worrying about Zak and Jane.'

'Okay.'

I wasn't convinced that Douglas was right to encourage me not to worry, but he was right that I needed to focus on the experiments. 'Douglas, when can I tell him about us being half-siblings?' I asked.

'Not yet. You've just said how temperamental he's being. Wait for a while. We'll know when it's right. Has he mentioned the Holy of Holies at all?'

'Not that I know of. Is it important?'

'No. But do tell me if he does. I'd like to know,' said Douglas, folding his arms.

'Sure,' I said, taking the hint not to press for more detail. 'I haven't seen Linda for a while. Is she still around?'

'She's gone to Bangla-Town, as far as I'm aware,' muttered Douglas.

'Can I talk through the experiments?'

'Fire away,' said Douglas, but we were interrupted by a bearded man in glasses appearing on the eWall.

'Sir,' said Douglas, pulling himself up straight and tucking his whisky under his chair.

'Who is that with you?' asked the mystery man.

'She's just leaving. I was getting an update on Aled,' said Douglas.

Douglas gestured to the door and I got up and left the room wondering who this mysterious "Sir" could be. As the door closed behind me, I overheard him asking Douglas if he'd destroyed that bloody so-called proof yet.

21

Aled

August 2037

I'd been back from China for two weeks and it was the last day of my training.

I was lying in bed, thinking about how it had been much more difficult than expected. We'd made great progress but I'd only just finished learning how to control my neural patterns and I was desperate to get on and rescue Zak.

One of the problems we kept running into was me getting distracted by something unforeseen. It kept happening. About a week into the training, I was sitting in the pool wearing the neural-imaging helmet with six Ds – Disintegrates – piled up around me. By watching the visor screen and concentrating on the neural patterns in my Ventral Tegmental Area and my Substantia Nigra, I was learning to control my slide into the abyss. I could use the presence of the Ds to inch to-and-from the edge for up to three hours without succumbing. I'd been sitting there for about thirty minutes when I got wholly absorbed in the painfully dystopian film, *Never Let Me Go*. It brought back pre-war memories of me and Simmone clutching each others hands, transfixed by its unfolding terror. My brain activity was registering normal because the overwhelming desire to bathe in the narcotic treacle of Disintegration was happening through a neural route we didn't monitor. Grey, observing the big screen from inside the booth, didn't realise that I was taking a neural dive into the whirlpool and it wasn't until the end of the film that she realised I'd gone. In the vague distance, through the haze, I gradually realised that she was holding my hands and slapping me around the face. As the haze cleared a little I became aware that she was trying to bring me back. I latched on to The Project, and Grey in particular, like a drowning man and, grasping for the normal neural patterns I'd learnt to visualise, I clawed my way up the slow climb out of Disintegration. It was an important lesson to learn. We stopped using dystopian films because they pushed the Ds even further into the pit, rather than shocking them out of their catatonia as we'd hoped.

We spent another week pushing the boundaries further and further until we got to the point where, as Carlos with his over-developed sense of drama put it, 'You're dancing with the Devil on the edge of oblivion – toying with his hell that's masquerading as heaven.'

I was able to control the impulse to go Disintegrate by feeling, rather than seeing, my brain activity. I no longer needed the helmet.

The time had come. I got out of bed and went down to the basement where fifty or so Disintegrates were propped up against the edge of the pool, like human husks. I sat down on the floor, waved to Grey in the observation booth, and dragged six of them on top of me. Instantly, I felt the tug of the whirlpool as my elements were drawn together and sucked towards the bliss of the vortex. I allowed myself to drift closer and closer to the edge, speeding up and slowing down at will, and after a few minutes I was ready. I brought myself back through the excruciating pain of returning from the edge, stood up and walked towards Grey.

'I'm ready,' I told her, as she came out from the booth.

'I agree,' she said.

The Project team had been busy preparing for our first attempt to change the course of history. They found and tagged two more of my friends – Dave and Jon – so that the CCTV network could monitor their behaviour. Grey had spent many hours going over and over the theory and the practicalities, but I wanted a final recap before we started.

'Grey, can you go over it one last time?'

'Of course, not a problem,' she said, patient as ever. 'So. When we're ready to start. The first thing is to put ourselves in the hands of God, using the singing bowl as we agreed. Then I want you to talk me through what you want to change – what you regret. Our theory is that it has to be specifically about you in order for God to pull your new reality through. Then we use the bowl again and, once you're happy that you're connected with God, you'll get as close to the brink of Disintegration as possible and your elements will be united. Start to unburden your regret and describe the alternative reality you want. Tell the story in as much detail as possible and at the point in the story where you want to make the change, invoke God's mercy and tell Her what you want. We'll see if She can…will…pull through your desired reality. Clear?'

I gave her the thumbs up.

'Ready?' she prompted.

'Yes.'

We'd discussed at great length what would bring us into the presence of God and had agreed that it was about my state of mind and the hum of the singing bowl would help me focus. I rubbed the edge of my bowl and as the harmonies began, I let my mind focus.

Douglas came into the laboratory and sat quietly beside Grey. She signalled that she was ready, so I began.

'We were in the pub talking about all sorts of different things when Zak started to take offence…'

Douglas interrupted me. 'Aled, be specific.'

I took a deep breath and started again.

'Every week, me, Zak, Dave and Jon would go to the Black Lion for a few pints, a catch up and a laugh and I still looked forward to it, despite the fact that things had been getting more intense over the previous few months. One Thursday evening, the same as any other, we were sitting discussing the merits of CCTV cameras…'

Grey interrupted with instructions. 'Aled, time to get into position.'

I sat back down with the Ds and pulled them to me. I let myself drift close to the lip of the whirlpool, concentrating on finding the perfect spot – where my elements were united but there was no trace of Disintegration.

I continued with the story. 'Zak was arguing that Absos, me included, wanted CCTV to make sure everyone obeyed the rules, rather than thinking for themselves. And because I was angry and knew he was hiding his fear that the cameras had caught him doing something he shouldn't, I used what I knew to destroy his argument and make him look stupid in front of his friends. I told them he'd been joyriding and was scared of being found out. My regret is that I drove a wedge between us and damaged the incredible trust we had in each other.'

Douglas's voice came out from the booth. 'And what do you wish would have happened instead?'

Grey chipped in, too. 'Focus again before that.'

I mentally balanced myself back on the lip of the whirlpool and rubbed the bowl until it resonated enough to make its beautiful hum.

I prepared myself for the first ever attempt to consciously invoke God into collapsing a multitude of realities to one single reality – the reality I desired.

I continued, 'I regret using the truth cruelly and selfishly. What do I wish it could have been like instead? I wish that when Zak had told me he'd been joyriding I'd said, and meant, that although I didn't approve, his friendship was more important to me than exposing him. I wish that when we'd been talking in the pub and he said, 'You've got to consider the context,' I'd agreed wholeheartedly and made the point that the only one that can see the whole context is God himself, and therefore I wasn't prepared to comment. I was one of the two people he truly trusted, so I want a future where his trust in me didn't change and he didn't take the path he did. That's what I'm asking for.'

I'd drifted away from the vortex and my core was torn apart once more. I moved myself back to the edge and my elements were brought back together. I could feel the power running through me. It was very similar to the narcotic delight of the vortex but, instead of a void, I felt fully alive and buzzing with anticipation. I looked up at Grey and Douglas, but immediately my mind, body and soul were ripped away from each other. I refocused. I inched my way back to the lip of the whirlpool, through the increasing power that was trying to blow me apart. The noise grew louder and louder, as if a battle was being waged at the centre of the Universe and all of heaven was screaming at me to hold on. Suddenly the noise dropped, the whirlpool slowed a little and the power pulling me away from it weakened. I lurched forward, just stopping myself in time from tumbling in.

Grey shouted from the booth, 'He flickered! Aled, he showed some life.' I looked up. I was able to look at Grey and still maintain my position. 'Aled…hold on for a few more minutes…it's looking good.' I edged back and forward, keeping the equilibrium in place, until Grey signalled me.

I stopped, crawled along the pool, climbed the steps and stumbled over to the booth, 'Sh…Sh…Show me,' I just managed to say, exhausted from the ordeal.

'Look,' she said, pointing to the CCTV feed.

Sure enough, Zak's eyes had life in them. He was looking around, no longer a blank lifeless husk.

'Do you think it worked?' I asked, my voice rising with hope.

'Looks like it may well have done. Well done that chap,' said Douglas.

Grey was standing still and silent. I tugged at her sleeve, 'Grey, what's up?'

'We may have done it,' was all she said.

Zak stood up, dazed. Douglas turned the CCTV display into a three-way split, showing Dave, Jon and Zak. Only Zak was reacting.

I screamed, 'Why? Why only Zak? It's not right. God, please…'

But nothing else happened. They were still part of the static sculpture of Disintegrates – lost to the world.

Grey came and put her arm around my shoulder, 'I'm so sorry, Aled. But look at Zak, it's incredible. I think we may have succeeded. This is so huge I can't believe…'

Douglas interrupted. 'Right, back upstairs. We need to regroup. And you two need some serious rest. It looks as if we are going to be able to do this after all.'

I collapsed on to the floor.

The next thing I knew I was waking up with the soft light of dawn outside my bedroom window. I stretched, got out of bed and left the room to find the others. I could hear voices from one of the downstairs rooms and made my way towards them. I looked through a crack in the door to see what was happening. A screen at the front of the room showed Zak, walking along the embankment of the River Thames. He still looked bemused but with an underlying curiosity in his face, betraying that deep down he was no longer Disintegrate.

'What can we do for him?' Grey asked Douglas.

'We're thinking of taking him to Whitechapel to be looked after. Do you know if he'd be okay there?'

'From what Aled has told me, I think he'd be fine. He used to spend a lot of time over that way so it'll be familiar and if we're right about what we just achieved, he'll be able to trust again. Trouble is, we'll lose all CCTV connection with him. Aled may never see him again.'

'I don't want Aled distracted from his task. We need to get Zak out of sight and out of mind,' said Douglas.

'I'm not happy, but I understand,' acknowledged Grey.

I burst through the door, shouting, 'I'm bloody glad you do. 'Cos I sure as hell don't!'

Douglas looked at me sternly. 'Aled, you always knew there'd be sacrifices. We can't look after him. And, more importantly, we certainly can't afford for you to be focussed on anything other than

The Project. You must understand…but if you're not happy we can take you back to China. If you'd prefer.'

'That's fine, carry on,' I said through a flood of tears. 'That's fine.'

22

Aled

August 2037

I stormed up the stairs, crashing into my room and making as much noise as possible, so everyone understood that I was unhappy. I threw myself on to the bed and continued weeping. Embracing the flood of emotion as it came spewing out. I could hear Grey as she followed me into my room, despite me slamming the door.

'Aled, he's focused on success. He might be a little insensitive but broadly he's right. You can't afford to be distracted, can you?'

I looked at her through my tears and opened my arms, inviting a repeat of the time in China. She came over to the bed, lay down and cuddled me. I looked in her eyes and kissed her on the lips, but she pulled her head back and, very tenderly, said, 'Aled, that's not going to happen. Please don't do it again.'

'I'm sorry, heat of the moment. I didn't mean anything by it,' I lied.

'Sure,' she said, giving me a light kiss on the forehead as a sister might pacify a younger sibling. We lay in each others arms for quite a while and my sobbing gradually decreased, like the tide receding as each wave gets smaller and smaller. Her precious and platonic presence comforted me, healing some of the pain caused by the loss of Zak. She was helping my frayed ends knit back together.

'Grey, we need to talk. Are you up there?' called Douglas, puncturing our cocoon.

'Yes. On my way,' she shouted back.

She kissed me once more on the forehead and, as she walked across the room towards the door, she looked over her shoulder and smiled a sad but intimate smile – a secret shared.

'Don't tell Douglas I freaked, will you?' I asked, more nervous than I let on.

'Just between me and you,' she said. 'Aled, there's something I must talk to you about later,' she added.

I stayed on the bed thinking about Zak. I didn't see why having him there would be a distraction. I thought it might even help to have an ex-Disintegrate to advise us, but it was apparent that this would not be sanctioned by The Project and so, if I was to do anything, I would need to do it alone and secretly. Surprisingly, that didn't feel wrong or frightening. But despite lying there racking my brains, I couldn't think of anything I should, or could, do.

Jane, one of The Project workers, stuck her head round the door and, in a business-like voice, announced, 'They'll be ready for you in twenty minutes.'

I got showered and dressed in my usual dirt-repellent trainers, jeans and t-shirt – my comfortable outdoor clothes. I made sure I had my Fabrication bag and my most recent gift from Linda, a Fabrication jacket. I was ready to go outside into the derelict world alone, should I want to. I made my way to the basement. Douglas and Grey were sitting in the big old-fashioned armchairs, regally placed on a small platform in the corner of the pool.

'We need to talk through the first major experiment and decide what to focus on,' said Grey as I sat down on the floor in front of them.

'I've been thinking about that and I'm not sure. Do you have any ideas? You chose me for a reason I'm guessing?'

'We did…' she started, but Douglas interrupted.

'Grey thinks you have some hotline to God.'

'Not exactly what I said,' replied Grey.

'I'm not so sure, but she's the expert, the Physitheist. No

matter. We know you were a key player in a number of major Absolutist events and we have some idea of a good place to start. Shall I kick off with a thought, and see if you agree?' he asked.

'Fine by me,' I replied, crossing my legs, intrigued to hear what he had to say.

'Aled, if I've got any facts wrong, please correct me,' he began. 'As we've said before, the root of Disintegration seems to be a lack of trust, nowhere to feel safe, where no one and nothing is certain – the world has been deconstructed and we don't know how to put it back together again. Working on that hypothesis, we've looked through the archive footage relating to the Absolutist movement and found what we think is a very interesting and pivotal moment. It's the time you represented them in court over the ruling on whether parents could make decisions on behalf of their children. I'm right that you were the key person for the Absolutists in that court room, aren't I?'

'Yeah…and you're probably right that it's something I regret and wish I could change. I guess that's where you're heading?' I asked.

He continued, 'It seems to us that this was a turning point in the trust we all had in our parents. And that's one of the underpinning social structures. A bedrock of civilisation. Losing it had a major effect on the fabric of society and we think it led, directly and indirectly, to further mass Disintegration across the country. And then, across the world. Did you know that other countries adopted the same law?'

'What do you think of starting with that court case then?' said Grey.

'I'm feeling picked on. Are you really trying to tell me that my contribution to a single court case was responsible for this mess?' I asked.

Grey was quick to respond. 'No, not at all…'

But Douglas interrupted. 'Yes. Actually we are. Well, almost. We're saying that this event, although not the first, was one of the largest and most widespread contributors to what you see today. We're not saying it was deliberate, but as the public face of the movement you did carry an enormous amount of influence. You were the movement personified. To be honest, looking back at the footage, you made such an appalling job of that court appearance, they had to rule against those parents. It was inevitable that a law would be introduced that would bring about this awful lack of trust. I'm sorry, but you were probably the key person in all of that.'

I grimaced and shrugged my shoulders. 'You don't pull your punches, do you? Actually…I prefer the direct and honest approach…so, thanks.'

Grey stood there waiting for my answer.

'It's easy for me to see where I went wrong and what I regret, so yes. Let's start with that one. Have you decided all of the situations in advance, or will I get some say?' I asked tetchily.

'We're fairly sure. But that's not to stop you having some ideas,' he answered calmly.

'Give me a few minutes to remember and then I'll start.'

'Sure. We want you to wear your helmet this time, so we can monitor how you are.'

'It's going to be a big one compared to Zak,' Grey called, already in the booth.

'And not forgetting Dave and Jon, of course,' I added, with a touch of sarcasm.

I made my way over to the other end of the pool where, as usual, an anonymous pile of Disintegrates were propped up against each other. A twelve-year-old boy running across a field of bright purple flowers appeared on the screen above the pool and the Ds immediately turned to watch. I sat down to gather my thoughts. This was not something I'd thought about for some time and, although the memory was painful, it was predominantly embarrassing.

'Put the helmet on so we can test the equipment,' called Grey, across the pool. I took the helmet from the side of the pool and put it on, pulled six Ds on top of me and allowed myself to drift towards the whirlpool, towards the enticing vortex. I edged back and forwards while watching the film until, after about five minutes, Grey called from the booth, 'Looks fine to me – shall we start?'

'Let's,' I answered, wondering if Douglas was still there.

The singing bowl was on the floor in front of me. I took the wooden mallet and carefully rubbed the outside of the bowl. Round and round until it was humming its perfect note. I was ready.

'I'll start on the day I was in court…I pushed my way through the crowd, a crowd that resembled a deep-sea creature whose body – a mass of screaming adults and crying children – had hundreds of tentacles held high in the air. Each with a phone attached at their tip in order to vStream the event to the world. It was May 2035 and this was being billed as the trial of the century. After a lot of jostling and haranguing, I managed to get to the gate of the old Desmond Tutu Primary School and buzz the intercom. The gate clicked. I pushed it open and stepped through, going from the crazy cacophony on one side of the wall into the serene silence of the other. For the previous sixteen years, since the demise of education in schools, these buildings had been hired for a variety of purposes, including court rooms. In the middle of the playground was a group of ten adults standing in a huddle with their heads bowed forward, as if they were about to play American Football. These were the *Frigid Five* – as labelled by the twitterati – with their lawyers. I grew up with them and now, in their thirties, they had brought a law suit against their parents. One of them spat on the floor as I walked past and, although it wasn't in my direction, I'm sure the timing was deliberate. A way of showing the contempt and hatred they had for me. As I walked up the steps into the school, I could hear the baying of the crowd outside the gate, drifting over the wall and across the playground. I thought of all the children since Victorian times when this school was built that had walked up those stairs with a thrilling eagerness to learn. Some, of course, would have had the same sort of dread I had then – wondering what might happen to them and how bad their day might be.

The legal system was almost entirely privatised and it was only when there was a case that might have a significant impact on the law of the land that the state intervened. In all other circumstances, the court was run by a private company that charged the loser for the costs of the case. If you couldn't pay, the company imprisoned you for as long as it took to pay back the court costs plus your board and lodging.

They thought this trial would only be a sensationalist trial with juicy, but innocuous tidbits for the masses and because it wasn't expected to challenge the law, it was being held in the privately-run courts. Those grown-up children must have been very sure of themselves as none of them were wealthy and no one brought a case unless they could afford to lose or were certain they'd win.

The school bell rang, calling the court back into session. I followed the flow of people back to the old school hall and, like a river finding its way to the sea, it was joined by small tributaries of people along the way. Sitting on the old school stage, at a nondescript table, were two women and a man. They were dressed in jeans and plain shirts, as a deliberate antithesis of the old style courts of pomp and power. However, they still easily conveyed their control over the room and the lives in it. The court reassembled itself, in the same way a theatre does after the interval – everyone politely finding their seats. Placed around the hall were casually dressed officials, all wearing similar jeans and shirts. Some of them had electronic stun-guns attached to their belts, re-enforcing the feeling that I was in a stateless court with no rules. They intimidated me more than if they'd been wearing official uniforms.

Over to the side of the stage were ten people in their fifties with bands around their wrists that would fire electronic shocks to their kidneys if they moved out of their seats. They were the defendants, the parents of the *Frigid Five*. One of the casually dressed but armed security guards came over and pointed to my seat in the front row. I was the next witness for the defence. An official told the court to be quiet – it was now in session.

The woman in the centre spoke and, despite the attempts to disguise her place in the social hierarchy, her voice, language and jewellery betrayed her privileged origins – hinting at the prejudice which often lurked beneath the surface of these presiding Justice Facilitators.

She looked in my direction and stated, rather than asked, 'You are Aled Griffen, a defence witness on behalf of the Absolutist movement.'

'Yes.'

I glanced over at the electronically-chained defendants and felt a great burden of sadness. These were the parents of childhood friends and before the War we'd loved, laughed and cried together. But, like so many others, they'd been taken in by the Liberalist propaganda and left the community – we'd not spoken for years.

The JF – Justice Facilitator – continued by giving an overview of the judicial system, explaining that there was no absolute truth, so it was important for witnesses to understand the context within which they were giving their particular version. She reminded the court that the defendants were accused of contravening sentient-beings' rights by taking actions that had led to their children being sexually inhibited and unable to fully function as members of today's liberal society. The specific charge was, that when the children were twelve years old these parents made a decision without discussing and negotiating it with them. They'd restricted access to knowledge, specifically sexual knowledge, that could be gained from viewing internet porn. She told the court that I was the same age as the defendants' children and that we were brought up together. Finally, after asking if there were any questions from the court, she instructed me to provide my testimony.

I stood up and began, 'I've known the defendants since childhood. When I was growing up, I always looked to them for spiritual and moral guidance. In a world where there is no belief in right and wrong, it's only proper that the elders of a community should provide the moral compass. I know that without it my life would have been miserable and chaotic, lurching from one disaster to another. Having to re-invent the wheel for each moral choice but in a vacuum of wisdom – the accumulated wisdom that these parents are accused of using to protect their children. I know that as a twelve-year-old I was not able, or willing, to stay still long enough to understand the implications of my decisions. The boundaries set by these wise elders were vital to my physical, emotional and spiritual well-being. And you have to understand that we were not kept separate from the world. In fact, my closest friends were not part of the community.'

I caught the eye of the elder who'd been my confidante up until the age of fourteen. The sting of betrayal I'd felt when she joined the Liberalists still hurt. The thought of what she knew about me and the difference between the theory I'd just explained and the reality I'd experienced made me stray from my well-prepared speech. I started to talk more to her than to the court, trying to re-inflict the same pain on her as she had on me all those years ago. It was my turn to point the finger at her adopted Liberalist beliefs.

I carried on. 'You only have to look around at the world we have created to see the damage that Liberalism has caused. People are now desensitised to the deep joy that having a sexual relationship can bring. They're transmitting and receiving sex as a trade rather than a sharing of pleasure. That's a result of the sexually liberated world we now find ourselves in.'

The JF stopped me and asked if I felt that my upbringing, which was the same as the plaintiffs', had in any way restricted or reduced my life. Her intervention threw me and, not stopping to think, I reacted with hostility. I could hear myself ranting – I sounded like Ma, when she really lost it.

'I don't know why you ask the question. We're all limited in some way or another by the hand we're dealt. If you're asking whether I would have liked to have had all sorts of bizarre sexual encounters with strangers. With men. With people I've only just met. Then I can say categorically that I find the idea disgusting and degrading. Why on earth would you want to take your own holy temple, your body, and prostitute it around for the pleasure of others who have no regard for you? And of course, the big problem with not knowing right and wrong is that all sorts of dangerous desires then become rampant, allowed to infest the soul of humanity and tear us away from God. There's no way those children should have been allowed to even know that sex existed, let alone see acts of degradation on screen. Ultimately, it's God's laws that must come first, before any piddling made-up human laws, such as this Sentient Beings Act. It's so blatantly obvious. I'm surprised you're wasting even a minute of your time on it. These people just want an excuse to ditch all responsibility and corrupt as many as they can with their unnatural desires.'

I pulled myself up sharp. I hadn't meant to let loose this tirade. My own fears, insecurities and pent-up anger with my confidante had got the better of me. I wish I'd kept to the script.

The trial continued, but all the media commentary said that my appearance had changed the public perception towards the issue. The Cumulus mood-vote that ultimately changed the law was overwhelmingly in favour of reducing the age of majority to eight years old. Giving anyone aged eight and over the right to make their own choices and, of course, with full access to the Cumulus for unbiased information about the implications of those choices.

I was devastated.'

23

Aled

August 2037

I made the bowl hum again and tuned my mind into its harmonies.

The battle between heaven and hell reignited, pulling me towards the vortex. The noise was almost too much to bear, but I was ready for it – thankful for the trial run with Zak. The angels roared as the multiple truths – the parallel universes – were reknotted together, to form a singular and final truth. I steadied my mind, my body and my soul as I circled the lip of the whirlpool – a surfer, nimbly bouncing along the edge of a wave.

Grey prompted me, 'What would you change?'

'Are you ready?' I shouted.

I felt a heady mix of erupting excitement and an incredible inner calm. I was ready for God. I was ready to change the course of the world. I started.

'I'm ashamed of my behaviour in that court room. The JF gave me an opportunity to be honest when she asked me about my upbringing. God, I'm so sorry that I lied. Please forgive me. Please change things. If I could go back, I'd tell them I was forced to suppress any desires that weren't considered faithful. I'm not saying they were good desires. But, if I'd been allowed to talk more freely about them, maybe they wouldn't have such a grip on me now. If only, in the court room that day, I could have admitted that suppressing my sexual desires prevented me from having proper relationships. When

I was a teenager, there was a girl I really liked and although she wasn't from my church we got along great. We liked the same books and the same music. We'd go for long walks around where we lived, just chatting about school and stuff. With the usual teenage angst, we tried to make sense of what we wanted from life. And then, one day she held my hand. I was pleased but awkward and unsure of how to react to the desires, racing through my veins.

The church encouraged me to talk about everything – because God knows it all anyway – but all I heard when I talked about her was warnings about sex before marriage. About saving myself and not being responsible for sending a non-believer in through the gates of Hell. I clamped down on my feelings and we were never close again. This pattern repeated itself, over and over again. The only sexual encounters I could cope with were brief and emotionally detached – I'd repent, be forgiven and move on.

Suppression was the real crime. The parents suppressed themselves and in turn their children. I'm not advocating that children should watch porn for sex education, but surely a culture of openness, which allows children to talk and express their feelings without being emotionally gagged and told they are evil, is a good thing. Over the years, I'd confessed my deepest and darkest desires to my confidante and she had consistently pushed me towards holy texts of hate and fear. Stoically describing God's pent-up punishment. That's why catching her eye in the court room jolted me away from my well-prepared script. If I had my way, that kind of blinkered suppression would be illegal, an abuse of human rights, but – and an important but – ultimately, I believe parents should have the right to make choices for their children.

I'm sure that if I'd been more honest in the court room then the vote – the aggregated mood-profile generated from the intonation in the voices of all the voters as they register their views – would have been more reasonable.'

I paused and rebalanced myself on the lip of the vortex but a mishmash of fantasy and memory came crashing in. Images of sexual encounters, real and imagined. A couple of years before war was formally declared, I was at a party celebrating the 2031 repeal of prohibition. MDMA was the drug of choice, far more popular than alcohol. The stuff that night was good, classified grade A by the authorities. I floated into the toilets, where the music was still pounding through the walls. A cubicle door opened and a blond man with a pretty face walked out, looked at me and then down at his hand. Cupping himself, he offered me his small, soft present. As he turned, I followed him back into the cubicle and held his hand, accepting his gift. The delicate skin became taut as I kissed him. He closed his eyes, lost himself in the moment until finally he exhaled, his body sagged and he kissed me on the lips in a farewell gesture…I saw Peace and Harmony lying naked together in a field – beckoning me to join them as they explored each other…I saw Peace undoing my robe, his strong body up close and tight against mine, clutching me to him…I saw Grey, her naked form sculpted by thin white cotton sheets…

Multicoloured explosions of neural activity lit up my visor. The pain increased. My core was being pulled apart and I couldn't keep myself from toppling into that dreamy pool of narcotic treacle. I was encased by an extraordinary, but ultimately destructive, bliss.

I felt the helmet being wrenched from my head as I was dragged by the feet across the pool. I felt the distant sting of a slap across the face and slowly I came round, groggily complaining, 'Is slapping me across the face really the only way to bring me back?'

'Aled, Aled. I thought we'd lost you. What on earth happened? Your brain went haywire. You seemed to Disintegrate with no warning. And, yes, it's the best way to get an instant connection with you before you go too far to be reached.'

'I need some fresh air and a little time alone. Please?'

'Of course. Can you unlock the door?' Grey asked the security guard.

I was outside, below street level, and there was an iron staircase up to the pavement.

I had a quick look at my uCumulus and two messages marked

private and urgent popped up. "Be careful Aled and trust no one" and "I know things you need to know. Zak."

One of the things that had attracted me to Zak was that he was direct and straightforward, which could sometimes be hard to take, but over time it became a precious part of our friendship. He wouldn't be so opaque, unless he felt he had to. It was great to hear from him, but his message and the Elder's repeat warning were terrifying.

This was my chance to find Zak and to find out what he meant in his message. I started to climb the steps but my energy suddenly drained away, as if someone had pulled my soul out through my mouth, deflating me. What the fuck was this project doing to me? Making me bring things back to life, things already dealt with and prayed out of existence. I should have stayed in China and let someone else, a Liberalist, sort this mess out. They'd really screwed up, thinking they could go against the laws of God. I punched the wall, time and time again, until the physical pain smothered the pain I felt inside. I sat down on the floor and held my sore head in my sore hands, wondering what I should do. I was in my outdoor clothes. I had my Fabrication bag and jacket. There was nothing to stop me just pissing off and leaving this behind.

I climbed the staircase and carefully opened the old iron gate. I looked around to make sure no one had noticed and moved cautiously on to the street. I ran to the end of the square and quickly turned the corner. Ducking in and out of doorways and abandoned shop fronts, I ran towards the Cleveland Street Workhouse. Curiously, there was a crowd gathering outside, but I resisted the urge to investigate. I turned into Foley Street, doing a double-take as I ran past the King and Queen – a pub full of people that I was sure had been deserted a few days earlier. The streets were empty as I carried on south. I turned the corner into Oxford Street and was confronted by a gang of old-people blocking my way. I turned around, only to find another similar gang blocking me from behind.

'What do you want?' I shouted, putting my hand in my jacket pocket, pretending to have a knife or even a gun.

A man with greying temples and a slight stoop stepped forward and started to speak. 'We want our grandchildren and our children back.'

'And what do you think I can do about that?' I shouted, turning my head from side to side, to keep an eye on both gangs.

He shouted back, 'That's what we want to find out – you're different and you're running from something, aren't you? What is it?'

'I get scared on the streets alone,' I answered in a quieter, more passive voice.

A gang of children came flying round the corner – none of them over fifteen and some as young as eleven.

'Give us back our parents!' they screamed, over and over again.

I used the distraction to slip across Oxford Street and into Soho – I was off to find Zak.

I walked briskly, keeping to the edge of the street – a shadow within shadows. The streets were empty but, as I turned into Frith Street and looked towards the Soho Square encampment, a young girl stepped out from her own refuge of shadows and sheepishly approached. She was dressed in rags and could quite easily have come straight out of the Cleveland Street Workhouse, if it weren't for the fact that her torn clothes were modern.

'Excuse me…Can you help…I'm looking for my dad.'

'If I can, I will,' I answered, but kept my distance.

'He's the only person I trust. It's been ages since I've seen him. I think he's living in a commune round here. I've been up there but I couldn't see him. Help me,' she pleaded.

'You're young to be out alone.'

'I'm nearly thirteen,' she said defiantly.

'What job does he do?' I asked her, thinking that might help us locate him.

'He was a bus driver,' she said.

'Did he have any hobbies?'

'He loved art…specially old stuff…you know portraits of kings 'n queens 'n stuff.'

'There are people in the National Gallery who sit and stare at the paintings. We could try there if you like,' I suggested.

'Sure…why not?'

She followed me, walking slightly behind as if she was ready to run at the slightest hint of danger.

'So why are you looking for him now?' I asked, curious about all this activity. It was as if the city was starting to emerge from its coma.

'We fell out…he left me, wandered off and never came back, but I need him so much. I can't remember when it was or what we argued about. I don't think he knows I'm looking for him. I need him so much…I'm scared.'

'Let's go see if we can find him then. Stay close.'

We arrived at the National Portrait Gallery which was one of the few collections still on display to the general public. 'You need to walk in front so you can look for him. Don't be scared by all the people just sitting and staring – will you?'

'Why would I? That's normal,' she replied, rolling her eyes.

I followed her through the tall magnificent rooms, full of old and familiar paintings but with piles of static bodies clustered around them. It was as if these ancient artworks had come alive just long enough for their subjects to spill out on to the floor, only to be frozen again before they could escape any further.

'Dad!' she shouted at the top of her voice, pointing to a man on the floor. 'Dad. Dad, Dad…Dad…Dad,' she cried, getting quieter and quieter.

'It's all right,' I said, trying to comfort her.

I wondered if, between us, we could do something for him. It was worth trying. I'd nothing to lose. I took hold of her hand. 'Come with me,' I coaxed. We walked over and shifted him out of his pile and into a small side room on his own. 'Now, hold my hand and his and try really hard to remember what you argued about. When you remember, squeeze my hand. I'll close my eyes and while I'm doing it, you must think about what you did to upset your dad. Don't worry if you hear lots of noise, it's good. Understand?'

'Like this?' she asked, squeezing my hand.

'Yes, exactly like that. Good girl.'

We held hands – a triangle of innocence, hope and despair. Her face contorted with the effort and every now and again she opened her eyes, which were on the verge of filling with tears, and looked at me. Each time I smiled and whispered, 'Keep trying, you're doing great.'

It was my fault. I'd been the one who'd interfered with reality and brought her back into this world of pain. I couldn't just leave her, even though it was delaying me.

'It hurts. In my head,' she screamed and squeezed my hand tightly.

I closed my eyes and imagined the hum of the bowl. 'Think about what you'd change, if you could.'

The drag of the whirlpool was weak with only one D – her dad – to pull me in, but it was enough to get me started and then it was easy to get to the edge. Once more, I was surfing the lip of the vortex. My mind, body and soul at one with each other. A small voice whispered, 'Lydia,' and I could feel the movement of his hand as he came round. An aggressive noise filled the small room, as if that particular reality was shouting 'stop!' Desperate not to be extinguished out of existence.

I held on to their hands and kept surfing round and round until eventually he opened his eyes and simply said, 'Hi, darling. How nice to see you.'

I left them in each other's arms, bemused but crying with relief.

I quickly found my way out of the building. There were small groups of people standing around Trafalgar Square looking lost, like tourists who've completed their guide books and have no idea what to do next. I kept my distance, not because I felt threatened but because I wanted to get on and find Zak. The river was likely to be the safest city artery for travelling east, so I walked down to the Hungerford footbridge and ran up the moss-covered metal steps, two at a time. Half-way across the bridge I was stunned by the beauty of London – my home. I stopped and looked along the river, weaving its way passed St Paul's Cathedral and on towards the ruined skyscrapers of the City of London. The ruins stood as a reminder of the early thirties riots when the economy collapsed and the money-lenders – the financial Absolutists – lost the plot and ran riot across the city. Someone was coming towards me from the south side of the bridge and, although it was subtle, they held themselves differently to anyone else on the streets.

I didn't like it.

I turned around to walk back, only to see someone else with the same confident walk approaching from the north. I was stuck and not sure what to do. The river was a long way below and anyway, if I was to jump I'd either drown immediately or slowly freeze to death in the inky black water. Frantically, I looked around for another escape route, but there wasn't one.

24

Grey

August 2037

'That's incredible,' I said.

'Pretty damn amazing,' said Douglas.

'You're saying that the little trick that Aled just pulled off has changed the world?' asked Peace.

'Seems that way. Look at the Database of Influence, it's frantic. Look at the way the nodes are gathering around family structures,' I said.

'Strongest bonds, by far. We repaired trust in parents – so it's not surprising,' said Douglas, nonchalantly.

The tracker that Linda had built into Aled's jacket kicked into action, alerting us that he'd left the house. Surprisingly though, Douglas didn't want to stop him. 'Grey, I want you to look around that virtual museum and see what you can find. Anything that might give us a clue about what he intends to do. See if there are any hints of who he might be in touch with. And try to find that damn Holy of Holies. When you find something, let me know straight away.'

'Of course. But won't he know I was there?'

'Peace can help with you with a ghost identity,' he replied and then left the room.

'What's all this ghost identity stuff then?' I asked Peace.

'It's a way of taking someone else's – a dead person's – identity.

We'll need to choose someone who was born about the same time as you and replace their image with yours in the database. Then, all the other systems that use that data think it's you,' said Peace.

'Firstly. You can't simply hack into the main Citizens' Database. And secondly, it can't be that simple to change my identity.'

'I can. And it is,' said Peace. 'Pass me your uCumulus.'

'Whatever you want. Boss,' I said, smiling and enjoying him being back in control.

He stroked the screen for a few minutes and then passed it back to me. 'How d'ya fancy this one?' he asked. 'Grace Cadogan. She'd have been thirty years old now, if she hadn't died when she was five. Born in South Wales, in Newcastle Emlyn. Disappeared on an educational trip to the United States – presumed dead.'

'She's perfect,' I said.

Peace nodded. 'Her whole family died, so it's unlikely that anyone will question her coming back to life.'

'And with Disintegration so widespread, even if there was still someone alive that knew her, they probably wouldn't notice,' I added.

'Shall I ghost her then?' asked Peace.

'Please.'

He stroked the screen for a few more minutes and then passed it back to me. I was now officially Grace.

I rolled out the mat and put on the helmet and gloves that Douglas had shown me how to operate. 'AGP Museum, please,' I said into the mouthpiece.

The front entrance to the museum appeared, like someone carefully unfolding a large sheet of paper, doubling its size, time and time again. I was offered entrance as a guest, a registered visitor or an existing member.

'Register, please.'

The museum warned me that it was taking my details from the uCumulus in my hand and then asked me to take a photo of my face, so it could authenticate me against the Citizens' Database. "Grace Cadogan – authenticated" appeared above the museum entrance. The door opened and I was offered the scent module. I accepted. I dragged my foot from the front of the mat to the back.

I was standing in a virtual street – a generic thirty-year-old female avatar, wearing a smart black dress and a t-shirt with a big green tick on the front. Ahead of me were half-a-dozen steps up to a circular building surrounded by tall narrow pillars that supported another circular platform. On top of them, another set of pillars and a platform. All topped off with a magnificent spire.

I loved circular buildings, and this one was splendid. I whizzed my hand diagonally upwards through the grid of beams and my avatar – Grace – lifted off the ground and flew around the spotlit spire of All Souls Church. I flicked my finger and dropped back down again. I walked her through the front door and into the church. Inside, the white walls and gold pillars took the wedding cake likeness to another level. It lifted my spirits. On the floor, in front of the altar, was a museum guide. I flicked through its screens, until I came to Cathedrals.

'St David's, Pembrokeshire,' I said, wondering if it had been Aled that had made sure something of Wales was here.

An opening in the side wall appeared and I walked through. Rather than waste time using all the avatar options to personalise her, I'd left her as generic as her creator had made her. Barefooted, but with a bottom that wiggled in a way that made it look as if she was wearing high heels, I walked through the gap.

I was in a grass field, sprinkled with the yellow heads of daffodils. The scent module mixed together the base scents of fresh grass, flowers and Welsh air. It was fantastic. I loved the feeling of being outdoors and in an ancient place. At the end of the field was a long single-storey old stone church. A central tower stood tall and proud in its middle. I dragged my foot time and time again, running faster and faster across the field to the cathedral. I flicked through the guide pinned to a notice board – sermons, library or treasury.

'Treasury,' I said.

I walked into a white room, lined with exhibition cases. A

plain gold ring with five notches formed the centrepiece, sitting alone and alluring in the middle of the room. As I approached, the audio commentary started.

'This simple gold ring is thought to date back to the thirteenth century. It is believed that the notches are there to remind the wearer of the five wounds of Christ.'

I walked over to the ring and stroked the notches. I had a limited amount of time before Aled might return and, although under normal circumstances I'd have soaked up every piece of information, I didn't have time.

'Holy of Holies.'

Nothing happened, so I requested the main entrance. I was back in the centre of the wedding cake. The cathedral screen of the museum guide was still active.

'Stephansdom.'

I was flying high above Vienna and in the distance, surrounded by low-rise houses, was the most magnificent building I'd ever seen. Two spires flanked the front of a stone barn-like building. Its roof of glazed tiles formed a mosaic of a double-headed eagle, bordered with diamond-shaped patterns. At the other end was another spire, twice as high, and this one was all spindly and spiky like a dragon's tail. The whole cathedral was bursting with opulence – the tiles, the spires and so much stonework that served no other purpose than to impress – it was my sort of place.

I dropped to the ground. In front of the cathedral were thousands of static avatars. The rich were living their Disintegration virtually – sitting static in the real world wearing their gloves and helmets, but standing in the virtual world, transfixed by the awesome majesty of the Cathedral.

Inside was equally magnificent. A multitude of statues lined each side of the long central aisle, its arches lit by the most exquisite gold chandeliers. The musty smell of old stone buildings hung all around.

'Holy of Holies.'

I was disappointed that nothing happened, but was still

determined to complete Douglas's mission. 'Main entrance,' I said and was dutifully transported back.

'Where's the Holy of Holies?' I asked.

A list of items, relating to the First Temple, appeared as icons. 'Bible Lands Museum,' I said and was whisked off again. I landed outside a glass-fronted building that was about as inspiring as a wet weekend in Wales. The artefact I was presented with was a Royal Seal from the First Temple Period. The description was weak – it may have been a jar to collect taxes or it may have been a measuring jug. But it wasn't the Holy of Holies.

'Main entrance. Tabernacle.'

Once more, I disappeared and then appeared somewhere else – the Bijbels Museum in Amsterdam. I was standing in a marble entrance hall at the bottom of an oval spiral staircase. I lifted myself just above the floor and glided up the staircase to a room at the top. A scale model of the Tabernacle – the fore-runner of the Holy of Holies – stood proudly as the only exhibit. 'This model was built from instructions in the book of Exodus. For thirty credits you may 3-D-print an exact replica,' the museum informed me. The door banged as Douglas came back into the real-life room.

'Wow! What a model. Come and have a look,' I gasped as I moved further into the room.

He ignored my excitement. 'We need to get out of the Museum in case Aled logs back in. Find anything?' he asked.

'No.'

'Me neither.'

'Exit,' I said, and evaporated into a cloud of white mist. The museum refolded itself. I took off the helmet and turned my attention to the eWall, to Aled. He was standing on a bridge with someone in front of him and someone behind.

25

Aled

August 2037

A tall elegant man stepped out from behind the now static figure on the south side of the bridge – it was Peace.

He walked slowly and deliberately towards me. 'Come with me,' he ordered quietly.

'How..?' I started to say, but he held up his hand.

'Later. But honestly. Did you think we'd lose you?'

I didn't see why I should do as Peace said, so I walked around him and crossed the bridge. I passed the sentries and trotted down the moss-covered steps on to the South Bank. Surprisingly, no one followed me. I kept walking steadily, not turning back, not slowing down, not speeding up. I hoped they'd leave me alone, that my job was complete and the world would now get on and repair itself.

Being close to the river had the same calming effect as the mountains in China. It was as if an invisible hand was stroking my forehead, whispering silent melodies to my soul. I hurried along the side of the snaking river as it slithered its way east. I reached the iconic Oxo tower and its small wooden pier where I paused, taking time to remember this once cultural seam of London, a stepping stone between the stilted make-believe of Covent Garden's theatre-land and the mundane reality of the urban lives to the south. It was some of our direct-action here that prompted the media – entirely owned by the Liberalist elite – to portray us as in-bred killjoys. They popularised the myth that we were unable to face the realities of the modern world.

I heard footsteps behind me and I quickly turned, but there was no one there. It was dangerous to stop, so I put my memories and fears to one side and continued east. As I walked, my mind started to wander away from the immediate danger and on to the trade-off between the security of The Project and the remote chance of rescuing Zak. I didn't even know if he needed or wanted rescuing. Was I being completely selfish? Had I convinced myself that I was doing this for Zak, when really it was to relieve the guilt I felt about the War? Or maybe it was to avoid more experiments? But it was risky, and if I was being selfish, why would I take such risks? Did it matter? I always found it hard to know why I did what I did, but even more so at that moment. If I was standing in front of the God that knows me better than I know myself – how would I explain what I was doing?

I stopped, leant on the river wall, looked longingly at the inky dark water and let my mind drift like flotsam on the snaking river's back as it wriggled its way down past the city and into the North Sea – finally escaping its constraints. Oh, how I wished I could float along without a care in the world.

But, I had to find Zak. I was desperate to find out if he was okay and what he needed to tell me. Then, I could leave him where he was. Or the two of us could tuck ourselves away, hidden from the responsibilities that were crushing me into the ground.

I ran along the river bank with a renewed vigour, determined to reach the East End of London before sunset. As I raced along I could see the shadows moving as if the ghosts of London were tracking me, darting in and out of hidey holes as I moved through their world. Was I a mad man running away? Running away from saving the world? Running towards a hostile community? Was I hurtling towards death – my physical death, my spiritual death? I ran as fast as I could, trying to outrun the questions, past the old-old landmarks of London – the Cutty Sark, the Golden Hind, the Globe Theatre and the Clink Prison – reminders of my dear city's resilience. It had outlived a multitude of onslaughts. It had suffered and yet still thrived. It was like an old man, invigorated by his grandchildren as he sits patiently watching them try new things. He knows that only some of their childhood experiments will become part of his family's heritage and he knows that most will only be temporary distractions. He understands that the ancestral gift of genes will grow quietly, like a tree steadily gaining in stature. He knows that if you were able to cut through the trunk of his family tree, you'd see the rings created by each generation, as they add to the girth of their ancestral inheritance. So it was with this city. Layer upon layer of history had created a wide trunk with deep roots, strong branches and glorious bursts of energy that blossomed, died and ultimately fed the tree. As I turned the corner there was Southwark Cathedral, standing elegant on the side of London Bridge. It was surrounded by the silent masses who remained faithful to the Church, despite Disintegrating. They stared up at this imposing stone edifice reaching for the sky. A macabre medieval frieze of churchyard stone angels with pained expressions, worshipping this inanimate representation of God. Behind them, the feral middle-classes scurried around Borough Market.

In the distance I could see the one-hundred-and-seventy-year-old Tower Bridge that crossed the river to the Tower of London – the greatest of all London's ancestors and part of Londoners' lives for thirty generations. In contrast to the silhouettes of ruined glass-and-steel skyscrapers, it was solid and untouched. They were both stark reminders of how different generations of the rich had chosen to make their mark on the city. Some built fortresses to establish roots for their descendants, oppressing and crushing the opposition and firmly stamping their authority into the ground. Others pillaged and bled the city dry, using temporary glass towers to dazzle and distract. Both created prisons in their own way. The Tower once held prisoners that disagreed with the ruling aristocratic class and more recently the City of London shackled us with the chains of the ruling consumerist class.

Both were evil, but, ironically, they were now irrelevant.

I arrived at the bridge, panting and out of breath, but packed so full of adrenalin that I couldn't have sat still, even if I'd wanted to. The two halves of the bridge were raised, as if they were saluting one another. There was no way to cross. North was separated from south. I looked around, desperate to find a way over. There were tall stone towers at either end of the bridge, linked by two narrow walkways forty-five metres above the river. I wondered if the door to the staircase was open. I approached cautiously because, although I'd not seen anyone since Borough Market, this would be an ideal place for an ambush. I found the door to the staircase and carefully pushed. It creaked open. Keeping to the side of the staircase, I nervously worked my way to the top and into one of the narrow walkways. Through the steel girder lattice I glimpsed the stunning view across the city as I stormed to the other end and down the stairs. I burst out on to the north side of the bridge, the adrenalin leading me recklessly out into the open.

I found a sheltered place to rest in the lost world of the smash-and-grab tyrants. Squatting inside one of the shattered skyscrapers, I unrolled my mat and put on my visor and gloves. The museum validated my identity and connected me. Worryingly, there had been an unidentified visitor that had spent an hour or so in the members' area of the museum. All of us had our own identity and so, if they were unknown, they were not an Absolutist. I checked the defences but couldn't see anything more than the usual automated bombardment of the site, attempting to make it crash. I made my way to the inner temple. There were some digital thumb-prints. An attempted violation of the most Holy of Holies that we, the elders, were sworn to protect. I took a look inside and thankfully the *New Natural Philosophers' Proof of Existence* was untouched. Only an expert attacker could get that far without leaving a traceable footprint. If Zak had been there, we'd have been able to follow the digital breadcrumbs back to the attacker's lair. On my own, I didn't have a clue how to find them.

Covering my tracks behind me, I flipped the switch which

reconfigured the network topology and reset all the digital trip wires and alarms. I said a prayer of protection and weaved my way out, into the main museum. As I put the rolled-up mat back in my bag, I encouraged the fabric to fold around it and hide it from casual investigation. The bag obliged.

I looked up and wondered what the empathic Christ would have made of all this. Would he have been pleased about the ruined city, echoing his distaste and disgust at the commercialisation of the temple? Would he share the silent scream of the Disintegrates as they collectively coalesced around their shared hysteria? I was sure he felt an agony like theirs when he was ripped from his home – his heaven – crippled, crucified and screaming, 'Why have you forsaken me?'

The hopelessness of the world was overwhelming, but I had to keep moving towards Zak and away from the depressive desire to stay and dive head-first into the narcotic treacle of Disintegration.

I walked along the street with the same caution as earlier in the day. The low sunset backlit the ruins, casting long shadows on the streets and adding to the eerie post-apocalyptic atmosphere. There was some movement to my side and I caught a glimpse of two dark overcoats as they emerged from one of the ruins and ran off towards my destination. They sparked a memory of the Jack the Ripper tours, banned by the Liberalists for refusing to make explicit links between the murders and the society that had ostracised and depersonalised sex workers.

A loud voice from the top of the minaret of the local mosque cracked through the veneer of my imagined isolation. 'Stop. Stop, right there!' boomed this unseen oppressor, from yet another tower attempting to impose its will on the people. A multitude of dark figures scattered and scurried into buildings and alleyways, like a horde of rats scared by the rat-catcher. I dashed towards an old warehouse. As I got closer, I could see through the open door that the warehouse had been converted into a home. Inside, a family were huddled together. The mum and dad were gripping each other's hands and staring at the eWall in terror, as if it was about to order them to kill each other. A girl sat watching them. She was dressed in the high-fashion style of a wealthy, pre-war London teenager – an antique black Victorian mourning dress and jet-black hijab sprinkled with tiny spider motifs.

'Who are you? You from over there?' she asked. 'I'll defend my Mum and Dad. Whatever I need to do. So be bloody careful, mister.'

I was shaking from the exertion but managed to reply in a fairly calm voice, 'Sorry. I didn't mean to barge in like that. I'm looking for a friend.'

'I just found my mum and dad,' she said, 'and I don't want to lose 'em again, but they don't seem to be all here.'

'I might be able to help…if you'd like me to?'

'Yeah, right,' she said sarcastically, but her eyes betrayed her desperation.

'I know a little about how to help them out of it.' I was careful not to give away too much detail, partly to protect myself but mainly because she seemed so fragile and I wasn't sure she'd be able to take it. 'What's your name?' I asked gently.

'Nisha,' she replied sharply.

'Well, Nisha, shall we try something?'

'If you want.'

'I do. Hold my hand.'

She held out her fragile little hand. I was touched by her openness. I had no idea why she trusted me but didn't ask, in case she changed her mind.

'We need to ask God to fix things. You okay?' I whispered, fearful of frightening her. 'I'm going to ask God to change the way things are and if it works you'll hear the most horrendous noise. Don't be frightened.'

I closed my eyes, to get ready. This time without the aid of the singing bowl. The promise of communion with God was incredibly enticing so, using the power of her parents' Disintegration, I drifted to the lip of the whirlpool. There was a loud crash, a splintering noise and lots of shouting and screaming. Nisha gripped my hand tight. To start with I thought the noise was the heavenly war as the multiple realities were being brought together, but then I felt a sharp pain run down my leg. I opened my eyes and there was a group of young Asian and White lads holding cricket bats and silently staring at the four of us. One of them stood over me, prodding my leg with his bat. A raw memory of being bullied at school flashed into my mind and all the years of fantasising about what I should have done back then came flooding through and something snapped inside. I leapt to my feet and shoved my face within inches of his. I stared wildly at him.

'What the fuck are you doing here?' I screamed.

He looked taken aback and another of the lads stepped forward, lifting his bat slightly as if he was about to hit me.

'Get the fuck out of my face, you little shit!' I screamed again.

Our noses touched and I tapped his forehead with mine. Through gritted teeth I talked quietly, pronouncing every word precisely: 'Fuck. Off. Now.'

I walked forward, pushing him backwards with my forehead. He pushed back and while we carried on with this human cock-fighting, I was desperately trying to think of a way to break the deadlock. Finally, it dawned on me – I prayed silently and, still holding Nisha's hand, I caught her eye and mouthed, 'Pray'.

There was a deafening sound in the room and the lads jerked their heads left and right. Their mouths were moving but there was no sound coming out. They raised their bats and then…whoosh… the sound subsided and a great calm descended. They dropped their bats and left the room, walking past us as if we didn't exist. A scuffling sound from behind snapped me back to my senses and I spun round. Nisha's parents, still in a daze, were scrabbling to their feet. Nisha pulled them close to her and they responded by hugging her tight. I was sure they'd be fine.

I slipped away, leaving them to their reunion. Out on the street I carried on towards my goal, sticking to the shadowed crevices of Whitechapel. The adrenalin was pumping so hard I was finding it difficult to be cautious. I wanted to shout and scream, 'It's me against the world!'

An explosion of intense loneliness burst in my head and I no longer cared. I ran as hard as I could down the middle of the road, exposed and vulnerable. Eventually, I ran out of steam. Deflated, I collapsed. All the adrenalin and anger had drained away.

I curled up into a ball and sobbed uncontrollably.

26

Grey

August 2037

'What can you see?' Douglas asked Peace.

'Nothing. They've taken him and I can only see a few hundred metres inside. I can move nearer if you like. But I might get spotted,' replied Peace, through Douglas's uWatch.

'Damn Linda and Rahman,' said Douglas. 'Stay where you are, but feed the helicopter camera into our eWall.'

We were sipping Douglas's whisky from the comfort of his office, having watched Aled trek along the Thames. I'd been uncomfortable spying on him, but Douglas had assured me it was for his own good. Douglas was adamant that, although The Project wouldn't stop Aled leaving, it certainly wanted to make sure he was okay.

'What on earth do you think happened in that warehouse?' I asked Douglas.

'Not sure, but it scared the hell out of those young lads. And out of Aled. Did you see the look on their faces as they came out?'

'Can I show you something else that's worrying me?' I asked.

'Of course, my dear,' he replied.

I connected the CCTV equipment to the eWall and punched in N43LDB5.

An empty street of identical four-storey houses appeared on the screen. A few shredded cardboard boxes lay on the pavement.

'C6,' I said. The camera turned south and a block of flats appeared. There was no sign of life.

'I want to show you what it's like for ordinary people, day after day. Rewind to ten-thirty,' I said.

A man pushing an old-fashioned supermarket trolley stopped on the corner. He took three cardboard boxes out and placed them on the pavement. As soon as he'd gone, a mum, dad and three sons appeared. The mum was the most striking, in her butcher's apron splattered with blood and her matted hair piled high on her head. The tallest of the sons lifted the boxes on to a knee-high wall while the others kept watch, casually knocking their metal clubs against the wall. A shrivelled-up woman, wrapped from head to toe in black rags, shuffled over from the flats. The rags on her feet became dislodged as she got closer, revealing a mix of old scabs and new cuts on her dirty toes. She inched her way to the butcher-mum and held out a pair of sturdy boots. The tallest son took them, made a show of inspecting them, and then gave the woman a loaf of bread. A man appeared from one of the houses across the road. He was dressed in an expensive, but torn, suit. He held his head high, turning it away with an exaggerated gesture as he passed the woman in rags. He stopped in front of them and held out the palm of his hand. Something glistened as the sun caught it. The man continued to hold his hand open in a gesture of subservience while butcher-mum whispered to the tallest son.

'Zoom in,' I said to the camera. It was a gold wedding ring. She nodded, beckoned him forward and took the ring from his hand. Her son lifted a box off the wall and placed it on the pavement. The man picked it up and walked proudly back to his house.

A few people were milling about on the street, bartering with household items such as kitchen knives and saucepans. They moved around with their heads bowed, desperately avoiding eye contact with each other. A girl with long brown curly hair, wearing a short green leather skirt and a tight black t-shirt, stood next to the dad. Every now and again, she would lift her t-shirt and reveal her thin pale flesh but the butcher-family and their hungry neighbours ignored her. A boy swaggered out from one of the houses opposite. He was carrying a string bag with two live kittens jostling around inside. Their little legs were getting tangled in the holes as they fought and scratched each other. He gave them to the butcher-mum and the dad pushed the girl in the boy's direction. They held hands and wandered off into the flats. The bustle of the street continued until the stock of bread and vegetables had been bartered away. The curly-haired girl returned and said something to the dad, who took one of the kittens out of the bag, smashed its head against the wall and gave it to her.

'Oh my God!' I said, taking a deep breath.

'Law of the jungle,' said Douglas.

I switched off the camera equipment and sat back in the leather chair. I was feeling a bit sick, so I took a large swig of whisky.

'It's like this all over. If we don't do something, it's going to get worse. We need Aled back to carry on with the experiments,' I said.

'Grey, the world is fixing itself. There's going to be pain to endure, but the weak will bow down to the strong and eventually an equilibrium will be found. If you'd have seen some of the things I saw on my field trips, you wouldn't be so worried about this little blip.'

'But we're not getting the reality we asked for.'

'People have free will to make of their world what they will. That's what's happening. Stop fretting.'

'I want him back,' I replied.

'Yes, I know. But not for the reasons you're giving me.'

'Yes, for those reasons. As well as the other,' I said.

Douglas swivelled his chair away from me and spoke into his uWatch. 'It might be useful to allow him into his museum so I can track where he goes. He's bound to head for that Holy of Holies, eventually.' He looked at his watch and then swivelled back to face me.

'Is that the only reason to bring him back?' I asked.

'Pretty much,' Douglas replied. 'But if you want to go over there and try to get him, be my guest. Peace is there already. See what the two of you can do. But if you're not successful then I want you to stop pining for him and get back here to help me in the next stage. Agreed?'

'Agreed.'

I called one of The Project cars to the house and we set off for Whitechapel's Bangla-Town. On the way I called Peace to bring him up-to-date and ask him to help me. Peace told me that Douglas was allowing him no more than thirty minutes with me. After that he was to return to the skies and keep watch on activity inside the wall. We arranged to meet at the spot where Aled had collapsed.

The car sped back along the same roads we'd used to come from the City Airport. This time, though, instead of the deathly post-apocalyptic silence, there was a faint buzz on the streets. The strange thing was that although there were groups of people moving around, each group generally consisted of two adults and several children.

At Tower Bridge, I asked the car to stop and let me out on to the north end of the bridge – I had a strong urge to relive Aled's experience. I liked being alone, walking towards Peace and feeling close to Aled. The hauntingly beautiful-but-tragic skyscrapers sparkled in the sunset, reminding me of the evening when we'd heard about the riots. It all seemed so long ago. I was a different girl then, besotted with Clive and unaware of Douglas or The Project. Things had seemed complicated, but in comparison they were a lot simpler and I didn't like the way I'd become Douglas's lackey. It had to change.

The air was filled with the smell of burning flesh as domestic animals, bred to eat, were barbecued. I walked through one of the city quadrangles that operated as an open-air food market. The range of food was amazing and appalling. There were cats, dogs, snakes, rats, guinea pigs and rabbits. All of them alive and crammed into tiny cages. Ready to be slaughtered at the point of purchase, so their meat was as fresh as possible. Samples were pinned out on wooden tables, their legs splayed apart and their skin peeled back to reveal the pink flesh beneath.

I stopped to look into the warehouse that Aled had departed so dramatically. A couple were snuggled up together on the couch, watching a re-run of the pre-war best-selling crime thriller, *The Temple Quakes,* and a teenage girl was busy washing vegetables at the sink – the perfect middle-class family. I knocked on the window, they saw me and a look of fear passed across their faces. Immediately, shutters came down on the outside of the window to protect them. I carried on to meet Peace as arranged.

He was waiting for me, lounging against a brick wall as if he hadn't a care in the world. I adopted my best casual walk, strolled over and leant my back against the wall and tucked up my left leg.

'It's great that we're having another adventure together,' I said, clasping hold of his hand.

He smiled but took his hand away. 'C'mon. We're here to rescue that lovely brother of yours. Remember?'

I raised my eyebrows, wondering if the two of them would ever openly admit the attraction and at the same time reminding myself that Peace was simply another unsuitable man.

Before we could connect the uCumulus to the cameras, two men appeared. One of them cupped my elbow and the other cupped Peace's, guiding us through the gate into Bangla-Town and to a small garden, growing an abundance of kale. Linda and Rahman were sitting on a park bench, watching and waiting.

Linda spoke. 'Why are you here?'

I sat down on the bench facing them, but Peace remained standing. 'We're here for Aled,' I said.

'Are you now?' said Linda. 'And what makes you think he's here?'

'Give us some credit,' said Peace.

'Okay. He's here. But he stays,' said Rahman.

'Linda, the world's getting worse. There's gangs. Girls are prostituting themselves for a piece of meat. We need Aled to finish what he started,' I said.

'No you don't. That's not why Douglas wants him back. Is it?' she said, looking up at Peace who shrugged his shoulders.

'I want Aled back. I need him back. Even if the world can repair itself – eventually – why wait? We don't have to rely on the slow process of evolution. We can bring about any alternative reality we want.'

'Linda. Let me,' said Rahman. 'You cannot trust DeSouza one inch. The Project is not what you think it is. If he is no longer interested in Aled, we should all be very concerned. It means he's close to getting what he wants. You'll be next, Grey. And then you, Peace. Him and his lot discarded me years ago. They've finished with Linda, too. That's why he sent her here. They will win. But I won't let them have my little corner of the world. This will be a safe haven for whoever wants it. Do you understand?'

'Can't Aled decide for himself?' I asked.

'He has,' said Linda. 'And, by the way, Zak is recovering very well under our protection. In case you're interested,' she added.

They stood up. The guards gripped our arms firmly and moved us back the way we'd come.

'Don't just walk away like that. It's not up to you,' I shouted, but they'd gone. The interview was over. We were politely but firmly escorted out of Bangla-Town and the gate was closed behind us.

I ran at the wall and kicked it, shouting and screaming for Aled. My hopes and dreams were crumbling.

'C'mon. I'll take you back,' said Peace.

'Fuck! Off!' I screamed at him. 'Go and find some young lad to impress.'

I stormed off on my own, but Peace soon caught up, grabbed me and handcuffed my arms behind my back.

'Sorry. Douglas insists you get back safely. By whatever means necessary,' he said.

The helicopter landed in Fitzroy Square and Peace uncuffed me. We walked side by side in silence, across to the house. I was in a state of shock. I'd lost Aled. I'd lost Peace. I'd lost my dignity. And now I was being dragged back like a naughty schoolchild. Maybe Rahman had been right about Douglas.

'I am sorry. Please believe me,' said Peace, as he left me with one of The Project guards.

I looked at him coldly and didn't answer. He'd broken my trust. I was escorted to Douglas's empty office. I was told to make myself comfortable and wait. I poured myself a large measure of his whisky and sat down. The smell of smoky peat was divine and the comforting taste of wood-ash lingered in my mouth. But I was so angry that, even as I felt the nectar burning my throat, I knew I wouldn't get drunk, no matter how hard I tried.

I ran my finger along the spines of the books that lined his den. All I really wanted to do was sink into drunkenness and get lost in the pages of some of his old classics – *Animal Farm, Great Expectations, Say It Like It Is, On Liberty, Brave New World and Midday Dread.* Instead, I sat and waited.

The door opened. 'Grey. We seem to have a misunderstanding,' said Douglas's disembodied voice from outside of the room.

He came in and sat down in the chair opposite me and poured himself a drink.

'What's that then?' I asked.

'I must apologise for Peace. He took me a little too literally.'

'So, I can go back and try again?'

'No. We don't need him. The secrets we need are in his Holy of Holies. It's much better if you and I focus on that. I know what I'm doing.'

'But what about the mess out there?'

'We don't need to worry. Do we? It's sorting itself out. And anyway, I'm sure you know enough to carry on the experiments without Aled.'

'We need him. He's the only one that can connect to God in such a deep way.'

'Don't you think there's as much chance that the experiments are working because of the power of a determined Human mind? Once it's convinced it can do something, there's no limit.'

'I don't know. But you promised me Aled, if I helped you out. You'd better keep your promise.'

'Had I?' he said, putting down his whisky. 'Guard,' he called. 'Show Ms Davies back to her room, please.'

He called after me, 'Everything is in place. Do not interfere.'

27

Aled

August 2037

Smells drifted across the room, settling inside my nose, like pollen left behind by a visiting bee. I could smell garlic and onions, cumin and coriander. All blending to form an evocative backdrop. The chink of glass, the ding of a cash till, the street chatter of buying and selling and the laughter of children floated around the room, like feathers escaping from a torn pillow.

I was lying there with my eyes shut, soaking up this cornucopia as it crashed into my senses. I felt full of life, as if the sounds and smells of the street were clothing me, encasing me in the sensuality of normal human beings. It was the antithesis of the Disintegrated world. I nurtured my fragility and reached out, as if to embrace this new world, letting it seep into my pores. I wanted Grey there. I wanted Zak there. They needed to feel this, to taste it, to immerse themselves and bathe in its luxury. I opened my eyes slowly and pinched myself to see if it was real or just a dream.

The last thing I remembered was running very fast, screaming, and then collapsing into a heap of despair and exhaustion. I had no idea where I was, but I guessed that I'd been taken there by someone who'd found me collapsed in the street. I knew this couldn't be any of The Project buildings because they were all ostentatious and this room was small. It had a low plain ceiling and was draped in red, yellow and purple hangings dotted with sequins that sparkled as the sunlight caught them. I pulled back the covers. I was fully clothed, except for socks and trousers.

There was a small window on the other side of the room through which the sunlight, sounds, and smells were finding their way in. I got out of bed and poked my head out of the window to look for clues. I could see down into a busy vibrant street with lots of people, all in fairly similar clothes – a bit like the photos I'd seen of pre-superpower China in the twentieth century. They were scampering to and fro, bartering with an exuberance for the food on display that I'd not seen since coming back from China. For all intents and purposes, it appeared to be a normal market street in a poor part of a city. I guessed I must be inside the Whitechapel enclave. I was getting more attuned to the sounds of the street and could pick out background noises of animals – horses and dogs mainly – mixed in with the shouts and cries of the market. The tinny sound of a pre-electric scooter echoed along the street, its pitch ascending and then descending as it rushed by. I needed to get dressed and get out of there because I had no idea how friendly or hostile a place it was.

Standing with my back to the window, I frantically scanned the room, searching for my clothes and in particular my bag. Under the bed I found everything except my boots and hastily, but silently, got dressed. I checked the uCumulus for any alerts from the museum – there were none – and then crept across to the door and gently turned the handle. My brain was fizzing with questions. Where was I? How did I get there? Was I safe? Thankfully, the door opened silently and I crept out, desperately hoping that I wouldn't alert my rescuers or captors – whichever they were. My boots were placed neatly just outside the door and I grabbed them as I made my way to the top of the stairs. I could hear voices downstairs. I picked my way very carefully, one step at a time, and, although I didn't know which stairs creaked, my teenage experience told me to keep to the edge of each floorboard. The voices were muffled so I couldn't make out what they were saying, but there were four distinct voices, two men and two women, and they were arguing in that loud yet anger-free way that some cultures seem to have perfected. There was an open door leading to a small back yard and, with as much stealth as I could muster, I moved across the hallway, into the yard, out through the gate and into the busy street. During the War, I learnt that the best way to blend in is to walk confidently, no matter how scared you are, which is exactly what I did.

There was a faintly pink tint to the sky and a nip of cold in the air. It was early morning but the market was buzzing with activity. I could sense people surreptitiously looking at me as I walked past. I was acutely aware that in these clothes I stood out as different – very different. Children ran up to me, nudging each other and giggling. Sitting on doorsteps and at café tables were old men and women, staring and shaking their heads. So much for blending in. I walked for five minutes, getting used to the buzz of the street, the playful interaction of the children and the wise stares from the elderly inhabitants. I was actually enjoying taking a slow stroll and studying the sparse contents of the shop windows. I recognised the railway bridge across the road – I was on Brick Lane, in the heart of Whitechapel. Memories of being there with Zak came flooding in. Days spent hanging around the outdoor cafés and long evenings spent with friends over luscious Indian banquets. To my left was a large space that was once an outdoor bar, but was now a thriving garden. The smell of the earth and the smells of the street food made me hungry, so I stopped at one of the food stalls that lined the side of the busy street. The smell of the lovely fresh parathas and thick lentil dahl captivated my taste buds, 'How much is the breakfast?' I asked the teenage boy running the stall.

'One hundred takapounds,' he replied, pointing at a hand-written sign ornately displaying *breakfast ৳£100*.

'What's a takapound?'

He showed me a normal ten-pound coin. 'Ten takapounds!' he said slowly, as if he was talking to a young child.

'That's just normal pounds.'

He shrugged and drawled, in the off-hand manner so typical of teenagers. 'Takapounds. D'ya wanna buy breakfast?'

I looked in my bag to see how much money I had. Sadly it was only fifty pounds, which wasn't going to last me long in a world where the pound was worth a twentieth of its actual value. I rummaged around to see what else I might have. I offered him a small carving of a dragon which he willingly accepted. We traded our respective crafts and I walked off with two parathas and a large plastic bowl of rich lentil dahl. I sat down and relaxed on the steps of a building, eating my food and taking in the atmosphere. I'd not felt this peaceful since I left China.

An old man, dressed in the same cream tunic and trousers as almost everyone I'd seen since I'd been there, came and sat down next to me. He had a soft way about him and I warmed to him immediately. It may have been because I was lonely and desperate for some company, but I think it was more likely that the place was rubbing off on me.

'I'm Rahman,' he said. 'How did you come to be here?'

'I don't really know. The last thing I remember is collapsing on the ground. I was running at full-belt along the Whitechapel Road towards the mosque.'

He nodded sagely. 'I'm an elder of the community. We don't often let someone in. We've a policy of keeping people out, unless they can make a positive contribution. They must have thought you fell into that category.'

'I was helping a little girl and her family. They were being attacked by a gang of youths.'

He nodded vigorously. 'That would certainly make you eligible to be welcomed.'

'Where am I?'

'Bangla-Town. It's a secure area a mile long by half-a-mile wide, with main roads on all four sides – Commercial Street to the west, Bethnal Green Road to the north, Cambridge Heath Road to the east and Whitechapel Road to the south. The only real weakness of our walled city is the railway line that runs through the middle, but it's high up, visible and barricaded at both ends. So far it's been secure. We use the railway line as our main entrance and exit. It allows us to take a horse and cart out to Chingford station.'

'Why Chingford?' I asked.

'That's where we meet the farmers of Epping Forest. They're growing food and hemp for making clothes. I'm really sad we have to appear hostile to the outside world to keep people away, but we can't cope with looking after many more.'

'Why did you decide to seal yourselves in?'

'In the early days of the War, the elders of the Bangladeshi community were uncomfortable with the direction the Liberalists were taking the country. They feared for their children and their families' moral well-being so they gradually withdrew. At that time they were starting to grow their own food and become more self-sufficient. This became a focal point for the two main sections of the community – the Bangladeshis and the trendy middle class. Together, they converted the City Farm and Weavers Fields into vertical city-farms, growing vegetables from their stock of rare seeds – seeds that were not genetically modified. As the two groups worked together, they started to bond around a vision of sustainable self-sufficiency. In time, they became convinced that this was their only way forward.'

'Seems a bit extreme to lock yourselves away,' I said.

'They grew frustrated with the Liberalists' world view and increasingly felt alienated until eventually, with the help of the aged George Galloway, they declared independence, as Bangla-Town. I joined them and we disconnected all incoming media channels, such as the internet and cable entertainment, and the young techies found a way to block all airborne signals.'

'I understand. I was in China. I loved the simple life of eating, carving, sleeping and chanting.'

'We watch the lost souls from the minaret. We don't really understand what's happening.'

'They're known as Disintegrates. They've had their inner being ripped out and have lost all trust in the world.'

I could see a tear in the corner of his eye.

He was getting fidgety and I presumed he wanted to leave.

'Have you seen my friend, Zak? Long red beard with a knot in the bottom.'

'Why don't we meet up here again? Tomorrow at dawn. After the Fajr prayers.'

He stood up as if he was going to walk away, but instead adopted an old man's pose, hands clasped behind his back. 'Tell me more about what happened with the cricket-bat lads.'

'Like I said, I was helping a little girl and her family. They were being attacked by a gang of youths.'

He smiled. 'You'll tell me when you're ready,' he said quietly. With obviously stiff and painful limbs, he walked off down the road.

I'd noticed that during our conversation, the market-stall holders and passers-by had been giving us sideways glances. As if they'd spotted a celebrity and didn't want to intrude, but none-theless were intrigued. I continued to sit on the doorstep, letting my mind drift back to The Project. I'd no idea how well the world was repairing itself outside of this comfortable haven and I wondered if I could affect anything by dropping a tracer-prayer into the whirlpool. I mulled this over for some time. Influenced by the patience and politeness of the old man and the contentment of those around me, I came to the conclusion that there would be no harm in trying to create a quantum ripple on my own.

I made my way to a stall that was selling bits of old broken furniture. I rooted around in my bag to find another carving and asked him if he'd be interested in selling any of them. He said he would and that a carving of that size and quality would fetch around three hundred takapounds, so he'd be prepared to pay me one hundred and fifty. That explained why the young lad had agreed to trade a carving for breakfast so readily.

We bartered for a while and settled on the one hundred and fifty offered, if he gave me pieces of broken furniture for free. I was starting to find my feet in this new world. I asked if there was a local church and he pointed me to St Matthews, which was near to Weavers Fields, at the mid-north point of Bangla-Town.

I turned around and walked back up Brick Lane, under the

railway and as far as the northern boundary. Down the centre of Bethnal Green Road was a twelve foot high wall made in the same way as dry-stone walls. The carefully selected debris from the shattered skyscrapers fitted together like pieces from many different jigsaws, slotting together to form a jumbled mess. The shards of shiny metal, large chunks of sharp-edged glass and crumbly-edged concrete made an imposing barrier to anyone thinking of trying to get into Bangla-Town. I walked along beside the wall until I reached St Matthews Row. Tucked away down this tree-lined side street was an austere-looking building with a tall tower in its centre. This was the church. This was my refuge.

The doors were open but it was empty. I retreated to the gardens, sat down and started to carve a minaret from the table leg given to me by my stall holder. I was in the best of both worlds now – all the appeal of the good bits of China but in a place that spoke my own language and had a church. I finished the carving and put it away carefully in my bag. Hopefully this would earn me a few days food. I got out the uCumulus to check the museum, but as it failed to connect, I put two and two together, realising what old Rahman had said about blocking all signals. I was truly cut off from the outside world.

Back inside the church, the light was streaming in through the arched windows, creating a heavenly aura. I prostrated myself in front of the altar and for the first time in a long while worshipped without asking for something. The enormity of what I'd been involved in hit me as I lay there and wept with joy. I was in absolute and utter awe of a God that is outside of time and space and yet forensically involved in the humdrum of everyday living. I tried to speak but couldn't find any words that could do this justice. His presence washed over me, wave after wave, cleansing me from all the spiritual dust and rubbish I'd accumulated since I left for China. I was ecstatic with relief.

I lay there for quite a while. It was time to release the tracer-prayer into the whirlpool, to see if God was able and willing to use it to repair the world a little bit more. Being in the church made me think about my visit to the Vatican. I lay there, prostrate in front of the altar, and, having churned it over, I prayed a simple prayer. 'Please change this for me. And for the world.'

I thought back to the structure that Grey had so often and patiently outlined for me. I had to describe the reality that has been, connect with and invoke God and then ask for the reality I would like. I felt deeply connected after my afternoon of prayer. All that remained was to fire up the part of my brain that created the whirlpool and describe my alternative reality. What could be easier?

The silence in the church was absolute, making it easy to activate the necessary neural patterns and invoke the whirlpool. I talked directly to God. 'How I wish we hadn't been so confrontational. I wish I'd been more patient with the Pope and tried to persuade him that a sensible review of the ancient texts could lead to a new religious age. It might have been difficult to sell back home, but I think I could have done it. Christ hated the Pharisees and their love of the rules. At least St Peter, the Pope's spiritual ancestor, tried to be honest. Even if he did get it wrong every now and again. It's fine to question what should and shouldn't be in the holy texts. Isn't it? So long as you're not simply following the zeitgeist and pandering to the popular evil desires of the day?'

I carried on circling the edge of the whirlpool, waiting for the loud crashing sounds – nothing. There was no indication that anything had changed. It had been worth a try and, although I was disappointed, the connection with God was reward enough.

I lay prostrate for a few minutes more and then leapt up, full of the joys of life, and strolled out of the church as happy as a Liberalist playing consequences.

28

Aled

August 2037

I wandered along the side streets of Bangla-Town, not bothering to keep to the edges, not feeling at all threatened. Brick Lane was west, so I headed towards the setting sun, zig-zagging through the narrow, winding streets. I was confident that at some point I'd cross the Lane and then I could find my stall-holder, sell my carving and supper would be in the bag.

I was vividly aware of the different architecture. Some ancient, some early-twenty-first-century and some in-between. Sure enough, I came to Brick Lane where I met an avalanche of cooking smells and the hectic sounds of the end-of-day bartering. The vibrancy of the street had moved up a gear since the morning. I walked past the young lad that sold me breakfast, gave a cheery wave, and then carried on to my other stall-holder, who merely glanced at my carved minaret, nodded his head vigorously, and handed over the agreed ฿£150. Back on the street, I was bombarded by a wealth of different curries and breads. It seemed as if every possible vegetable that you could think of had been sliced, diced and spiced for my pleasure. I kept on walking down the street, resisting the clumsy attempts by the young lads drumming up trade to pull me into their cafés. I sampled most of the curries on offer and studied all the menus as I went. I wanted to make sure that after I'd finished my meal, I didn't find a better café round the corner. I was amazed that there were so many people buying prepared food rather than cooking at home, even though communal eating was an integral part of their culture. A black-skinned lad of about twenty years old offered me a small dish labelled curried goat. It was very spicy and tasted like beef, but had the texture of liver. It was enough to tempt me into his café. The inside was very simple, with the same type of wall coverings that I'd woken up to the day before but in red, gold and green. A ragbag collection of office tables and chairs were randomly spread around the room. Scavenged from the destroyed city skyscrapers on the other side of the boundary wall. I looked around the café and everyone was deep in conversation. My spirits plummeted as I got an overwhelming sense of being an outsider. Rather than sit there on my own and let that fester, I decided to buy my food and take it back to St Matthews. I desperately wished I had someone to share this surreal experience with – walking home with a take-away meal.

On the tree-lined side street stood the church like a monarch at the heart of her court – the other buildings subservient and inferior. I skipped up the path to the front door, unable to believe my good fortune. A church, no Disintegrates and delicious food, enticing me to kick back and relax into the evening. The meal was delicious but I missed Grey and I wished I could find Zak. These were longings that I was sure, in the fullness of time, would be satiated as well.

I sat down in front of the crucifix hanging on the wall: the emaciated figure of Christ hanging in absolute agony. I was shocked that the church had kept it despite the ban by the Liberalists, who saw it as an implement of torture, rather than a religious symbol to be revered. I picked up the holy text I was reading earlier and inside the front cover was a piece of text headed, 'Statement on Truth by the United Worldwide Church'. I was certain it hadn't been there earlier.

The language was flowery and complex, but the Statement boiled down to the fact that the UWC believed that the revelations of God through the Holy Texts were not set in stone and, in the same way as science sets out a hypothesis that can be tested, the UWC believed this was the case for spiritual truths. It concluded that it takes centuries of acting as if these were absolute truths to fully test their validity.

I was speechless, staring in awe at the crucifixion of Christ and as transfixed as one of the stone statues near the altar. We were in a different universe. One in which the Holy Text had not been fixed at a single point in time, and then defended at any cost. I was stunned. The magnitude of what I'd done made me extremely anxious.

I woke up, still curled up in front of the crucifix, stretched my body and let the events of the previous day gradually percolate their way to the edges of my brain. God changed the world for me, I met a man that could take me to Zak and I found this refuge. I felt ready for the day and everything it might bring.

Already I could feel habits forming. On my way to meet old Rahman I'd collected a piece of wood from my stall-holder, bought the same breakfast from the same stall as the day before and sat on the same doorstep to eat and carve. The sky started to light up, as if someone was turning up the planet's dimmer switch until the orange disk appeared, signifying the start of another day of events, another day of spinning around inside the solar system.

I could see old Rahman strolling down the street on his way to meet me. He stopped to have a brief word with most of the stall-holders and acknowledged the rest with a tilt of his head. Once again, his calm and steady manner pulsated around him, producing smiles on everyone he passed. Every now and again, children would run alongside him, chanting 'Rahman' to a beautiful and repetitive melody.

After his long majestic walk he arrived in front of me. I stood to greet him but he motioned for me to sit back down. I welcomed him with a smile. 'Good morning. Peace be upon you.'

'And peace be upon you also,' he replied, lowering his stiff body to sit beside me.

My enthusiasm spilt over, a little too rudely, exploding with a question that sounded like a demand. 'Take me to my friend, Zak. I need to see him. I need to make sure he's all right.'

'Patience, my friend. First I would like to hear a little more about the encounter with the boys and their cricket bats. I've consulted with the border guards and they tell me that after a rather inelegant stand-off, you closed your eyes and without speaking or any physical contact, the boys simply walked away, as if you didn't exist. Can you explain this for me?'

'I don't think you'd understand or believe me. Better just to accept that they decided not to pursue their attack. Maybe I scared them off. So where's Zak?'

'Aled. It is Aled, isn't it?'

'It is…but how did you know that?'

'It's not important. Aled, you have to tell me what happened out there before I can put you in touch with Zak. He is a little scared of you and thinks you are probably caught up in something very sinister with "The Project". What can you tell me?'

I carried on carving, grateful for the distraction. How on earth would Zak know about The Project and why was he so close to this old guy? I was the one that should have been scared. Not Zak.

'I don't see how that's relevant to either you or Zak, to be honest,' I replied.

'I think you probably can, if you are honest with yourself, Aled.'

'I'm happy to tell you and Zak at the same time, if you really can take me to him. I don't see why I should trust you just because you're a friendly old man.'

He shifted his body, as if he was about to stand, and two men I'd not realised were with him, stepped out of the crowd and put a hand under each of his arms, helping him to his feet. They looked at me with a level of distrust I'd not experienced since I'd been there. As he walked off down the road, they nudged me, guiding me to walk alongside him. And then they fell into step behind us. The children and old folk that had been so intrigued, playful and friendly the previous day, averted their eyes as we paraded past.

29

Grey

August 2037

'Sort it, DeSouza.' said a voice from the eWall as I entered the office.

'Okay, sir,' said Douglas and he switched it off.

The guards left the room. He sat there fiddling with a uCumulus, looking at the blank eWall as if the image of whoever had been giving him a hard time remained. I stood just inside the room and didn't utter a word; I was still angry with him. He returned my stare, as if he was trying to make up his mind about something.

After what seemed like ten minutes, but was probably only thirty seconds, he came and stood in front of me.

'You give me no option,' he said.

'Or maybe "Sir" gives you no option,' I replied.

'Oh for pity's sake, don't make me laugh,' he said. 'Sit down. Please.'

There was no point in trying to have a face-off – I wouldn't win. I sat down and waited to hear what he had to say. He switched the eWall back on and fiddled with his uWatch. An elderly woman dressed in stretchy black trousers, a polo-necked jumper and sensible shoes was sitting with her legs crossed, surrounded by sheets of paper and at least a dozen wafer-thin microcapsule screens. Her hands moved elegantly, stroking them as if she was conducting a virtual-orchestra. She looked beautifully poised and in control. Every now and again, she'd pause, pick up one of the sheets of paper, scribble on it and then continue with her solitary activity.

'Aunt G,' I said, under my breath.

'Yes. Surprised?'

'What's she got to do with this?' I asked.

'Nothing. Yet. But that's your choice. She's in your hands.'

'Sorry. I don't understand the connection,' I said.

'You're the connection. You and your half-sibling.'

He focussed closely on to the one screen that she'd not yet touched. 'See the code in the corner – GD2098335?'

'Yes,' I replied, still no clearer.

'Access GD2098335. Override all protection protocols. Leave no trace,' he said into his uWatch.

Aunt G's screen was replicated on the eWall. On it was a collection of datasets with formulae linking them together. I recognised some of it as the research that had made her famous back in her early career. Douglas smiled, acknowledging that he knew I recognised it. He zoomed out again, letting me see the whole room. She was in her bedroom, the place she chose to do her most secret work. She'd once told me I should always make sure I had a space to think, a space that belonged to me and no one else. The closest I'd ever got was outside of St James's church, sitting with the Disintegrates.

'Sound,' said Douglas.

'What the hell's going on?' cursed Aunt G. 'There's no way I made a mistake like that. It's just not possible. Someone would have noticed. I'd have noticed.'

She got to her feet, picked up the offending screen and left the room. The image on the eWall followed her as she walked along an off-white municipal style corridor. She paused by a pale wooden door with a glass panel at head height. The sort of door that can be found across all public buildings with a concern to ensure that passers-by, or those in charge, can easily see the occupants and find out what they are up to without the inconvenience of having to ask. She tucked the screen into a Fabrication pouch on the back of her jacket. She'd obviously upgraded her clothes since I'd last seen her. It closed and almost completely disappeared, melting into the jacket fabric – she'd upgraded with the highest spec available. The eWall flipped from her back-view to her front-view as she walked through the door. Douglas zoomed out so we could see the whole room. Four women, two in their early twenties and two in their late fifties, sat in low grey padded chairs. Talking easily, they were obviously comfortable in each others' company. All four of them were dressed in pale-green lab coats with the ancient microscope logo of the company that Aunt G worked for embroidered on to the lapels. Out of each of their top pockets poked a different coloured board-marker. At the far corner of the room was a large shiny-white wall covered in multi-coloured letters, numbers and symbols – a sure sign of active research, of a place where individuals scribble their half-formed ideas for others to add comments and corrections.

'Geraldine. Where have you been?' asked the twenty-year-old nearest the door, crossing her bare legs as she spoke.

'I needed some space to think,' replied Aunt G.

'Three days?' asked the other twenty-year-old. She was wearing a headscarf covered in tiny images of a glucose molecule.

'Yes,' said Aunt G, sitting down on an empty chair.

'We were worried that you'd gone outside to get provisions,' said the bare-legged woman.

'You were worried,' corrected the fifty-year-old holding a blue board-marker in her hand.

'I needed some space,' Aunt G repeated.

'Please let us get the provisions,' said the twenty-year-old with the headscarf. 'It's scary out there. You'd be surprised what goes on.'

'I know, and I'm extremely grateful that you take such risks for me,' said Aunt G, smiling around the room. 'Has anyone noticed anything odd with any research data?'

'What do you mean?' asked the fifty-year-old with the blue marker.

'Data you thought was saying one thing, now appearing to be giving different conclusions.'

They all shook their heads.

'Oh well. Forget I said anything. It's probably a result of being cooped in here for so long. We need some outside contact. Any luck with the Cumulus?'

'Nothing yet. Maybe we're the only scientists left after the outbreak,' said the fifty-year-old who had been quiet so far. She walked over to the shiny-white wall, but carried on speaking. 'You say it's changing out there? When you go to get food?'

The bare-legged twenty-year-old spoke. 'Yeah. They don't just stare into space any more, but the aggression levels seem to be rising. Not sure if it's for the best, but we can now get food and, so long as we avoid the gang-families, it's not too bad.

'We'll run out of drugs to trade at some point, though. And then what?' asked Aunt G.

'That's a way off yet – six months at least,' said the head-scarfed twenty-year-old.

'Let's hope we find the cause and a cure in the next six months then,' said Aunt G.

'Let's,' said the fifty-year-old standing next to the shiny-white wall. 'We were just saying before you arrived, though. We still don't actually know if it's a biochemical problem.'

Aunt G spoke in what I recognised as her most soothing motherly voice. 'Of course. But that's our expertise, so what choice do we have? And, if nothing else, we can make sure all this research, and all our past research, is documented and remains as a valuable legacy for generations to come. And, on that note, I'm going back to my work. I suggest you all do the same.'

They all stood, put their empty cups and plates in the sink piled high with dirty crockery and followed her out. Douglas used the cameras to follow her back to her room and once she'd sat back on the floor, in the typical cross-legged Aunt G pose, he muted the eWall and turned to face me.

'Your problem, Ms Davies, is that you have to make a choice. I must gain access to the Holy of Holies in Aled's museum and you're the only one he trusts enough. And yet, you put a non-rational attachment to him above humanity's evolution. That gets in my way. You give me no choice. I have to help you choose.'

'Humanity is evolving without my help,' I replied, 'and Aled can make that happen even more.'

'Yes. Yes. But, he holds something that must be destroyed in order to help move humanity along.'

'What's that then?'

'Irrelevant. You must get me access to his Holy of Holies. If you don't, I'll continue to feed false data into your aunt's research. Once it gets out that she falsified results in order to prove the theses that made her name, she'll be disgraced. Now and for ever. Her legacy will be that she was a fraud. As I say, your choice, Ms Davies. Do you need an escort back to your room while you think it over?'

'No. I can find my own way thanks,' I said as I stood up.

There was a knock and Peace stuck his head round the door. 'Boss. Switch on the eWall. Problem with Aled.'

Douglas brought the screen to life and there was Aled being walked through Bangla-Town.

'Time to rescue him,' said Douglas, smiling at Peace. 'You have about an hour to decide, Ms Davies. When we return, I want you to welcome him back into the fold and carry on with the experiments. Get me access as quickly as you can. You know the alternative.'

30

Aled

August 2037

We walked in silence towards the distant boundary wall. They were either taking me to the mosque for questioning or were going to dump me outside, back into the world I'd escaped from only two days before. I pulled my bag close so it moulded to my side, offering me a little comfort in what was turning into a hostile and alien place. We were about a hundred yards from the end of the road when old Rahman slowed down, as if he was resisting whatever was about to happen. A figure stepped out from a side street – it was Zak. I stopped, wary of him now that I knew he was part of this. The two men who'd been following us gently but firmly pushed me.

'This is proof that I can be trusted,' said old Rahman.

'Trusted to try and intimidate me,' I replied, trying to show a braver face than I felt.

I took a deep breath and stepped forward. A loud high-pitched screech, mixed in with a low rumble, burst into the air. The locals ran or hid behind their stalls, knocking things over as they rushed to disappear. The staccato of the screech increased. Old Rahman jerked his head up to the sky, visibly shocked. I followed his stare. A helicopter was approaching, piercing the sky with its malevolent form, its blades cutting their way towards us, filling the world with its presence and pushing all else into insignificance. I turned to look at Zak, who was running towards me, in the opposite direction to everyone else. Old Rahman stood still. I moved towards Zak, but I was snatched from the floor and left dangling, like a forgotten puppet. I couldn't see into the helicopter. I couldn't see who'd grabbed me and was slowly winching me up. I came level with the open door and Carlos helped me inside. Douglas was waiting for me. They'd found me.

As we passed over Zak's head I shouted, 'FITZROY SQUARE. THE PROJECT.'

Douglas thrust a pair of headphones at me.

'What the fuck gives you the right?' I shouted over the noise. I put the headphones on and the noise of the blades softened as they moved us swiftly across the rooftops of London. Quieter, but still angry, I asked again, 'What gives you the right?'

Douglas spoke sternly and with a hint of irritation in his voice. 'Aled. We're trying to save the world. We put all that time into finding and then training you. You owe The Project.'

'I want you to take me back to China. As promised. No questions asked.'

'I'm afraid you forfeited that option when you broke our trust and disappeared. And don't think you can simply skulk around in your Holy of Holies.'

I'd seen how they treated the Ds; there was no point in replying. I was now a Project prisoner and no matter what I said or did, nothing would change that.

'What do you want me to do then?' I asked.

'Wait until we've landed and I'll tell you. But in the meantime, look down there. Since you woke up the Ds they've been running wild. There's no law, and even less order than before.'

I looked down. Lots of people were out on the streets, moving around in gangs. A man and woman came crashing out of a church. They were being chased by eight people – a mix of men, women and children – and the children were closing in on them. The youngsters clubbed the couple across the knees as they overtook them and then blocked the street. The adult gang-members closed in from behind and the couple fell to the ground, begging for mercy. The whole gang, adults and children, beat the couple around their heads.

We started to descend towards the street but Douglas called out, 'Do not go down there. Let them sort it out themselves. It's not our business.'

The pilot spoke through the intercom. 'I can buzz them? Scare them off?'

Douglas muttered, almost under his breath, 'Let them kill each other. They want to be with their God anyway.'

The pilot turned round. It was Peace. 'Yes, boss.'

He took the helicopter back up and after a couple of minutes we landed and stepped back into Fitzroy Square. Two security guards came out from The Project house and stood either side of me, discouraging me from attempting to escape. I was taken straight down to the basement, to the old familiar pool.

Grey met me with her usual enthusiasm. 'Hey, Aled. It's so cool that you're back.' She had a big grin on her face, but her voice seemed strained.

'Really?' I asked, sarcastically.

Douglas and the two guards left us on our own.

'How are you?' she asked, with more genuine affection than when Douglas had been there.

'I was fine until you lot snatched me. What gives you the right?'

'We were watching you from the helicopter. It looked as if you were getting into a spot of trouble – being marched down the street with guards either side.'

'And it upset you that they weren't your guards, I suppose?'

'I was worried for you, but I have to admit Douglas didn't seem that bothered. He's gone a bit weird since you left. I overheard a couple of calls where he was reassuring someone that he could get you back at any moment. That he'd know when the time was right. He seemed strangely anxious, which is unusual. The strain of fixing a crumbling world must be getting to him. I don't see so much of him any more. He even had me escorted back to my room, calling me Ms Davies.'

'And what do you think of kidnapping me?'

'It had to be done, Aled. We need you. Didn't you see the chaos out there?'

'Sure. Horrible. But what can I do?'

'We've traced another pivotal moment in your time-line. We need another intervention.'

It was strange to be back in that room preparing for another monitored encounter. When, out in the real world, I'd done it without all the equipment. Mine had been a bit random, though. Whereas The Project researched them thoroughly, looking for key moments in time where a single change to my time-line could invoke a significantly different future. Although, when we made one change, such as repairing the trust in parents, we seemed to generate another problem, such as the gang-families I'd seen on my way in. And it was unlikely that we could keep sending our universe back for a better one. Even His patience would run out, eventually.

Grey interrupted my thoughts. 'Remember that time you were involved with the police – the suicide bomber?'

'Yes. Is that what we're changing?'

'Sure is, Maestro.'

I put the helmet on and pulled the Ds up close. Once again preparing to change the world – Project style.

'Back in 2035, a few months before the Pope resigned, I was called to a suicide-bomb incident. Our great diplomat of the time, Lord Makaarim, was at the opening of a synagogue. An offer to meet with the Liberalist diplomats had been sanctioned by our senior council in the hope that we would find an end to the War. We'd leaked some of the detail, hoping to warm things up before-hand. This was before the court case with the children and before any great Disintegrations started, but we could see the cracks in society already starting to form. And, we could see we were losing.

A suicide-bomber, who had decided to stop the meeting, managed to take Lord Makaarim hostage. I'd been called to the scene because the bomber was an Absolutist. I arrived to find a paralysed police unit – unable to make decisions – and a suicide-bomber getting more and more agitated. The units of twelve armed police had to have a majority decision of ten before they could take action. The rule had been introduced in response to the many indefensible knee-jerk killings by the police. The crux of that particular police unit's quandary was that Lord Makaarim had convinced them that life was more important than dogma and, therefore, to take the life of the bomber was wrong. However, this conflicted with the rule that you must kill a suicide-bomber if they are a possible danger to anyone, or to themselves – which of course translated as "kill all suicide-bombers". The police couldn't reach a majority decision, no matter how hard they tried. Eventually, the bomber killed herself and Lord Makaarim. The loss to our movement was immense and we never did find anyone to replace him – or at least anyone that stood as good a chance of making peace.'

I paused and looked at Grey, who put her thumb in the air to signal that we were ready to carry on. Finding the edge of the whirlpool was as easy as letting go of the handrails of a swimming pool and sinking under the water. The pain returned. Grey nodded to the singing bowl.

'I don't need it,' I said.

I concentrated and instantly I was back on the lip of the whirlpool. Begging for a different past, a different present, a different future.

'I wouldn't want to contradict Lord Makaarim, but I wish the police had shot the bomber. That would have been a good decision.'

One of the project workers called over from another corner of the room, 'We seem to have something. The police are back on the streets and there's no apparent resistance.'

Grey came bounding over. 'Aled, we've done it again. This is fantastic. We must…'

I felt trapped. I didn't like being told what to say to my God – so I cut her short, 'Really? I'm so pleased for you.'

31

Aled

August 2037

I lay on my bed staring at the ceiling, with no enthusiasm for what we'd done. I was deeply disappointed that Grey hadn't been to visit, even if it was only to tell me how successful the last experiment had been.

The room was stifling me – as if a large transparent pillow was being pressed down, slowly but surely expelling all the breathable air. I studied the ornate plaster work around the edges of the ceiling, thinking back to Bangla-Town, to Zak and how free I'd felt walking along the river. Now I was confined and under the control of The Project.

Absent-mindedly, I opened my bag and rifled through its contents – the uncarved chair leg, the TakaPounds, the robe from the monastery, the rolled-up virtual mat and the bulge of the uCumulus, protected like a baby kangaroo in its mother's pouch. I gently persuaded the bag to release it, giving the fabric enough time to be sure of who I was. I connected to the Cumulus, only to discover that everywhere except the museum was off-limits.

I unrolled the mat and put on the visor and gloves, feeling a bit nervous about being caught. I wandered around inside the museum, using the artefacts to remind me of better times. I meandered along the virtual corridors, reacquainting myself with the paintings of the great moments from history – Moses as he left Mount Sinai with the Ten Commandments, Christ on the mount giving us the timeless beatitudes, and in my lifetime, the great sermons of Graham Browne and Daphne Hicksworth. Each artefact was in its place, the floors were clean and tidy, and there were no visitors so there was no furniture cluttering up the corridors. The cleanliness and order of the museum soothed my soul and brought back a spark of life. I ambled along the corridors, gazed at the walls, revelling in the familiar and yet still magical aura of this home-from-home. Gradually the intimidation of The Project faded.

A scrunched-up piece of white paper, discarded in the corner of the room, shocked me out of my comfortable daydream. There had been a visitor with sufficient access rights to change the museum, to create and leave a new artefact. Albeit a piece of litter. There were only a handful of us with that level of security clearance and it was unlikely that any of those would be so crass as to litter the place. We must have been hacked.

Cautiously, I examined it, conscious that someone might be watching me. The edges were torn, indicating that another visitor, with an authorised thumb-print, had picked it up but failed to open it. It must have been encoded for a single specific recipient and one with the highest security levels. I brushed my thumb, in the shape of a hexagon, across the museum floor. This was my secret thumb-code which the museum automatically added to anything that belonged to me.

The paper unravelled itself, revealing a clock counting down from "25:12:35", one second at a time. Underneath was a message. 'I'd tell the world what I think, but would you destroy a page to conceal my truth?'

It reminded me of the arguments that Zak and I had often had over the morals of removing negative customer comments. I'd argue that there was only one truth and therefore it was wrong and he'd argue that you've got to manipulate lots of truths to push your own truth to the top.

I needed to find the visitors' book. I hurried to the museum's exit as quickly as I could, but resisted using my unique option to fly. I didn't want to attract any attention, in case the other visitor wasn't Zak, was hostile and was still there. I found the book and casually flipped through its pages. Nothing. Nonchalantly, I carried on flicking through the remaining empty pages. Three pages from the end was another message. 'You helped me from my tomb, so now let me help you from yours. Leave the entrance open and I'll come find you. Lazarus.' The reference to Lazarus and the clumsily coded message were both Zak's style. There was no mistake it was him.

I screwed up the page, along with the other message, and by flicking them on to the virtual floor, I signalled to the museum that I wanted them destroyed. They turned to ash the moment they hit. A small robotic cleaner entered and swept the ash into its incinerator, puffing a cloud of smoke to reassure me that there was absolutely no trace left. Anywhere.

I left the museum and rolled up the mat. I had just over twenty-four hours to wait.

I'd been feigning sleep for a long while. It was time to make a move. The guards had left a few hours before and I hadn't heard any replacements. I opened the door cautiously. I crept along the corridors and down the stairs to the kitchen and, not hearing anyone inside, opened the door. Thankfully, it was empty.

There was a small patio outside with steps leading up to the street. This would be the best way for Zak to get into the house. I switched the kettle on to give me an alibi and then edged around the central island to the outside door. Surprisingly, the key was in the lock. I unlocked it, praying that no one would notice. I hesitated, because it all seemed a little too easy but, as I didn't have any better ideas, I carried on and made my way back as carefully as I'd come. I lay down on the bed.

Waiting.

32

Grey

August 2037

Aled had really hurt me. I didn't understand why he'd been so sarcastic when we'd achieved yet another triumph. The Project had brought us together, but I was worried it would drive us apart, for ever.

I sat on my bed with the pillows arranged so I could look into the square. Carlos appeared, pulling a flat-bed wooden handcart, grimacing as the wheels caught in the grooves of the pavement and bounced the cart from side to side. He lowered the front legs to the ground, wiped his forehead with the back of his hand and disappeared. A few minutes later he reappeared with Jane. They each carried a black metal rectangle with the quantum computer floating in the space between them. They were dismantling the labs, using one of the few anti-gravity prototypes ever built.

I sat and watched, confused by what they were doing. How could they take it all apart when we still needed to heal the world? Douglas might have questioned whether God existed, but he'd admitted we still needed to do more to help. Our latest excursion had repaired trust in the police, which was a huge step forward. But we still needed to fix the trust in Science, in Technology, in History – to name a few. Without us, it would take centuries to return to the pre-War level of civilisation. And, on top of all that, there was still so much we could do for individuals. Repairing tiny pieces of their broken lives.

I banged on the window, but they ignored me. I tore off my dressing-gown, throwing it on the floor, and grabbed a pair of dirty knickers from the bed. I dragged them on, stumbling as I lifted my left leg and got it caught in the twisted material. I grabbed a pair of burnt-orange corduroy trousers that were hanging on the back of the door and, as I stormed out of the room, I pulled an all-in-one Fabrication shirt-and-bra over my head.

Douglas's office door was open. I slammed it behind me, striding across the room. He was watching Jane and Carlos floating the eWall down the front steps.

'You can't do this,' I said.

'Do what?' he replied, turning to face me.

'You're dismantling The Project before we've finished.'

'I'm moving it.'

'And were you going to tell me?' I asked.

'I'm not sure you want to come with us,' he said, moving away from the window. He motioned to the chair next to me. 'Shall we be civilised about this?'

I accepted his offer and dropped into the chair.

I could smell the mustiness of my clothes and suddenly I felt dirty and dishevelled. 'Douglas, please tell me what's happening,' I begged.

'As I said before, I don't think we need Aled any longer. We're not still pretending to call on God, so why would we need that religious freak?' he replied.

'How can you say that?'

'Easy. It's true. The real question for you is whether you want to carry on?'

'I do. But with Aled.'

'It would seem to me that your answer is no then,' he said, getting up and walking back to the window, dismissing me by turning away.

I went and stood alongside him.

'Does it matter how it works? Surely the fact that it does is enough?' I asked.

'Of course it matters. We can't develop it further if we don't have a concrete basis to start from. Unless it can stand the scrutiny of scientific testing, it's worthless,' he replied.

'But what exactly are we testing for? And what if we're not clever enough to know what the test should be?'

'Process of reduction, my dear.'

'By then it might be too late to save Humanity.'

'Ridiculous. We need to stick to the fundamentals of scientific methods above all else. Fewer, but rational humans is better than perpetuating a profligate but flawed irrational Humanity. Surely?'

Douglas's uWatch vibrated and he waved out of the window in the direction of a white car with the gorgeous sleekness of a turn-of-the-century classic – a first-generation Prius NHW10.

'Must go. The choice is yours,' he said.

We left his office and at the foot of the stairs we parted company. As soon as I got into my room, I took my clothes off as fast as I'd put them on, and stepped into the shower. I ran the water for a long while. It washed away the surface dirt on my skin and some of the layers of guilt I felt about the state of the world. I dried vigorously, which refreshed me even more. I put on my warm Fabrication dressing-gown and it hugged my body with its soft richness. I folded my tweed suit and placed it at the bottom of my trunk. I took all my clean clothes out of the wardrobe and put them on top of the suit with my brogues on either side, their soles touching the sides of the trunk. Next to the bed was Barbie. I picked her up and stroked the two cuts on her arm, remembering my own which were now covered by more recent scars from self-harming bars. I wrapped her in a clean t-shirt and put her in the trunk with the *Silver Chair*.

I paused for a few seconds, empathising with the torment of my *Madonna*. I lifted her off the wall and carefully wrapped her in a towel. Lastly, I put all my dirty clothes in a laundry bag and closed the trunk lid.

I pulled the chair across to the window and sat down, watching the trail of Project equipment being loaded on to the cart, piece by piece.

33

Aled

August 2037

I was still lying on the bed, waiting, when Zak crept in and made me jump.

'How…' I started, but he put his finger to his lips. He moved across to the en-suite bathroom and signalled for me to join him. Once the bath was running, he relaxed.

'Don't ask. But it weren't easy,' he whispered. 'The folks in Bangla showed me a load of techie stuff. You need to know – someone here's been pushing real hard at your museum security, 'specially the inner whatsit. And they're solid at what they do, but no real wins yet so don't fret. Real big brains and dripping in cash, though, I'd say. Any idea what's going on?'

'No. But thanks for coming,' I said, giving him an understated punch on the arm. 'Is that what you meant when you said you knew stuff I should know?'

'Well…there's a few people been mooching around in there, but two stand out. One's a complete mystery, tip-top hacker I'd say, and the other signed in as Grace. On the way over here I traced her via her Cumulus Protocol address – her tag is Grey. She's good at hiding her real identity, though. I couldn't crack it – mean anything?'

I stared at him, not wanting to believe that Grey had been attempting to break into the most sacred part of my museum.

'She's here. She's a friend…I don't think it's her…'

'Well, let's see,' he replied, standing up to move.

'You won't find her. She's been spectacularly absent since I was dragged back here. Well, apart from one official experiment.'

'I got her marked. She's in the room two along from here and you're right – she's not been moving about much.

I looked at him quizzically. 'How do you know all this?'

'Long story, but it's an old geezer in Bangla you should thank. He's a star. And very sharp on the techie stuff. Used to be a bit of a city whizz, so he says.'

'I'm in your hands, mate.'

Zak placed some weird home-made device on his head. It looked like a bicycle helmet with an extendible rod attached to the front and then a small screen at the end of that. On the screen I could see a sketched-out map of the house, showing one stationary green light with two red lights close by and a blue light moving around in another part of the house. 'We're red, she's green and Douglas is blue,' said Zak, beckoning me forward. 'Come on.'

I followed Zak out of the room, along the corridor and into the room with the green light. Grey was sitting in a battered Georgian chair, looking out over the square. She was wearing a long dressing-gown with her hair tied up, as if she was about to get into the bath. 'Grey. Are you okay?' I asked, quietly.

'Of course…just thinking,' she said, as she turned. She froze. 'Zak?'

'Yeah,' he replied. 'We caught you out. Sneaking around trying to destroy Aled's museum.'

'Slow down Zak. Please,' I said. 'Grey. Were you in the museum?'

She couldn't take her eyes off him and didn't seem to be hearing a word I was saying. All the colour had drained from her face. She moved her head as if it weighed a ton. 'Aled, I'm so sorry. I don't know what to do. I'm glad you came. It's all getting out of control. I didn't know what to do next, so I came looking for you in the museum. I hoped you'd be there.'

The Grey that stormed around China, led the experiments

and was a tower of strength to me had vanished. A fragile Grey had taken her place.

'Do you want to tell me about it?' I asked, putting my arm around her shoulder.

'She's a traitor. Dangerous to us both,' hissed Zak, under his breath. He poked her arm. 'What've you been up to, you shit?' he said, with a shocking amount of bile. 'We know you've hidden your real identity. And, sweety, that's not the act of an innocent.'

I signalled him to stop and then turned to Grey. 'What's going on? You've not been to see me since the last experiment. I now find out you've been stalking me in the museum and you're sitting here as if you've given up on life altogether. Which, quite honestly, is odd for someone whose theory of mixing God and quantum physics seems to be working. What is it?' I asked.

She turned around. 'There's so much…I don't…I'm not sure…Aled, I can't…will you hate me?'

'Tell me, or we'll never know,' I said as I hugged her a little closer.

Through uncharacteristic sobs, she started to explain. 'Aled, I've not been honest with you…'

'Again?' I interrupted.

'There's a secret reason I wanted you to be the one I worked with…I don't think you'll ever forgive me…I can't…you won't understand…it's not my place…'

I held her hand. 'Grey, we've been through quite a lot. Haven't we? You can tell me…you have to tell me…how bad can it be?'

She inhaled deeply, sucking the sobs back inside herself. 'My dad is your dad,' she splurted.

'We both have a father in heaven,' said Zak sarcastically.

'Zak. Shut up!" I snapped.

'Dylan Griffen was my dad. I only met him twice. The second time he told me I had half-brothers. Douglas found you for me. We have the same dad.'

The sarcasm dripped off Zak's tongue. 'Coincidence you're both here then.'

'Actually, I put my neck on the line to make sure I got Aled,' she sobbed.

I looked at Zak to see his reaction. 'Unlikely,' he said, rolling his eyes.

'Cheating, lying bastard,' was all I could manage in response.

'I'm not,' she said, sobbing louder.

'Not you, him…Dad…Bastard…'

'What ya doing believing her? She's Project through and through,' chipped in Zak.

'I can tell when she's lying and she's not. So shut your gob for once.'

'Yeah, right. Like knowing she was creeping around in the museum?' he said, his voice once again thick with sarcasm.

'When I told you about me and my brother arguing and er… went a bit far…no wonder you behaved oddly.'

She nodded, still crying gently. We sat in each other's arms, just being together. Me in the knowledge that she was my sister and her in the knowledge that I knew. After a few minutes she said very quietly, 'I'm really sorry. I wanted to see if we could bring Dad back.'

'We could try…' I said, hesitantly.

'Sorry to spoil this special moment, but not now you can't,' interrupted Zak. 'Douglas is on his way and I'm guessing we don't want him to find me here. Or you two all loved up. Right, Grey?'

She shook herself, as if to wake from a dream. 'He can't find us – there's something really wrong going down with him. He's becoming more and more sinister. He also seems to have Peace completely in his pocket. I'm scared.'

'But there's so much I want…need…to ask you about. You can't drop a bombshell like that and then leave it.'

'Later,' she said forcefully.

'Aled, mate. We need to find out who's been tramping around your precious museum, trying to break into the centre of centres.'

'Holy of Holies.'

'Whatever. Mate, he's on his way to your room.'

'Right. I'll go back and see what he wants. You two see what else you can find out about these break-ins. Okay?'

When Douglas appeared, I was sitting up in bed with the uCumulus on my lap browsing CCTV footage. I greeted him cheerfully. 'Hi. Looks as if things are on the up, all round the world.'

'I am very pleased with the progress The Project is making,' he said, in his soft rounded tones. He continued in a business-like manner, 'Our usage panel detected a surge of activity from your room, which made me wonder what you were up to, locked away up here. Is it only the CCTV footage that has drawn your attention? I can redirect bandwidth from elsewhere to increase yours. For activity I approve of, of course.'

His body language oozed confidence and I was sure the usage panel was as sophisticated as they came. He knew exactly what I'd been up to.

'I've been wandering around inside the AGP Museum, reminding myself of all the beauty and truth it contains,' I replied.

'I know. And what did you find most appealing in there?'

I had to think about how to answer him, so as to tell him enough but not too much. Memories of meeting him in China came flooding back.

'The great moments of revelation, I guess. Moses, Christ and, although nothing in comparison, Browne and Hicksworth,' I said.

'What else is in the Museum? Are there things that the general public can't see? Are you able to wander the secret corridors?'

I could almost taste his impatience. 'There are some places I can go which are not open to the public. Why do you ask?'

'There were conspiracy rumours that there's a Holy of Holies that holds top-secret documents. I presume it's beyond your level of seniority.'

I quoted the press-release we'd prepared years ago, when these rumours first started. 'Interesting idea, but simply misguided speculation by ill-informed meddlers.'

'You won't mind if I have a look around for myself then, will you?' he asked.

'Of course not. Be my guest.'

'You scratch mine and I scratch yours. I'll expand the bandwidth in here and fully open up your access to the Cumulus. You can go and do whatever takes your fancy,' he said, with a condescending smile that I think was meant to look friendly.

34

Aled

August 2037

As soon as Douglas left, Zak and Grey joined me. 'What'd he want?' asked Zak, crashing straight in.

'Weird, but he seemed to be trying to be friendly. He's opened up my access. But he also wanted permission to explore the museum. Oh, and he was asking about the Holy of Holies.'

'What is it with this Holy of Holies?' asked Grey.

'It's where we store the precious artefacts. I think that's what Douglas is after. I suspect he wants to destroy them,' I said.

Grey put her hand on my arm. 'He's said he doesn't believe that God has anything to do with the experiments. He's also said we don't need you any more. And he does seem increasingly obsessed with the Holy of Holies. I had a bust-up with him earlier and he started spouting off like an abso-scientist…'

Zak interrupted her. 'Don't trust him one little bit. Reckon he's gonna latch on and try to piggy- back you. He might be able to jump the security. I can set up a decoy Holy of Holies. And a detection system if you want, but you'll have to operate it. I'm gonna have to make myself scarce and hide for a bit. I don't wanna be found.'

'Zak, that sounds great. And of course set it up and then hide. But how will we contact you?' I asked, worried about losing him all over again.

'I've got this funky little device Zak's given me,' said Grey, holding up a small black cube.

'Right. That's the false Holy of Holies done. I reckon you should head on over and see if anyone follows. Your uCumulus is also configured to detect any piggy-backing. Wait. Look, someone's just gone in. Let's check…yup that's the same thumb-print as the one I just lifted off your door handle. An' it's not yours, mate.'

Zak sat back triumphantly, as if he'd solved all of our problems.

'Explain,' I said.

'Took a copy of Douglas's thumb-print from your door handle. You know you need to register your thumb-print to get into the museum? Bingo. Douglas has just gone through the front door. Wow…and look at the way he's moving around. I recognise that pattern I'm sure…hold on a mo'…'

Zak flicked a switch on the side of his home-made screen and various graphs, numbers and letters appeared. Rising and falling as if they were monitoring a patient's life signs.

'What's that?' I asked.

Without taking his eyes off the screen, he answered, 'When people visit places, they tend to follow the same pattern of behaviour. It's a bit like watching someone you know enter a pub – there's always one that'll go straight for the seats, one that'll scout round to see who's there and one who'll head for the bar. This little beauty is cleverer than that, but basically it builds a profile of Cumulus behaviour to distinguish one person from another.'

'Does it work?'

'Gets better each time you track someone. This is about ninety-five per cent accurate for the museum regulars and improving,' he said.

All three of us went quiet for a few minutes while Zak concentrated on the screen. And then he announced, 'Got 'im. Douglas is our mystery intruder from before. We got him bang to rights. Use your uC to see if he's following you into that false Holy of Holies. You'll see I've set up a tracer to alert you to who's creeping around or piggy-backing.'

Zak nodded towards Grey. 'Be careful,' he mouthed silently to me.

Grey spoke directly to him. 'You know you can trust me. I thought we sorted all that out while we were waiting for Aled and Douglas to finish. You said you'd make sure Douglas didn't destroy Aunt G.'

'Sure…well I trust you far more than Duggie down there so…yeah…Hey…I better scarper for a while so I'm not caught. They may 'ave spotted me already.'

He left the room, surprisingly quietly for him. I looked at Grey. It was the first time we'd been alone since she dropped her bombshell. We smiled. I shrugged my shoulders and she shrugged hers back.

I broke the silence. 'So…Sis…what should we do?'

'We have to find out what Douglas is up to, don't we…Bruv?' she said, grinning.

'Seriously though, Grey, this might get very messy because I will do whatever it takes to protect the Holy of Holies. And I mean, whatever. You can duck out now if you want – I'll understand.'

'Might you kill him?' she asked.

'I hope not, but if I have to…well…and don't forget there are far worse things than death.'

'I'm with you,' she said.

The last time we'd seen Douglas's blue dot on the screen, he was in the basement. We made our way downstairs towards the laboratory. We stopped in an alcove outside the lab door and I unrolled the mat and put on the visor and gloves.

'Let's see if he follows us,' I said.

I entered the museum through the front door, registering as myself and giving Douglas as much chance to see me arrive as possible. I wandered along the corridors towards the false Holy of Holies. The tracer picked him up. He changed direction and came towards me. I moved faster and he responded by doing the same. I opened the door to the false inner sanctuary and stepped inside. I left it open and waited. He was close.

Douglas's avatar joined mine in the virtual room. I signalled to Grey that I was going into the real lab to confront him. I flung the door open.

'Why are you following me around the museum and why have you let yourself into a room marked private?' I shouted as I stormed across to where he was standing.

He took off his visor. 'Aled…and Grey. How touching. So glad you could join us,' he said, looking over our shoulders. 'Say hello to our guests,' he continued.

'Hi again,' said Peace.

'Peace. Disable these two irritants, please,' he said, with an undertone of malevolence that made me shudder.

'Sure, boss,' replied Peace.

'Hold on a minute,' said Grey, 'before you go disabling us – whatever that means – don't you want to know what your boss is up to? Sneaking around mysteriously in the AGP Museum. Going to such great lengths to remain anonymous.'

'You know me,' he replied.

'I do. And, I know that beneath that superficial monotone is a decent person. Hear us out, at least,' she said, with a slight twinge of begging in her voice.

'Okay. Boss – what's this about?' asked Peace.

'You don't need to know. You're employed to do what I tell you, so get on with it,' demanded Douglas.

'I don't need to remind you, do I, that I'm a mercenary not a slave? If I want out, I'm out. If Grey says there's something I should know about, then I want to hear it.'

'If you knew who you were dealing with, you wouldn't talk to me like that,' snapped Douglas.

'In which case, I definitely want to know who you are and what's going on,' demanded Peace.

Douglas stood up and faced him. 'You are so out of your depth, my little toy-soldier. You think we're a bunch of abso-scientists, but ours is an organisation of the world's elite. We're more powerful than the combined forces of Christianity, Islam and Judaism. We're dedicated to the destruction of all religion and false hope. Your petty war was beneath us – but we tinkered with it from time to time.' He turned towards me. 'I particularly enjoyed nudging you to destroy the Catholic Church. Now, I'm going to destroy the filthy contents of your so-called Holy of Holies.'

'Why?' asked Peace, as straightforward as ever.

'Because we need to free the Human Race from the shackles of superstition. Those bloody new-age philosophers and their proof that God exists – as if.'

I was startled. 'How the hell do you know about the *Proof of Existence?*'

He smiled but didn't answer. He continued, in the same malevolent tone as before. 'We will set the world free to become the best it can. To explore the Universe without being suffocated by the lies and control of your religious nonsense.'

Peace interrupted. 'But the experiments rely on God?'

'Bloody fools. They are pure quantum physics with a false veneer of mumbo-jumbo for our two beloved colleagues here.'

I interrupted. 'They worked for me without your equipment. God is at the heart of this. Admit it.'

'My dear deluded boy. You may think you can keep the masses sedated with your irrational morals, but we will destroy you. A world built on pure rational thought will be our legacy.'

Grey held my hand and stared at him in disbelief.

'Do you realise that if you succeed you could throw the whole world into something even worse than Disintegration?' I asked him. 'And you know the Holy of Holies has three layers of protection?' I added, quickly recovering.

'Tell me about them,' demanded Peace.

'The first layer protects against a serious but unsuccessful attempt to penetrate and destroy any of the contents. It sends a shock wave of disruption around the Cumulus as a warning to back off and randomly corrupts and collapses some non-essential servers. A second attack would launch a comprehensive shut-down of all non-essential servers across the world.'

'What's non-essential?' asked Peace.

'Anything that is not relied on by the Police, Fire or Ambulance. We considered the military to be non-essential.'

'And the third?'

'The third shuts down everything. On the assumption that, by then, the essential services have been taken over. I doubt the Cumulus would survive the first, let alone the second or third, the state it's in at the moment.'

'I agree,' said Peace, looking at Douglas. 'What have you got to say to all this?'

'Poppycock. And anyway, like I said, there are some things that are more important to the survival of the Human Race. We need to pull down these false Gods and reveal these purveyors of magic potions for what they are.'

Peace walked over to me and, holding me by the arm, guided me to the far end of the room.

'Lock him in the control booth,' Douglas shouted after us.

Peace took me down into the pool where the others couldn't see. 'Let's talk,' he said.

'If you agree he needs to be stopped, then I've an idea. But it's severe and unpleasant,' I said.

'What is it?' he asked.

I explained and he agreed with me that it was unpleasant, but necessary. We returned along the side of the pool together, Peace no longer guiding me by the arm.

'Traitor,' Douglas sneered.

35

Aled

August 2037

Peace walked over and lifted him up. 'Come with me.'

'What on earth do you think you're doing?' demanded Douglas.

I called across the room, 'Grey. Can you find the film of Orwell's *Nineteen Eighty-Four,* please?'

'I'll see if we have it. But I thought we agreed that those kind of films didn't help?' she said.

'Depends on what you're trying to do.'

Peace took Douglas down into the pool, tying him to a chair in the corner furthest from the booth.

'Beating me up will get you nowhere,' Douglas shouted. He was being aggressive, but he wasn't fooling me. He was obviously scared.

The door into the basement opened and Zak wandered in. 'Saw you were all here, so I guessed I should come join the party,' he chirped.

'Got it,' called Grey, as she came back into the room. 'Oh, hi Zak, good to see you,' she added.

'Yeah, what's been occurring?'

'Shut up. Please. I know you're scared, but I can't afford to be distracted by all this banal banter,' I said. 'Right. This is not going to be pleasant. If anyone wants out, then please, please, leave now.

Don't interrupt me, or try to stop me, once I've started.'

'What the fuck? Bit serious, aren't you, mate?' said Zak.

Grey moved next to Zak, 'You're freaking me out, Aled. What are you talking about?'

'I have to try and stop Douglas and his organisation. If you don't agree that we must stop him, whatever it takes, then it's best to leave.'

They joined me, the look of intensity on their faces betraying their deep concern. I took a deep breath and steadied myself. I was going to need all the concentration, conviction and commitment I could find.

'Grey, put the film on and have it ready at ninety minutes from the start. Peace, bring those Ds in from next door and surround him with them. Zak, can you record this and keep an eye out to make sure no one disturbs us?'

They all hesitated, but then moved. Doing what I'd asked.

I sat cross-legged in front of Douglas, opened the uCumulus and stared him in the face. He stared back with an incredulous look.

'You do realise what…who…you're messing with here, don't you?' he said.

'Aled, what on earth are you doing?' shrieked Grey.

'I told you. It has to be done. Back off.'

'You've gone all weird. Like him,' she said.

I looked over my left shoulder and up at her. 'It'll be fine,' I mouthed.

I turned back. 'Now. Douglas. You were asking if I knew what I was doing. I think I realise only too well. A man once warned me about you, and that's why you're going to tell me how to stop them.'

He sat still. Staring and silent.

I spoke into my uCumulus. 'Novel, Orwell, Nineteen Eighty-Four, room one-o-one,' and up came the text.

Douglas took a deep breath.

'Room one-o-one, the room of the worst thing in the world, for you,' I said.

I read the passage aloud.

I stopped, letting it sink in.

'I'm guessing, Douglas, from the intellectual superiority you so obviously believe you have, and from the contempt you've shown the Disintegrates, that becoming one of them is your worst thing?' His eyes widened and sweat appeared on his upper lip, betraying his fear.

'Tell me how to stop – them. And I'll stop – this,' I whispered.

'I can't,' he muttered.

'Try.'

I propped six Ds against him and stood behind him. I put the helmet on his head and cupped his face in my hands.

'Look at the screen,' I whispered as I moved his head. 'Can you see that lovely brain of yours working away?' There was no answer, but he shuddered. I was pleased.

I leant in close to his left ear. 'Watch the film and think about Disintegration. Don't forget, holding up one finger means you're ready to do what we want.'

'Your God won't let you.'

'I think He will. Peace, make sure he's watching the film.'

I held his hands, took a deep breath and let the Ds cloak me with their nothingness. The whirlpool was easy to find, but I made sure I went there extremely slowly. Douglas's neural patterns began to change, showing the gradual decline towards his own Disintegration. I took him nearer and nearer. I could feel my body, mind and soul being pulled apart. His brain waves were going haywire and he was emitting small frightened animal-like noises. We circled the vortex, moving close and then drawing back, alternating between the real world and the void.

He grappled for something in his pocket. Peace grabbed his arm, wrenching it away from his trousers. 'Oh no you don't, matey. Let's take a look at what's so important, shall we?' said Peace, shoving his hand into Douglas's pocket. Peace held up a small black cube, similar to the one Zak had given Grey. 'Very snazzy,' he said.

'What's that?' I asked Peace.

'Location device. Top of the range. But still inactive, thank God.'

'Please, Aled, this is too dangerous. I'm scared,' said Grey.

I pulled Douglas's head back, forcing him to watch the film. Winston was betraying his beloved Julia – begging them to torture her, instead of him.

'See that. Orwell knew that everyone has their breaking point. Disintegration is yours.' I lowered my mouth to his ear. 'You know how to make this stop,' I whispered.

I took him back down to the vortex, pulling him back and forwards.

Torture. Relief. Torture. Relief.

We returned to the surface.

'Please. Don't,' he said.

'Tell me how to stop them.'

'No.'

I took him back down. Dragging him to the edge. I could sense he was panicking. I brought him back up.

'Tell me,' I said.

'No.'

'Next time, I'll leave you there.'

'Project twelve two o-nine,' he said.

'What's that?'

'The portal.'

'Not enough.'

'No more,' he said and looked at the floor. 'Please, I'm begging you.'

'You have a choice,' I whispered.

'I don't,' he screamed.

Before his scream ended, I dragged him back into his pit of despair and kept him there. As if I was drowning him. The words of the duffle-coated man came back to me. 'You'll know when it's the right time to release it to the world.'

'*Proof of Existence*,' I said into my uCumulus. It pulled the document from the museum and brought it up on screen. 'Look at this, Douglas. This is the *Proof* you've been so desperate to see.'

I showed it to him, scrolling very slowly, allowing him time to absorb it. His eyes widened and he pushed back in his chair, as if he was trying to get away from it.

Still he said nothing.

Grey gasped. 'Is that real?' she asked. I nodded.

I turned back to Douglas. 'Have it your way,' I said. In we went again. To the lip of the whirlpool and over the edge. I was careful not to go beyond the point of no return. I could feel him giving up. I brought him back. There was a pungent smell of sweat, piss and shit.

Zak put his finger under Douglas's chin and lifted his head. 'Aw, man. What've you done? Did Duggie poo-poo himself?'

Silent tears flowed down his face.

I could feel him desperately trying not to succumb. His inner core seized hold of mine and attached itself, welding my fate to his. I was being dragged further and further into Disintegration and I had to go down with him.

I wanted to find a way to disconnect from him. I wanted to leave him there and avoid my own private hell – an existence devoid of God. The pain and torment was overwhelming, but I had to make an example of him. As a warning.

I beckoned to Zak.

'Fuck. You all right, mate?' he asked.

It was hard to form the words through the mist, but I forced them out…'I'm fine…can you replace…their Portal…with vStream of this…? Send it viral…label it…*A warning.* Include the *Proof of Existence*'

'Sure, no problem. But, I'm not gonna leave you attached to that piece of shit.'

He grabbed my elbow. I managed to shout at him…'No. Go away…you'll only…end up…with me…DO NOT DRAG ME BACK.'

I could hear a distant scream, echoing around the pool.

I thought it might be me, but I was down inside the vortex and I couldn't really tell. And I didn't really care.

I was terrified and yet strangely relaxed; I imagined committing suicide felt very similar.

I could just about feel the floor beneath me, keeping me connected to reality. I knew I was Aled. I knew I was fading and I knew it was my choice; I had to stop him. I had to drop my soul into this chasm of despair and drag his with me. But was it enough?

The whirlpool was slowly drawing me in and with each minute that passed it was becoming more difficult not to succumb. The prospect of letting go, once and for all, was enticing; to stop striving, fighting for my beliefs, was a trap I was increasingly drawn towards. The narcotic treacle was calling.

I couldn't speak or move, but I could hear what was happening.

Zak ignored my command. 'Peace. Help me!' he shouted.

'Zak. Don't release the *Proof*. It's too dangerous,' shouted Grey.

They dragged me clear. I came back up enough to see them place the Ds around Douglas. As if they were making a pyramid of logs for a bonfire, a toxic pyre. I closed my eyes, wavering on the edge of the abyss.

'Douglas is recovering,' shouted Grey, 'Look at his patterns. Zak. Get me the Database of Influence up on the screen.'

'Douglas DeSouza,' said Grey. 'Show all his high-rated connections.'

'What are you up to?' asked Zak.

'Watch. Look at all those top influencers breaking their connections to him. I reckon that's his secret comrades running away. He's being hung out to dry.'

Grey spoke to Douglas. 'Look. Can you see how low your influence rating is? You're finished. Look at yourself plummeting. You're becoming nothing,' she said.

'Grey,' said Zak.

'Hold on. Wait,' she said. The intense silence was broken occasionally by a small whimper from Douglas.

'He's gone,' said Peace. 'Now, Aled. Let's sort you out.'

They carried me across the pool. I could just make out what Peace was saying. 'I'm taking him back to China. That's where he'll stand the best chance of recovering. He knows enough to be able to bring himself back from the brink, given the right circumstances.'

'Agreed,' said Zak.

'Agreed,' said Grey.

'Zak. Get that piece of scum cleaned up and then lock him in that box-room at the top of the house,' said Peace. 'And can you arrange round-the-clock security to make sure he isn't rescued?'

'Yup. Will do.'

'Can we give him something to look at?' asked Grey.

'There's a souvenir from one of his anthropological trips – a painting of brightly-coloured stick-figures on dark-brown parchment. Give him that. As our one and only act of kindness,' said Peace.

'Please take good care of my brother,' said Grey.

Peace took me in his arms and carried me out of the basement. 'My pleasure,' he said softly.

36

Grey

September 2037

Peace gave me an update from the monastery each day. Aled's neural patterns were improving and stabilising. Using the revitalised Cumulus, I joined Aled in the museum. His avatar walked around slowly, and apparently aimlessly.

One day, he spoke. 'I will come back,' was all he said, but it made all the difference.

He clawed his way back, manipulating his brain waves to form their normal pattern, resisting the urge to wallow in the dream-like state of the D. I was so proud of him, totally impressed by his strength and determination.

We were standing in front of the virtual St David's Cathedral when he started to speak again. 'Grey. Can we go to where I grew up?'

'Of course. Whatever you want, 'I said, thrilled that he'd taken the initiative. 'CCTV. London. E151LX.' The museum streamed 3D footage of a pub.

'He spent a lot of time in there,' said Aled.

'Who?'

'My dad. Your dad.'

'Looks a bit rough.'

'Not really. Quite warm and friendly once you're accepted. I miss him.'

'He never even knew me, to leave me,' I said. I was pretty

much over the fact that he'd slunk off when he couldn't stand the complications of fathering two children at the same time and, if this was helping Aled, then I was happy to pick away at old scabs for his sake.

'I know. Still, at least we've now got each other. Eh?' he said, and then started to cry.

'Don't,' I said, 'you'll start me off.'

We both wept for a while.

'Aled, I'm so pleased you're back. It's all gradually fixing itself, you know. It's fragile, but hope is returning. Councils don't have to leave cardboard boxes on the street any more. Instead, community soup-kitchens have popped up all over the place. People are getting on with one another, and talking to each other. Without being afraid.'

His avatar nodded, acknowledging what I was saying. 'And, what about your aunt? Aunt G, wasn't it?'

'Yeah. She's decided to stay on and help the local hospital. Putting that stockpile of drugs to good use.'

His avatar gave me the thumbs-up.

'Didn't we make some amazing discoveries? I wonder, was She involved?' I said, with Douglas's statements still ringing in my scientific ears.

'God exists. Of course He's involved,' said Aled.

'We never quite got the universe we asked for, did we?'

'Further evidence of a superior intelligence. We should release the *Proof*.'

'No,' I said, 'it's convincing, but it's only theoretical. I can't allow it; releasing it would undermine so many of the common-held beliefs that are slowly and shakily returning. Having free will is a deeply cherished belief for most people. The *Proof* could rip that away from underneath them. If there's an ultimate observer choosing your life for you, free will doesn't exist. It might even cause another world-wide Disintegration.'

'Grey…'

'No,' I said. 'Anyway, I've been thinking about setting up

an Institute of Physitheism to teach others how to use what we discovered. To heal their own world.'

'Why don't we siphon off funds from the Project?'

'I'd love to. What a great idea.'

'Let's do it,' he said.

'I'll get Peace to help. Is he there?'

Peace joined us and helped me tap into The Project accounts. We extracted enough to buy the old RSA building for the Institute headquarters and took ownership of The Project house. As the last of the money transferred, we received a warning that the codes were changing and The Project miraculously disappeared.

Aled had been in China about a month when Zak found large shifts in the pecking order within the database. Something strange was happening. Academics were shooting up the list at an unprecedented rate and the algorithms couldn't provide us with an explanation. We all assumed that Douglas's organisation was on the move. We sat at screens day after day, painstakingly working through the data, desperately trying to understand what was happening. It was Zak that spotted the first link – there was a proportionate correlation between the rise of academia and the rising health of the Cumulus. Zak wrote some elaborate algorithms to see if there were also correlations between social-network activity and these shifts. We ran them for twenty-four hours but nothing surfaced. We were baffled, and then a strange thing happened. Dead academics started to rise up the list. Most of them had been presenters on the popular educational channels that had tried to replace schools back in the late twenties. It seemed that people's trust in education was returning.

Zak kept an eye on the Cumulus, looking for any sign of activity from Douglas's organisation. The footage of his torture in the hands of Aled had gone viral, its reach increasing at the same pace as the recovering Cumulus. Zak watched the Database of Influence, looking for any unusual or extreme movements.

*

The click of my leather soles echoed around Douglas's old office as I paced the parquet floor waiting for Aled's return. Jane and Carlos had done a good job of stripping the room of all the valuable equipment. The eWall was gone, the computers were gone and the filing cabinets were gone. All the exquisite rugs were taken, but I didn't mind. I lay down and pressed my cheek to the cold wood; I loved to feel the ancient strength of Mother Nature. The leather chairs remained, tucked in the corner near the window. Between them was one of those ridiculous carved elephant-tables. Barbie stood proud on its back, like a female Hannibal, the *Silver Chair* resting at her feet. *Madonna* hung above a three-hundred-year-old mahogany writing bureau, surveying her new domain.

All three of us were content.

On the wall, opposite *Madonna,* were Douglas's books. It amazed me how many there were, given that none had been printed for so many years. On the green leather drop-down-leaf of the bureau were my two most favourite of all his whiskies – his beloved Arberlour and a Benriach *Maderensis Fumosus.*

I sat in the leather armchair, sipping his Arbelour, pondering what the Institute should do. I didn't want to simply carry on the experiments as before. I didn't want to let the world stumble along, slowly finding its own imperfect way. We had to give it direction and we'd so much to offer from everything we'd learnt. It seemed to me that the best way to protect against Douglas's organisation was to speed up the healing process, to focus on individuals, rather than big key events; dramatic turning points were too unpredictable.

I took a deep breath, touched Madonna's cheek to steady my thoughts and walked to the basement. Sitting in the pool were the first six recruits. I stood in front of them.

'Welcome to the Institute of Physitheism. You were invited because the algorithms selected you. Thanks for accepting. What I'm about to tell you will sound weird and at times unbelievable. It's true. And, it's the best chance we've got to put things right…'

Epilogue

Grey

November 2037

He's coming back. It's been three long tortuous months, but at last my little brother – younger than me by two weeks – is coming home. I pour a glass and add a tiny drop of water using Douglas's silver whisky-pipette. Today must have gravitas. To complete the preparations, I need the perfect book to complement my signature tweed suit, brogues and the peated smokiness of the Benriach.

A whole shelf is dedicated to first-editions and, whisky in hand, I slowly run my finger along the spines of these rare antiques. Pausing at those I recognise, I try to decide.

First editions of Darwin's *Origin of Species* and Tolstoy's *War and Peace,* remind me of the vast wealth Douglas had access to. I settle on Lewis Carroll, *Through the Looking-Glass.* It'll be the perfect backdrop to the closing scene of these bizarre few months.

I'm in the middle of reading about the *garden of live flowers* when my uWatch buzzes, alerting me to the imminent arrival of Peace and Aled. I drain my glass, return the book to its rightful place and stand awkwardly in the middle of the room, waiting. The door opens and in walks Aled. He looks tired, fragile and somehow smaller, but I've never seen him so happy.

'Hi, Bruv,' I say.

'Hi, Sis.'

We link arms and silently cross the room to look out into

the garden. We stand there for a few minutes, soaking up each other's company. Comfortable and at ease. I've been waiting for this moment for a very long time.

'Aled. The recruits are ready. They're waiting for you to take them to the whirlpool for the first time.'

'I know,' he said.

'Are you still okay to do it?'

'Yes,' he says, gripping my arm a little tighter.

There's a crash as the door slams open, making us both jump.

'Grey, look at this,' says an excited Peace, as he comes running into the room. 'It's mass migration across the world. Loads of people are moving. They say they're off to where they feel the most at home. Look.'

Peace gives me the uWatch and takes Aled into his arms. A constant stream of short messages, drawn from the Cumulus, is scrolling across the screen:

Mum, I'm on my way home.

I loved my years of travelling.

Should never have left you and the kids.

I'm coming back.

Sorry, I want to be single. I'm leaving.

I look at Aled. He smiles back at me and melts into Peace's embrace, as if he finally knows where he belongs.

Thanks

I'd like to thank all those that have helped me and most of you know who you are. I hope. Special thanks to Penn, Gail and Kim for each of their unique contributions.

And a big thank you to those that encouraged me along the way: Angeline Igoe, David Walker, Emily Snowden, Gill Venn, Jane Walker, Kate Hutson, Manu Koeb, Mayla Hardaker, Paul Wilson, Pete Blissett, Rachel Melville-Thomas, Roberta Smith, Rupert Smith, Tony Briden and last but not least the insightful Hilary Johnson.

ALSO BY STEPHEN ORAM

Fluence

Imagine a world where your influence on social media determines
your job, your home and your friends. A world without
politicians, where the corporations run the country.

Set in a dystopian London, *Fluence* is a story of aspiration and
desperation and of power seen and unseen. Amber is young and
ambitious. Martin is burnt out by years of struggling. She cheats
to get what she wants while he barely clings on to what he has.

It's the week before the annual Pay Day when strata positions
are decided by the algorithms. The social media feed is frenetic
with people trying to boost their influence rating, while those
above the strata and those who've opted out pursue their own
manipulative goals.

To what extremes, and at what cost to their families, will Amber
and Martin go to achieve the Fluence they desire?

Eating Robots

The future is ours and it's up for grabs...

Step into a high-tech vision of the future with author of *Quantum Confessions* and *Fluence* Stephen Oram. Featuring health-monitoring mirrors, tele-empathic romances and limb-repossessing bailiffs, *Eating Robots* explores the collision of utopian dreams and twisted realities in a world where humanity and technology are becoming ever more intertwined.

Sometimes funny, often unsettling, and always with a word of warning, these thirty sci-fi shorts will stay with you long after you've turned the final page.